Taming Jerei

'Amazing,' he gasped, relaxing his grip on Tia and helping her sink back to the grimy floor. 'What have you done to me?'

'I'm the one who should be asking that question,' Tia retorted. 'Before you, I never would have had sex in a courthouse closet. Not in a million years.'

'Oh really? Then you probably wouldn't have put up with this, either.'

Mark began stroking her again through the gap in her panties, much more gently this time. It was incredible, how his state of arousal transformed his touch. Earlier he had been pawing her with all the finesse of a grizzly bear; now his fingers were exploring her folds as softly as a moth's wings. Good thing, too, because the treatment he'd given her had left her so sensitive that a more aggressive contact would have hurt.

'I want you to come,' he said. A guttural order.

'I can't. Not with those women outside listening...'

'That's why you have to come. Come so they know it. I can't disappoint my audience.'

Taming
Jeremy

Anne Tourney

In real life, always practise safe sex.

First published in 2006 by
Cheek
Thames Wharf Studios
Rainville Road
London W6 9HA

Design by Smith & Gilmour, London
Printed and bound by Mackays of Chatham PLC

ISBN 0 352 34030 4

Chapter One

Meet Boy Wonder

One of these days, someone would have to probe Tia's subconscious to find out why she devised her wildest paintings when she was asleep and restrained. Monday, before sunrise, Mark had her tied to his bedframe, her wrists bound with the sash of her emerald satin kimono. A morning man to the core, he was drinking his daily stimulant from the well between Tia's thighs while scenes from a weird art-sex dream still jangled her subconscious.

In her dream Tia stood in front of a cement wall beside the convention centre downtown, holding a wet paintbrush in one hand as she studied a mural she'd just painted: a Gaugin-like image of three muscular blue men making love to a voluptuous ochre woman under a papaya tree. Tia was wearing a leopard-print bra and matching panties that she'd seen in a Frederick's of Hollywood catalogue, but had never dreamt (until now) that she'd wear. It was morning rush hour, and thirty or forty commuters had gathered to gawk at Tia's painting. Out of the crowd stepped Mr Wilkins, her high-school driver's ed teacher, who had somehow been transformed into a modern-day Adonis. In reality, he had looked like the Skipper from *Gilligan's Island*.

'Tell us what you've done here, Tia,' said Mr Wilkins, in the fawning tone of an afternoon talk-show host who's scored a celebrity he doesn't deserve.

Tia stepped back and surveyed her work. Pretty spectacular, she had to admit. She'd never painted anything like it: crazy, vibrant, outrageously sexual. The golds and sapphires and crimsons were sexy in their own right; the colours made you want to lick them.

'This isn't just a mural, it's a sex spell,' Tia explained. 'I wanted to call up the primitive eroticism of the stressed-out, overworked, modern female.'

Mr Wilkins was hanging on Tia's every word, but his eyes were wandering up and down – mostly down – her body. She suddenly felt a draft down south and realised that her panties were crotchless.

'So what do you call this masterpiece?' Mr Wilkins asked.

Tia tilted her head and tapped her chin thoughtfully with the handle of her paintbrush. 'It's called *The Temple of the Crotchless Papayas*.'

'Wow. I always knew you were gifted, but I had no idea you could do anything like this,' Mr Wilkins breathed, getting down on his knees. 'Speaking of temples, would it be OK if I worshipped at yours?'

'Of course,' Tia said.

Mr Wilkins parted Tia's lips, which were already ripe for attention, and nibbled adoringly at her inner flesh. The yuppie audience, holding attaché cases and Starbuck's cups, murmured their approval.

Tia roused herself with a moan. She opened her eyes to see Mark's head between her legs, his hair caressing her thighs while his tongue lavished attention on the knot at the heart of her folds. She was a bit disappointed that the mural wasn't real, and that she wasn't actually a genius, but she didn't mind seeing her hunky lover down there instead of a man who looked like the Skipper.

Mark lifted his head. Though her eyes were still unfocused, Tia could see the expression on his face: the fanatic grin of a control freak.

'Don't say a word, Tia. You're still mine.'

Tia shifted her arms, but her wrists were restrained.

That didn't surprise her. Mark was an expert at stealth bondage, and Tia often woke up with some part of her tied to the furniture. What did surprise her was how close she was to a climax; she could already feel the wavelets gathering into a tidal wave. A few more licks, and she'd come crashing down on Orgasm Beach. Her nipples still ached from the things Mark had done to them last night, and the nubs throbbed as Mark's tongue drummed at her clit.

Sensing the tension in her muscles, Mark cupped Tia's bottom in his hands. He drew her into his mouth when she rose into her climax, her body curving in a quivering bridge. She hovered there for a few seconds, coasting along on the spasms, then sank back down and came to rest on Mark's mattress. Just then, Mark's alarm went off, a chorus of liquid rainforest noises and exotic animal calls. Mark didn't need any electronic screeches to wake him up in the morning. He was always up before sunrise, and he proved it to Tia, sliding into her with one slow, capable motion. He was going over his allotted time, but Tia wasn't about to complain.

She raised her legs and wrapped them around his lower back, coaxing him deeper inside her. They rocked together at a sweet, unhurried pace, until the friction set off a wildfire. Tia loved the way his face looked when he was about to climax: his eyes widened at first, then squeezed shut, as if he were about to sneeze. With the birds in his alarm clock still hooting in the background, he exploded into Tia.

'Who's Mr Wilkins?' Mark asked, as they were catching their breath. 'You were mumbling his name just before you woke up.'

'Don't even ask,' Tia shuddered. 'I don't want to spoil the afterglow.'

Mark glanced at his clock. 'Sorry. It's past six.'

'I know. You kind of spilt over your time,' Tia said, giving his butt a playful smack. Mark reached up to untie Tia's wrists. She watched his cock, still half-hard, swing heavily as he climbed out of bed and padded off to take his shower.

Mark and Tia had an arrangement. Twelve hours out of Tia's day belonged to her, and her alone; the other twelve belonged to Mark. From six in the morning until six in the evening, she did whatever she had to do. After six p.m., all bets were off. She had to follow Mark's instructions, no matter how kinky, shaping her time to his desires. Tia's law-student roommate thought the arrangement was outrageously weird, 'a throwback to authoritarian patriarchy', Noelle said. But, to Tia, her deal with Mark was a form of behaviour management, not so different from what she did at work. As an art therapist, she had to help her patients find outlets for their thoughts and urges. She gave them a space where they could go wild, at least with tempera paints or salt dough. It was the same thing with Mark. She was channelling his dominant drives, giving him a safe area to get crazy without letting him take over her life.

'Tia! What are you still doing in bed?'

Mark was stepping out of the bathroom. He'd towelled his body dry, but his skin was still ruddy and glowing from the hot shower. His blond hair, dark with water, was combed back against his head like an actor from an Italian porno movie, and his sleek goatee glistened with droplets. His tightly knit muscles showed the payoff of his memberships at two different gyms. His pendulous cock, hanging long and loose, was the cherry on top of the sundae. Forty minutes from now, Mark would be standing in front of a portable whiteboard, telling a gaggle of city officials about his plans for a new annex to the downtown public library. Right now he was looking a lot like Tia's breakfast.

'Waiting for you,' said Tia. 'Get over here.'

She sat up on one elbow and lowered her eyes to Mark's pride and joy. The thick root was stirring, and Mark was walking towards her, already hypnotised. Tia loved being able to do that to him. Mark might be a control fiend, but the offer of a morning blowjob could turn his whole body, with one critical exception, into putty. When the tip of Tia's tongue met the tip of his erection, he groaned and sank his fingers into her messy hair. Tia sucked him, feeling him stiffen against her lips. Even after he'd showered, Mark couldn't totally wash away the flavour of his sex. His musky scent set off another rush of juice between Tia's legs. When he came into Tia's mouth, her body got warm all over, in a flush of pride. Tia couldn't exactly put 'expert fellatrix' on her résumé, but she counted it as one of her most valuable skills.

'You're in for it tonight,' Mark warned. 'I'm going to be late for my meeting.'

'Too bad.' Tia stretched like a cat and smiled up at him. 'I guess you'll have to punish me, Sir.'

'Damn right I will. And you won't be smiling about it, young lady.'

Young lady. She'd be hot over that all day. At 28, Mark was two years younger than Tia, but you'd never know it from the way he bossed her around.

'Wear your purple bra and panties today,' he said. 'And the pink T-shirt I like, the stretchy one with the buttons.'

'We're on my time now,' Tia reminded him. 'And the bra and panties you're referring to are "eggplant", not "purple", if you must know.'

'Hey,' Mark said, spreading his hands innocently. 'I'm just a guy with a suggestion.'

'OK. I'll wear the bra and panties, but I'll have to wear something decent on top. Tight T-shirts aren't the thing to wear on a locked psych unit.'

'I see what you mean,' Mark said with a grimace.

Sometimes Tia got the feeling that he didn't like her job, but he knew better than to say anything. The sour look vanished when he bent down to kiss her goodbye.

'I might have to work late if my afternoon meeting

runs over. But I'll be calling you at six on the dot. Be ready.'

'Oh, I'm ready already,' Tia said and laughed.

As soon as Mark left, she would have to do something about the swelling warmth down below. No matter how many times he made her come, Tia never seemed to get her fill these days. Three months ago, before she met Mark, Tia never would have guessed that her weekly quota of orgasms would climb up to the double digits. Who would have thought an art geek with a weakness for overpriced lingerie could get so lucky?

If she'd known better, Tia never would have unwrapped her nude body from Mark's Egyptian cotton sheets. She could have called the hospital and told them she had a nasty, contagious stomach bug; the nurses could have filled in for her with a group therapy session. But she'd promised Kim that they'd be painting ceramic turtles on Monday, and Tia had sworn to herself that she'd never break a promise to a patient.

When Tia showed up on the inpatient psych unit, the charge nurse told her that Kim had been placed in seclusion. She'd had a rough night, had broken her safety contract and wouldn't be painting any turtles while she was in four-point restraints. Tia managed to round up three other patients, but the session didn't go well. Frank wouldn't touch the plaster turtles because their blank white eyes frightened him (Frank had phobias about everything, but apparently albino turtles held a special terror). Samantha, an incessant talker whose manic repartée usually lent a cocktail-party atmosphere to therapy, was broody and distant. Darrell was enthusiastic for once, but he insisted on painting his turtle pitch black and decorating its shell with a blood-red pentagram.

While Tia was making a note in Darrell's chart about the satanic turtle, all hell broke loose in the day room. Kim, still in restraints, started screaming about her civil rights, which escalated two of the other patients, who were already mad because they'd lost their smoking privileges. Soon the morning snacks were flying around the room and, before Tia could run for cover, she was hit on the side of the head with a boomerang banana. The fruit was green enough to cause some serious pain, and one of the nurses insisted that she should go downstairs to the ER and have it checked out.

'You might have a concussion. Unripe fruit can be a deadly weapon,' said the nurse in an ominous tone. 'I'll have to talk to Dietary about that.'

She sent Tia packing down to the ER, where Tia waited for the triage nurse to call her name. The waiting room was packed with people, most of whom looked like their only emergent concern was a need for air-conditioning. On a sweltering summer day, a lot of patients didn't mind waiting for two hours, but Tia couldn't spare the time. She had just decided that the gentle throbbing in her skull wasn't worth the trouble, when she spotted a familiar figure crossing the waiting room. You couldn't mistake Leo Baines; he was the only man in town wearing a fat green parka in the middle of July. Tia flagged him down.

'Leo! Over here!'

The psychiatric resident looked around the lobby with his characteristic expression of curiosity mingled with irritation. When he recognised Tia, he hurried over, each step counterbalanced by the weight of his bulging leather briefcase.

'God,' he sighed, plopping down in the seat next to Tia. 'I hate consulting in the ER. I just had a psychotic teenager scream obscenities at me for forty-five minutes. Someone should have put Haldol in her Froot Loops this morning.'

'Sounds like your day is worse than mine,' Tia said, rubbing her temple. 'I got hit in the head with a green banana. The nurse sent me down to see if I had brain damage.'

7

'Let me take a look.' Leo pulled a pen light out of the depths of his parka and shone it into Tia's eyes. Then he waggled his fingers in the air on either side of her head, touched her nose, and made what looked like a priestly benediction in front of her face.

'What was that?' Tia asked.

'A neurological assessment. You're fine,' Leo said. 'Drink three stone-cold martinis and call me in the morning.' He sat back in his chair, pulled off his glasses and rubbed the bridge of his nose. 'Tell me, Tia, why are we here? I should have followed my mother's advice and become a professional violinist.'

'And I should have been an artist,' Tia agreed.

'You're still an artist. You haven't stopped painting.'

'You mean I haven't stopped *trying* to paint. I haven't done anything that I like in months, except in my dreams.'

'How many months has it been, exactly?' Leo asked, stroking his chin. 'Three, maybe?'

'If you're implying that I stopped painting when I started dating Mark, you're absolutely wrong,' Tia declared. 'I've been taking a break. Getting a new perspective on my art.'

'Mmm, hmm. You know, Tia, I could revolutionise your perspective, if you'd let me.'

Leo's myopic eyes lingered on the top button on Tia's blouse. No doubt he was remembering the steamy make-out session that the two of them had had after sharing a pitcher of margaritas at the hospital's Christmas party. The hospital really should stop throwing parties, Tia thought. The state of American healthcare was bad enough without encouraging the staff to get drunk and grope each other. Actually, she had always known that Leo could be cute if he would burn his beloved parka and stop letting his mother cut his hair with a mixing bowl. From what she recalled of that tequila-fogged evening, he had looked almost handsome without his glasses.

'Don't go there, Leo,' she said. 'We've already been there. We don't want to go back.'

Leo sighed and got to his feet. 'One day you'll see the light. Mark is just too ... organised for you. You're a free spirit. Too much structure will suffocate your soul.'

'I'm thirty years old. I need a little structure in my life.'

'A little structure, yes. A golden cage, no. Now, my pretty nightingale, I really have to run.'

Leo lifted Tia's hand and kissed it, then lurched away, his briefcase keeping him off-balance. What did he mean by 'organised'? Tia wondered. Was he implying that Tia was disorganised? And what were those cryptic references to cages and nightingales? Leo would make a great Jungian analyst some day, if he survived his residency.

Tia realised that she was chewing her nails: a definite sign that she was thinking too much – and that she was starving. She should take the rest of the day off; no one would notice if she slipped away for a four-hour lunch. But, as she stepped out of the ER into the hot summer day, she ran head first into the charge nurse, who reminded her that she was supposed to evaluate two newly admitted patients that afternoon. The wait had eaten up Tia's lunch break, so she bought a Hershey bar with almonds (protein bonus) from the vending machine and gobbled it in the elevator on the way upstairs. The first patient she evaluated scored so low on cognitive function that she thought he might belong on the neuro floor, and the second refused to be tested at all.

'I don't belong in this pigsty,' he announced. 'There's no one here but a bunch of nut-jobs. I am from the Lost City of Atlantis.' He looked at Tia's neck, then folded his arms and turned his back on her. 'I'm not even going to speak to you,' he announced. 'You don't have gills.'

Like all bad days, this one finally limped to an end. When Tia got back to her apartment, the first thing she did was take off her high-necked paisley blouse and straight black skirt. She tossed her sedate work clothes on the floor of her closet and put on her favourite pair of jeans and the pink T-shirt Mark liked so much.

'Hey, Tia. Can we talk?'

Noelle leant against the doorframe. Something about her casual slouch made tiny hairs bristle on the back of Tia's neck. Red alert: Noelle never did anything casually.

'I'm not much in the mood for talk,' Tia said. 'I had a rotten day.'

'Really? What happened?' Noelle cooed.

'Cut the crap, Noelle. Just tell me what you want.'

Tia's roommate drew back with a sharp little sniff. 'Why do you assume I want something from you? Don't you think I care about your day?'

'Nope.'

'Well, all right,' Noelle grumbled. The Selfless Friend act had already broken down. 'I need to talk to you about my brother.'

Tia looked up at Noelle in surprise. 'What brother? You don't have one.'

'Yes, I do. His name's Jeremy. I don't talk about him much.'

'You mean you don't talk about him at all. Why not?'

'Jeremy has . . . issues.'

'Such as?'

'He had a few problems at college. Dropped out. Disappeared. Lived on the streets, hitchhiked around the country, got arrested for painting bizarre stuff on public buildings. He's brilliant, and he's talented, but he's never been like other kids.' Noelle spewed all this information in a single rush, without taking a breath. 'He's back in the city now. He's got everything he needs to make things work. He's got a case manager and a therapist, he's taking his meds, he's committed to making his treatment work. He just needs a place to live.'

'And what else?' Tia prompted.

'He needs a friend. Someone who's not officially part of his treatment team, but who could keep an eye on his mental status. Someone who could watch his moods and keep him under control.'

'Co-dependent nanny, at your service,' Tia sang, clicking the heels of her mules.

Noelle held up her hand like a traffic cop. 'No, Tia. That's not it at all.'

'So what does he need me for? He has a whole team at his disposal.'

'You can help him find productive things to do with his time. Channel his creative energy. If he starts making weird art again, you'll be the first to know. You'll be right there with him, monitoring his mental status.'

'Look, if Jeremy ever ends up getting admitted to my unit and I work with him on a professional basis, I'd be happy to monitor his mental status. Can't you see how warped it is to monitor someone who doesn't know he's being monitored?'

'Oh, he knows,' Noelle said breezily. 'I told him what you do for a living. It's fine with him if you watch what he's doing. Jeremy loves to be analysed. His biggest complaint about his current treatment team is that no one wants to spend any time using his art to explore the depths of his psyche.'

'Well, I don't want to do that, either.' Tia burrowed into the sofa and gave the coffee table a petulant kick.

Noelle's ears pricked up as she heard the whine creep into Tia's voice. Her lips curved into a small, self-satisfied smile. 'Yes, you do,' she said seductively. 'Intensive analysis was exactly what you wanted to do when you decided to go into art therapy. When you wrote your dissertation on sculpture and psychosis, did you really think you'd end up in a grubby public hospital watching your patients paint ashtrays and make caterpillars out of egg cartons?'

Tia pouted. 'There's nothing wrong with working in

a public hospital. And stop practising your prosecutor tactics on me. You know how I feel about artists. Remember Steffen?'

After she broke up with Steffen, Tia swore she'd never get personally involved with another creative type. She'd done her time on the mood-swing trapeze and, besides, she couldn't take the mess. She'd never forget the day she came home and found Steffen using her favourite pair of French-cut silk panties to smear paint on a wall-size canvas. The sight of that intimate apricot scrap crumpled up in his meaty hand made her cry, especially when she saw the colour he was using. Burnt sienna: an exotic term for brown. Freud would have had a field day analysing that passive-aggressive manoeuvre.

Steffen had almost carried it off. He claimed he'd found her panties lying on the bedroom floor, and the texture of the fabric combined with the traces of her musk had driven him wild with inspiration. This romantic touch might have saved the day, except that Steffen got even more excited by the scent of turpentine than by the scent of Tia. Every clear surface in Tia's loft apartment turned into a grove of jelly jars half-filled with coloured water and paintbrushes. Crumpled pencil sketches overflowed his drawing table and drifted on to the floor, and chunks of charcoal littered the carpets like deer droppings. Tia managed to put up with Steffen's mess for the four months he lived with her but, when they stopped having sex because Steffen was 'exhausted by his muse', Tia swore off artists. When she found out that his muse was a chunky blonde figure model named Liesl, she almost swore off men altogether.

So it was out with Steffen, in with Noelle. After having Steffen as a room mate, Noelle was refreshingly sane, maybe a bit too sane. She was efficient and neat to the point of being scary, making Tia feel like a pink frosted flake by comparison. Noelle was a health-food freak, a devoted runner and the top student in her class at law school. That's why Tia couldn't believe that Noelle had a brother like Jeremy, much less that she was dumping him in Tia's lap.

'Steffen was totally different. You were romantically involved with him. Nothing like that is going to happen between you and Jeremy,' Noelle soothed. 'Look, won't you at least meet him before you make a final decision?'

'Fine.' With the world's heaviest sigh, Tia caved in. 'I'll meet the kid, if it will make you stop harassing me.'

Noelle stood up straight and crossed her arms over her chest. 'Great. Then we're set. Now would be the perfect time. He's upstairs, decorating his new apartment.'

'What? You mean he's going to live in the building?'

'Relax, Tia. He's on a month-to-month lease. I co-signed, just to reassure the landlady that things would be OK. If this doesn't work out, he's going straight back home to live with Mom. Trust me, if he thinks there's a chance of getting sent to Mom's, he'll be on his best behaviour.'

'You are such a manipulative bitch, Noelle.'

'Thanks. I do what I can.' She twirled on her bare foot as she turned to leave the room. She always executed that little spin after a professional victory, only it looked a lot more lethal when she was wearing her favourite pair of Ferragamo pumps.

If manipulation ran in the family, Tia was already in deep trouble with this boy.

Jeremy's front door stood partially open. Tia knocked but, when no one appeared, she decided to venture inside. The living room was empty, except for a pile of boxes, a sway-backed couch and a gaggle of mis-matched wooden chairs. Tia found Jeremy in his bed-room. He was perched on a stepladder, doing something to the ceiling. The first thing Tia saw was his bare back, taut and sinewy, heartbreakingly strong and young. Several inches of plaid boxer shorts rose above the waistband of his faded Levi's, which covered an ass so tight and firm that Tia had to do a half-pirouette to pull her eyes off it.

Noelle's brother, she reminded herself sternly. Noelle's wild, unstable baby brother.

'Hi there,' Tia said. Lame intro, but what else could you say when you were face to face with a backside like that?

Jeremy looked down. His hair, tied back in a blue bandanna, was black and wavy, the way Noelle's would be if she didn't discipline the spirit out of it with gel. In fact, Jeremy could be a younger, masculine duplicate of Noelle, *sans* glasses and tight-assed frown.

'Hey,' he replied. Shy pleasure with a touch of surprise. 'Wait a second. Let me get off this thing.'

Jeremy spread his arms, winglike, and leapt off the stepladder. He landed on the floor as gracefully as a gymnast and bounded over to Tia. He skidded to a halt only six or seven inches from her – poor sense of spatial boundaries, she noted, but at least he wasn't exhibiting any superhuman energy. He had a frank, gritty-sweet smell, like a child after a long day at the playground. She took a couple of steps back. His lean, ropy muscles were dewed with perspiration, and his pecs rose and fell with each breath. She could hear the air sifting faintly through his open mouth. Her knees almost gave way.

'What are you doing?' Tia asked.

'I'm making constellations,' he said, waving a sheet of glow-in-the-dark stars. 'These help me sleep at night. I pretend that I'm navigating on the ocean in the dark, like the Polynesians used to do in their canoes. Of course, it's more fun to navigate with someone else.'

'I hope you're not going to have too many overnight guests.' Somebody help me, Tia thought, I'm possessed by my mother. 'This is a quiet building. Your sister will go nuts if you start making a lot of noise.'

Jeremy laughed. 'Don't worry. I don't know very

many people around here.' He cocked his head and gave Tia an eager, assessing look, like a puppy checking out a new chew toy. 'Not yet, anyway.'

He was cute. Not just in a garden-variety way, but in a metaphysical sense: cute as an existential category. Way too cute, and too young, for Tia to be having the kinds of thoughts that were swirling through her brain right now.

'So what's your name?' he asked.

'Tia.'

'Oh, yeah. You're Noelle's best friend. She told me all about you. You're an art therapist. That's way cool. You're a real redhead, which is even cooler. You're lactose-intolerant, so, if I take you out for coffee, I should order you a soy latte with Sweet 'n Low. Your bra size is a 36D; you smoked clove cigarettes in college; you spend way too much money on underwear, and you've got a kinky thing for Russian sable – paintbrushes, I mean.'

Tia's jaw dangled. She couldn't say a word. She ought to be used to this kind of thing from kids like Jeremy, but his thumbnail portrait floored her. 'Noelle told you my bra size?' she managed to squeak.

'Uh, no. I guessed that part. It's a gift I have. I've been able to do it since I was twelve.'

'A gift,' Tia echoed weakly, wrapping her arms around her chest. Her nipples were hard, and her breasts felt warm and heavy and way too lush. 'You should be in lingerie sales.'

'Maybe I will be, one of these days.' Jeremy grinned. 'I'm pretty much capable of anything.'

Jeremy's right canine tooth was crooked. The cocky fang overlapped its neighbour in a way that strummed at her libido more than any set of perfect teeth. For Tia, sex appeal lived in the details of a man's face. A flawless surface offered nothing to cling to, nothing to snag her heart.

'Tia,' he said slowly, as if he were tasting the name

in his mouth. 'Like Tia Maria. I got wrecked drinking that stuff once. Tia means aunt, you know. Are you going to be my surrogate aunt or something?'

Or *something*. She definitely wanted to be his something. Tia didn't want to be an older female relative to this smart, sexy, metaphysically cute . . .

Tia's cell phone went off, playing the opening bars of Wagner's *Ride of the Valkyrie*. It was the special ring that she chose for Mark, who was an opera fanatic. In fact, she had bought the phone at Mark's request. She didn't need a cell phone for work – what would the hospital need to call her about urgently? A mass explosion of ceramic ashtrays? – but Mark wanted to make sure he could reach her at all times.

Tia's hand dove into the pocket of her jeans. Her fingers fumbled as she tried to answer the call; the phone felt slick and alien in her hand, like a transmitter from another planet.

'Hello?'

'It took you almost a minute to answer.' Mark's voice was rich, smoky, and deeply reproachful. 'How do you think I should punish you for making me wait?'

'Uh, I'm not sure about that. Why don't you tell me?'

'Imagine something cruel and unusual, something perfect for a naughty little redhead.'

Tia's face reddened. Her jeans felt too tight all of a sudden. She could feel her eggplant satin panties riding up between her lower lips. There was a reason why Mark wanted her to buy her panties a size too small. Jeremy was watching her, his head tilted again at that quizzical puppy-dog angle.

'How about a cauliflower casserole?' Tia suggested. It was the most cruel and unusual punishment she could name in front of Jeremy.

'Someone's there with you, right?' Mark asked. He sounded pleased. Tia could hear him revving up his engine.

'Right,' Tia chirped.

'You're not still at work, are you?'

'No . . . not exactly.'

Tia squirmed. Mark had touched a sensitive spot, one that she'd been avoiding ever since she caught the first glimpse of Jeremy's naked back. Would her time with Jeremy be considered work? Noelle wanted her to watch him, to manage his behaviour. That was basically what she did at the hospital. So did her time with him fall inside the bounds of professional behaviour?

God, she hoped not. Jeremy was too cute to be an ethical dilemma.

'Great. Are you wearing your pink cotton T-shirt with the button-down neckline? The one I asked you to wear.'

'Yes.'

'Good. Then I want you to run your finger down the collar. Play with the buttons till you get to the first one that's still fastened. Then I want you to unbutton it. After you're done with that one, keep undoing the buttons till the person you're with can see the top of your bra.'

'Mark, I don't think that's such a great idea right now.'

'One button, then.' His voice deepened. 'I've been waiting for this all day. You know how horny I get when I wait.'

Tia played with her collar, casually, as if she were scratching a bug bite under the fabric. Jeremy watched. She slid her finger down the neckline and hooked a pearly button. Here goes nothing, she thought, as the button sprang out of its hole, revealing a good inch of cleavage.

Jeremy didn't think it was nothing, apparently. He swallowed hard. Tia thought she heard him give a small whimper. Tia couldn't go on. This was too cruel and, besides, she'd already flashed her purple bra strap. That should be good enough for Mr Control.

'Done,' Tia announced.

'I hope the person you're with appreciates your assets.'

'I don't think that's a problem.'

'Good. You have amazing breasts,' Mark said. A lion's purr. She could hear him licking his chops. 'Guess where I am right now.'

'At the office?'

'Nope.'

'Starbuck's?'

'Closer. Keep guessing.'

'On the corner?'

'Getting warmer.'

Damn. He was somewhere in the building, probably prowling up the stairs. Tia should have suspected he was near by; the reception on that call was too clear. She crammed the cell phone into her pocket and gave Jeremy a brilliant smile. 'Why don't we get together tomorrow morning?' she asked. 'I've got to go – something just came up.'

'Sure. I'll be here.'

Jeremy looked confused. His full mouth drooped. Tia fought back the urge to kiss him on the cheek. He had a hint of dark stubble on his jaw. The contrast of that masculine shadow with his childish, crestfallen expression made a starburst of lust spread through Tia's loins.

'Or we could get together later, after it gets dark,' he suggested. 'We could look at the stars.'

Tia fought the urge to blurt out a big, sloppy 'yes'. She had to keep this situation under control. 'I think it's supposed to stay cloudy till tomorrow morning,' she said. 'It wouldn't be a good night for star-gazing.'

'I wasn't talking about the stars outside,' he said, motioning to the ceiling above his bed. 'You'll be able to see stars in here any time you want.'

'Right,' Tia gulped. 'I'm sure I will. Now I've really got to go.'

She wheeled around before Jeremy could give her another sexy, soulful look. He should have been born with a licence for those eyes; they were nothing less than sex lasers, the weapons of a supercharged wonder boy. Tia had always thought Noelle's turquoise eyes were stunning, but they looked washed out compared to Jeremy's. It had to be his brain that generated that dazzling light, reflecting those blues and greens and golds from the prismatic colours of his imagination.

As she clattered down the stairs, Tia tried to forget about Jeremy's eyes. She was too busy trying to think about how she would tell Mark about Jeremy.

'Sexual Overlord, meet Boy Wonder,' she muttered to herself, rehearsing the scene in her mind. Somehow, it didn't quite work.

Chapter Two

Public Solitaire

Mark was waiting on the landing outside Tia's apartment. Tia felt a catch in her throat when she saw him leaning against the banister of the old staircase. His hair fell in shaggy blond wings across his forehead and cheekbones, accentuating the planes of his face. His jaw was set at a hard angle; a woman who didn't know him might think he was seriously pissed off. Tia knew better. Mark had plans for the night.

She'd never forget the first time she saw the *look*. It was their third date, and Mark had arranged an extravagant evening for Tia, the kind of evening that had 'I'm determined to get laid' written all over it. A black Lincoln Town Car had picked her up at her apartment. The back seat of the car had been piled with pink and yellow roses, and Tia could barely make a place for herself in that bank of blossoms. The car had swept her off to Le Cerf d'Or, an ultra-exclusive French restaurant that was perched on the top floor of the city's art museum. Tia was such a pleb that she hadn't even known the place existed, until the limo driver took her upstairs in a glass elevator that rose above the urban skyline like a colourless balloon floating to heaven.

Living up to its name, the restaurant was a study in gold, decorated in shades ranging from the palest beige to a rich reproduction of the precious metal. If someone had blindfolded Tia and set her loose in this place, she wouldn't have known at first whether she was in a bank, a museum or an eating establishment. She wished she were back in her own neighbourhood, ordering a messy gyros sandwich at the Greek grocery store across from her apartment building. Fifty gradations of beige and gold didn't do much for her appetite.

As the maitre d' lead Tia through the maze of tables, where the city's wealthiest art patrons sat sipping martinis or Cristal, Tia felt like the poor little match girl in her calico skirt, jean jacket and sandals. She could have sworn that Mark had suggested she dress casually for tonight's date. The curious glances of the town's high-class fashionistas informed her that she looked more like someone who should be scrubbing their kitchen floors instead of drinking Champagne at a neighbouring table. But for some reason – probably because of Mark's reputation – the maitre d' took her to the table and sat her down without a word.

And there Tia waited. She waited for what seemed like forever, sipping water and picking at the rolls in the bread basket (the rolls were reassuringly simple, just mounds of baked dough that might have come out of a Pillsbury tube) and scattering crumbs all over the floor. Trying not to count the minutes, she studied the art on the walls. In the cultured, self-conscious atmosphere of Le Cerf d'Or, the paintings were exotic anomalies, violent spectacles of the imagination. One work in particular held Tia's attention: two nude women together, composed of thousands of sparks of colour. The nudes were interlocked by an energy that she could sense, but not define. She would have loved to paint something like that, if only she were brave enough.

She wasn't feeling brave tonight. By the time Mark arrived, she was a bundle of nerves, dead certain that he had arranged all this just so he could prove a point: Tia wasn't in his league, and never would be.

Then she saw him talking to the maitre d'. Mark was such a stunner that he caught the eye of every female in the room, but the only woman whose stare he returned was Tia's. Her heart stopped. Mark was incredible. He could have been climbing Pike's Peak that afternoon, or conducting a meeting on how to transform the entire city – you'd never know by looking at his athletic body and sun-streaked hair.

'Sorry you had to wait,' Mark said lightly, as he pulled out a chair for himself.

That's when Tia knew that he *had* meant to make her wait. He had orchestrated the whole scene as carefully as if it were an act from an opera, from Tia's casual outfit to the intimidating limo ride to the interminable, nerve-wracking minutes she'd spent at the table, tearing rolls and praying for him to show up.

Anger froze Tia's vocal cords – or maybe it was the presence of fifty or sixty members of the cream of the city's social set that wouldn't let her scream at Mark like a fishwife on a Saturday-night bender. If she could have screamed, she would have told him how much she resented him for tricking her into dressing for a hay ride instead of an elegant meal. She would have ripped him to shreds for leaving her alone and vulnerable in a room full of impeccably attired social sharks.

'Tia? Is something wrong? Your face is maroon.'

Mark calmly took a sip of a vodka martini that the waiter had brought him. The cool, superior look that he gave Tia over the knifelike rim of the glass sent her flying over the edge.

'You didn't have to go to all this trouble just to fuck me, Mark. We could have done that back at my apartment tonight. In fact, we could have done it fifteen minutes after we met the very first time! Why did you have to set me up like this? Why did you have to embarrass me?'

Tia's voice rose with every epithet as she accused Mark of everything from emotional manipulation to mental cruelty. The dining room had gone dead silent now, but Mark didn't even flinch. He leant back in his chair, sipped his drink and enjoyed the show. At one point, she got so carried away that she shoved her chair away from the table and stood up. Standing, she took more oxygen into her lungs, which meant that she could yell louder.

'Are you done?' Mark asked, when she finally stopped to catch her breath. 'Because I'd really like to order. I'm starving.'

Tia sank back into her seat. She slumped in her chair, feeling defeated. She hadn't accomplished a thing but deeper, darker humiliation.

'What do you want to eat?' Mark asked, looking at the menu again. 'Or should I order for you?'

'I want to go,' said Tia, in a small tight voice. Now that the purple mist of her anger had cleared, all she could see were the jaded, mildly intrigued stares of the restaurant's clientele. And of course there was Mark's face, bland and expressionless, nothing marring the smoothly tanned surface but a tiny shaving cut on his left cheek. Nice communication skills, Tia, she said to herself. She felt about as effective as a two-year-old on the downslide of a tantrum.

The waiter appeared again to take their order. Mark ordered for both of them in French; Tia, with her junior-high francophony, had no idea what she was getting. But then, she never did know what she was getting with Mark. This was only their third date, and he'd already proven he could bowl her over with sweet surprises, or yank the rug out from under her composure with a stunt like the one he'd pulled tonight.

Tia folded her hands on the table. Her anger was dwindling to a low simmer. 'Why did you do what you did tonight?' she asked.

Mark took a few moments to finish his drink. 'Why do you think?'

'You like to be in control. No, scratch that. You *need* to be in control. You're a big success at your career, you're one of the most eligible bachelors in the time zone, but being on top of your profession and on top of half the single women in town isn't enough for you. You'll never get enough accolades or power; you'll always want more. You need to be the director of every relationship you have, even if it's only your third date with an insignificant, no-name therapist who thinks she's an artist in her spare time.'

'Very perceptive,' Mark said. 'I'd say you're on target. I do like to be in control. I do enjoy being wanted and admired – what man doesn't? Power is a huge turn-on for me, and I do need to direct my relationships, especially with women. The only thing you're wrong about is your assessment of yourself. You're not insignificant. Especially not to me.'

'Then why did you make me feel that way tonight?'

'I didn't. A woman like you should be able to go anywhere, wearing anything, and be confident that she's the most extraordinary female in the room. You're not like the other women I've dated, Tia. You have a fierce, unrestrained spirit. I love that about you. I *want* that about you.'

Tia didn't know what to say. She occupied herself with pushing her breadcrumbs into a pile as she stared at the tablecloth. She'd been trained how to respond to any kind of verbal challenge; she'd had conversations with patients who were acutely psychotic, and with patients who couldn't sit still long enough to tell her their names, and with patients who spoke persistently in rhymes. Men who were as level-headed as Mark didn't usually leave her speechless. When she finally did look up, Mark was looking at her with a focused, almost predatory gaze that sent a shiver running through the most sensitive parts of her body, from her nipples to her toes.

'I have a proposition for you,' he said. 'You're going to think I'm weird, you might think I'm crazy, and you might get up and leave. That's fine, but I want you to hear me out before you storm out of the restaurant.'

'Try me.'

Mark leant forwards. 'You're an independent woman. You've got your life arranged the way you want it; you like to do things your own way. I'm proposing that for half of your day, twelve out of twenty-four hours, you live your life *my* way.'

'What do you mean?'

'From six in the evening until six in the morning, you do anything I tell you to do. And I do mean anything.'

'Such as?'

'The sky's the limit. I could ask you to take your panties off right now and lay them across my plate, so I could eat my dinner off them. I could ask you to follow that grey-haired gentleman over there, who happens to be a deputy mayor, into the men's room and show him that hot-pink merry widow you're wearing.'

'Hey! How did you know –'

'Shhh. I have my ways. Just listen. I could ask you to do all sorts of things, things that would stretch your imagination, push your limits. It would be incredibly challenging, but beautifully simple. You'd only have two rules to follow: one, don't say no. Two, don't even think no.'

'And what would be in it for me?'

Tia posed the question as coolly as she was able, but her insides were churning. None of her lovers had ever tried to take control this way. She'd been held under water by her teenage sweetheart, and pinned to the wall and kissed beyond reason by a grunge rocker. But those were isolated episodes in a love life that had been characterised by courtly politeness. Even when they were behaving badly, her lovers had been politically correct. Most of them could hardly master their own lives, much less control Tia.

'What's in it for you,' Mark said, 'is the hottest adventure of your life. Make a deal with me. Try it for six weeks. If having me push your boundaries drives you crazy, I'll stop. If you love it, we'll go farther than you ever thought was possible.'

Tia fought back the temptation to chew her fingernails. What did she really want out of life? Out of men? Whatever it was, she hadn't found it yet.

'Listen, Tia.' Mark lowered his voice to a deep near-whisper. 'I know I look like the total straight-laced professional, but I'm kinky. Under the right circum-stances, I can be very kinky. If you can handle that, you'll love what I can do for you. Or I should say, what I can do *to* you.'

Tia took a moment to digest this. The concept of the kinky urban professional had never occurred to her, but she liked it. Her body was already responding with enthusiasm; a tiny flare had gone off at the heart of her sex and, as she imagined the implications of Mark's offer, the flare blossomed into a flame that coursed through her belly, her thighs, her lower lips.

'I know what you want,' she said. 'You want to mind-fuck me.'

'And does that appeal to you?'

Now it was Tia's turn to make Mark wait. She ran her finger around the rim of her water glass, making a faint squeak. Then she picked up her glass and took the world's longest, slowest sip.

'Yes,' she said. 'I think I'd like to have you inside my mind.'

A smile, slow and triumphant, spread across Mark's face. He picked up Tia's hand and kissed her fingertips, one by one. Each time his lips touched her skin, she thought she would rocket out of her chair. Her legs were trembling under the table, and she felt distinctly moist between her thighs. She wondered if the whole res-taurant could see how aroused she was.

'All right then. We'll start now. Put your hand between your legs,' he said.

'*Excuse* me?'

'You heard me. Do it.' His voice, suddenly deeper and harsher, made Tia jump in her chair.

'Are you serious?' she whispered. 'Are you asking what I think you're asking?'

'You're a smart woman. Go ahead.'

Nervously Tia scanned the dining room. One by one, the faces of the other patrons became familiar to her. Mark had already pointed out the deputy mayor. The woman at the table next to him was one of the city's top news announcers and her dinner date was an outspoken lesbian book reviewer. At the table catty-corner from Mark and Tia sat a local sculptor whose work filled half the galleries and public gardens in town. Across from him was a distinguished couple who were heavily involved in local politics. Tia couldn't recall what the silver-haired man and woman did, or what party they belonged to, but they were famous fundraisers. More importantly, they reminded Tia of her grandparents.

The gig was already over. Tia couldn't masturbate in front of her grandparents.

'I'm sorry,' she said, pushing her chair away from the table. 'I'm not going to be able to do this.'

'Yes, you are,' Mark said. 'You'd be amazed at what you're able to do. Go ahead and try. Keep your eyes on me. Slide your hand under your panties. Pretend you're in bed at night, and you've just woken up from an erotic dream. It was an amazing dream, full of scenes that set your imagination on fire. You're so turned on that you're soaking wet; you're ashamed of how wet you are. You know the dream I'm talking about. Just thinking about it makes you throb.'

Tia didn't have to think very long to recall a dream exactly like the one Mark was talking about. Her last erotic dream had starred Mark himself. He was taking her on a tour of a brand-new building, guiding her through a labyrinth of empty rooms whose scaffolding was still exposed. At one point, he told Tia to walk in front of him and, as he followed her through the hallways, she could feel him getting closer, his physical presence so potent that she started to quiver with suspense. When they reached the end of the hallway, they were standing in front of an open window with a broad sill. The window looked out over the entire city. As Tia was taking in the view, Mark suddenly took her, bending her over the sill and roughly lifting her skirt, before thrusting into her with one motion that made her howl in her sleep . . .

'Go ahead, Tia,' Mark was saying. 'Touch yourself. You're not doing anything wrong. Just a game of public solitaire.'

To her own disbelief, Tia found herself following Mark's instructions. She tugged up the hem of her skirt, slipped her hand between her legs and discovered that she was way beyond juicy. Once she had broken the first rule – touching her private parts in public – it wasn't hard to drift into Mark's fantasy, coasting along on his words. Playing with herself in public for the first time was kind of like learning to swim. As soon as she got used to the rhythm, the motions, she glided unexpectedly into a state of grace.

'Faster,' Mark ordered. 'The food is going to come soon.'

'Me too,' Tia whispered.

She didn't care what anyone thought any more. The world had been reduced to a tight enchanted circle that contained herself and Mark, and at the heart of that space her fingers played a tune on her wet humming sex. In the back of her mind, she heard the shocked whispers of her mother, her grandmother, her aunts – *It isn't nice to touch yourself THERE. My lord, child, what are you doing playing with your hoo-hoo in such a fine restaurant? This nice young man will never want to marry you now* – but her mounting climax blew the voices away like dead leaves.

She knew Mark was watching her. His eyes hadn't left her since he sat down at the table. But she wasn't aware of the details of his features any more; like the rest of her surroundings, Mark's face was blurred by her excitement. She bit back a moan as her orgasm unfurled, the spasms all the more powerful for being suppressed. Rocking back and forth in tiny motions, she let pleasure subtly overwhelm here. Tia wasn't even aware, until she caught her breath, that there was a plate sitting in front of her. The waiter must have brought it while she was coming.

'I ordered oysters for you,' Mark said with a grin. He looked immensely pleased with himself. 'I was under the impression that you needed an aphrodisiac. I guess I was wrong.'

That was how it started, the first step of her adventures with Mark. If not for the fact that Noelle and Leo knew about Mark, Tia might have thought she was imagining this whole thing. She had known patients who dreamt up entire relationships, with complicated storylines that involved all kinds of bizarre activities. Mark's voice could be an exceptionally powerful auditory hallucination, telling her to do things that she never would have dared to do. But she knew that there was no way she was hallucinating his strong forceful body or his skilful hands or his beautiful thick cock. Mark was real, and so was the strange, thrilling journey that Tia had agreed to take with him.

That was the first time Mark ordered Tia to come in public and, in the mental scrapbook she was making about their love affair, it was still the most arousing.

Mark had a key to Tia's apartment, but tonight he'd chosen not to use it. Instead, he watched Tia clatter down the stairs in her platform shoes. She felt his eyes on her with every step. With his light trimmed beard and wire-rimmed glasses, he looked like a young schoolmaster waiting to deliver a brisk spanking. By the time she reached the bottom, she could hardly breathe. After three months, you'd think she would have got used to him, but Mark was a sex magician. Tia never knew what he was going to pull out of his hat. Or his trousers, for that matter.

'I've got something for you, Cherry Bomb.'

'What is it?'

'A small reward. For being such an obedient girl.'

Tia looked up at him through the red fronds of her bangs. 'This morning you said I was in for some punishment tonight.'

'Who says punishment can't be a reward?'

'Hmmm ... that's a deviant twist on operant conditioning. I'm not sure I should trust you.'

'I'm sure that you shouldn't. But if this can't shape your behaviour, nothing will.'

Mark held up a gold paper bag by its handle, dangling it in front of Tia's nose as if it held the world's most enticing carrot. Shimmering tissue paper foamed over the edges. Tia yelped as she recognised the elegant, curly D on the front of the bag.

'You got me something from Delana's?' she shrieked, jumping for the bag.

The elegant boutique was so far out of Tia's shopping turf that it might as well be on Mars. Delana's garments were the Fabergé eggs of lingerie, unparalleled luxury with price tags to match. Only kept women could afford Delana's; you had to be a human pet armed with American Express platinum to step through the door. Tia didn't even dare to window-shop at Delana's. Though her taste in lingerie could compare to any billion-dollar blonde's, her income was too meagre for her to fog up their glass with her bohemian breath.

'Whoa, there. You're going to have to work for this.' Mark laughed. 'This handful of cloth and thread cost me a week's salary. Now that I'm doing public contracts, I won't be able to afford too many of these.'

'Public contracts are good for your karma.' Tia snatched at the bag again, but Mark whipped it out of her grasp.

'You might change your mind when I'm buying you polyester panties from Wal-Mart.'

'Hey, if you've got the balls to walk into the intimate apparel section of a Wal-Mart, I'll be willing to wear anything you buy. Now could you show me what's in that bag before I explode?'

Mark reached into the folds of tissue paper. Slowly, he pulled out a ribbon of seafoam silk edged with creamy lace. He let the bodysuit unfold over his palm like the world's most expensive, sensual Slinky toy, then held it up for Tia to look at.

'Mine?' she whispered.

'Yours.'

She could already feel the pale-green fabric rippling down her torso, making exquisitely cool contact with her skin. The lace décolletage would plunge to her belly button, so that Mark would have unlimited access to the silk spaces underneath. Hemming the edges of the lace was a filigree of hand-sewn seed pearls, which trailed from the yoke of the bodysuit all the way down the bodice. The gusset itself was a scanty strip of cloth, barely wider than a shoulder strap.

'I assume you want to model this little beauty for me.'

'Not yet,' Tia said, looking at the skimpy gusset. 'I'm a bit, um, overgrown at the moment.'

'I noticed that this morning,' Mark said chuckling. 'My redheaded bush baby.'

'Do you want to come in and wait while I shave?'

'Absolutely not,' Mark said softly. He lifted Tia's chin and covered her jaw line with a trail of kisses. 'I've got that part taken care of. Come with me.'

Mark slid the delectable green confection back into its bag. He turned and headed down the stairs.

To her own surprise, Tia found herself holding back. She could feel her cheeks light up like a string of chilli-pepper lights. She and Mark hadn't reached the watch-ing-each-other-perform-personal-hygiene stage of their relationship yet. So far, Tia could still count the number of times she'd stayed over at Mark's apartment, and she still locked his bathroom door when she had to pee. As far as Tia was concerned, anything to do with grooming her bikini area was only a step above peeing. It didn't matter that Mark was already intimately familiar with the topography of the region; she wasn't ready to let him see her plucking, picking, peeing or anything else of that nature.

'Tia? You're on my time, you follow my orders. Remember?'

Standing at the foot of the stairs, Mark had a diabolical intensity in his face that set off warning bells in the frontal lobe of Tia's brain. She wanted to follow, but she felt like the platforms of her shoes were glued to the landing. How far was he willing to go to test her? He had already got Tia to wear a dog collar to the ballet, flash her black lace bra during a courtroom trial and play with herself in the government periodicals section of the public library. Up to now she'd managed to fulfil his orders without getting herself arrested, committed or disinherited, but Mark hadn't stopped pushing the envelope. In fact, according to Mark, the envelope hadn't even hit the table yet.

'At least tell me where we're going,' Tia said.

'Sorry. Can't do that.'

'Why not?'

'That would spoil the surprise, wouldn't it?' Mark held up the Delana's bag, with its precious booty, and swung it back and forth like a pendulum. 'Better hurry. I'm making off with your door prize.'

'Won't you give me a hint?' Tia pleaded.

Mark paused, stroking the short pale fur on his chin as he scrutinised Tia over the tops of his glasses.

'Women in glass boxes shouldn't throw stones,' he said.

'Huh? What's *that* supposed to mean?'

'*That* is the only clue you'll get. Now come on, we have an appointment.'

He pushed open the ornate Art Deco door of Tia's apartment building. For a second he was silhouetted in the open doorway, his tall dark form rimmed with a fuzzy outline of sunlight. He looked like the dashing villain in an old Western. Then he was gone. Tia heard his Hummer starting up outside.

'Controlling bastard,' she grumbled to herself.

After a day like today, she had no desire to leave her comfy old building. Noelle would be out most of the night with her study group, and Tia had hoped that Mark would come inside and spend a quiet evening with her. They would share a pitcher of extra-dry martinis while she cooked one of her specialities: grilled halibut fillets topped with fresh pineapple salsa. After dinner, he would 'punish' her with a leisurely over-the-knee spanking, followed by an even more leisurely lavender-oil massage. Instead, he was taking her away to an undisclosed location, to do something cruel and humiliating that involved personal hygiene.

Then she thought of the sea-green Delana's bodysuit, lying in its airy nest of tissue paper like a treasure waiting for a mermaid. And she thought of Mark's sculpted body, and how it would respond when she wore that delicious piece of cloth for him. After a moment, she bolted down the stairs. Mark might be a pain, but had his operant-conditioning routine down to a science.

'Teeee-yuh!' Mark bellowed out the window of his vehicle.

'Coming!' Tia shouted, bursting out the door.

'In United States v. Douglas, we have the classic example of a citizen defending his Second Amendment rights,' Dale was saying. 'I mean, we're getting to the heart of the Constitution here. You've got a guy who wanted nothing more than to live life his way, on a piece of property that nobody else wanted. Then the government comes along and tries to run him off. Who can blame him for defending himself?'

'Douglas blew the head off a mailman he mistook for a federal agent,' Kevin reminded Dale. 'He used a sawn-off shotgun at three feet. Big mess, Dale. I believe in personal freedom. You know that. But tell me how attacking the US Postal Service served Douglas's constitutional rights.'

Noelle sucked at the eraser of her mechanical pencil. She should have jumped into the debate at this point, but she was too busy watching the two men go at it. Kevin or Dale? Conservative pragmatism or liberal idealism? Which one of these studs would she rather strip naked and drizzle with hot fudge? She had good eye contact going on with Dale, who was detached enough from the argument to notice the tricks Noelle was playing with her pencil. Still, she couldn't deny the pull of Kevin's supercharged intensity.

Noelle didn't have much of a chance of going home with either one of them, but fantasy took her mind off her problems, the biggest of which was waiting for her back at her apartment building.

Jeremy.

Of course, her little brother had to reappear now, when she was just settling into her first year of law school. Noelle kept her eyes on Kevin's face, flushed with the heat of his conviction, but she couldn't stop thinking about the last time Jeremy had fallen off the face of the earth, only to reappear at the worst possible time. Stanford University, her first year of law school. A mellow Indian-summer sun illuminated the old sandstone buildings, and palm trees rose elegantly against a flawless blue sky. Everyone had warned Noelle that her first year of law school would be brutal, and it was. But Noelle loved every second of the torture. After a life of disorder and chaos, she'd finally found the linear, logical paradise that she'd always dreamt of. She loved her gruelling classes, and she adored her university. Everything at Stanford was so orderly, so perfect, from the Mediterranean architecture to the cool abundance of the libraries to the golden-haired third-year law student Noelle was dating.

Greg was an American blueblood, the son of a Silicon Valley software pioneer. Noelle couldn't have made a better catch if she'd used a harpoon; each morning that she woke up with her body spooned against his, she had to slap herself to make sure she wasn't hallucinating. Here she was, a first-year student, and she was practically engaged to be married, while most of her friends were still floundering in a morass of one-night stands, cheap wine and body piercings. Noelle herself was rising from the mud of her past – until Jeremy dragged her back down.

She could still remember that day, strolling across the campus, with Greg at her side and feeling like she held the world in her palm. They were heading for Green Library, where they planned to study for an hour or two before sneaking off into the stacks for a hot quickie. Greg was telling Noelle about his parents' winter home in Colorado, where the whole family went skiing every Christmas. He had just asked Noelle if she liked to ski, and she knew – she just *knew* – that he was going to invite her to Aspen for the nerve-wracking but essential parental review, which would lead to her becoming the lovely and precociously successful Mrs Greg . . .

A small crowd had gathered around the statue of Rodin's *Thinker* that stood outside the library. At first, Noelle couldn't see what had captured their attention, but something about the scene sent a razor-sharp shiver down her backbone. The crowd, mostly underclassmen, were laughing and jeering at the poor *Thinker*, who always seemed to be the victim of some vandalism or abuse, especially around the time of the annual football game between Stanford and Berkeley. As Noelle and Greg got closer, she saw that the kids weren't laughing at the statue. They were pointing at someone who was riding on the statue's back, a skinny dark-haired clown who was waving his right arm and singing the German national anthem at the top of his lungs.

That wasn't just any skinny dark-haired clown,

Noelle realised, with a sinking heart. As she watched in horror, an object flew out of the crowd and hit the singer on the side of the head. It was an apple core, and it was followed by a deluge of other flying objects: spitballs, pencils, textbooks, even some kid's Sketcher shoe.

'Fascists!' shouted the boy on top of the statue. He clung to the *Thinker*'s head as the spitballs flew faster. 'You wanna-be scum-sucking phoney Marxists!'

'Who on earth is that?' Greg chuckled. 'What a loser.'

Noelle stared at him, at his perfect, suntanned face, his sun-bleached hair. 'That's my brother, you jerk,' she said.

Greg's perfect features contorted, as if he'd just had someone offer him a steaming cow pie on a paper plate. 'You've got to be kidding,' he said and laughed. 'No way you're related to that idiot.'

'He's not an idiot. He's got an IQ of a hundred and eighty, and he's smarter than you'll ever be.'

'Right,' Greg sneered. 'You must be as whacked as he is.'

Noelle shoved at Greg with all her might, her blood on fire. Then she was running into the herd of freshmen, shoving and clawing and screaming, pushing a path through the crowd.

'Noelle! I came to see you!' Jeremy cried, flapping his arms like mad. Inspired by joy, he broke into a chorus of 'The First Noël'. His angelic voice silenced the ruckus for about five seconds, then the battery of flying spitballs and jeers started up again.

'On a cold winter's ni-iight that wuh-uhs so deeeeep,' Jeremy carolled, raising both arms to the sky. 'Look, Noelle! Snow in California. It's a miracle!' he cried, through the shower of paper missiles.

'Come on, Jeremy. Time to get down,' she said wearily.

The crowd had grown to include some worried-looking faculty members, and in the distance Noelle could see the campus police barrelling towards the library in their golf cart.

'OK.' Jeremy clambered off the statue without protest, as if the last fifteen minutes had never happened.

Off the statue. Off his meds. Until six weeks ago, Jeremy had been staying in an inpatient unit at a private hospital, trying to get his moods stabilised. Apparently, stability hadn't worked for him, though it had been working beautifully for Noelle. Noelle took Jeremy's hand and lead him away, as he bounced along at her side. Stanford was over. Noelle would take a year off, so that she could help Jeremy get back on level ground, then transfer to a school near her parents' house. Out of her whole family, she had always been the only one he would listen to. And, in spite of the fact that Jeremy had been screwing up her life since the day he was born, Noelle loved him so ferociously that he might as well have been her own kid.

Now it was the same story all over again, repeating itself like the rerun of a TV show that you'd never wanted to watch in the first place. Jeremy had been doing well at college, studying art and music and foreign languages and anything else that caught the light of his mind, until he pulled another one of his disappearing acts. When he resurfaced, it was his sister that he swam to once again, gasping and flailing like a surfer who's gone too far out to sea. Noelle's role, as always, was to hoist her brother up by his armpits and drag him out of the waves.

But this time, Noelle wasn't going to play the lifeguard game alone. Now she had a partner. Noelle twirled her pencil in her slim fingers and smiled to herself. Tia, with her mountains of lingerie and sexy shoes, thought she'd finally landed the perfect man in Mark, someone who would balance out her eccentricities and bring order to her life. Tia's life had got a bit too predictable, Noelle mused. The redhead could use a taste of chaos ... and for Jeremy, chaos was an art form.

Chapter Three

Beautiful Live Ladies (NUDE!) Behind Glass

Tia couldn't believe that Mark was taking his sweetheart – the four-wheeled one, that is – into the ghetto. Though his vehicle, a black Hummer, was built to withstand urban warfare, Mark rarely took his pride and joy out of his own uptown neighbourhood. Tonight, he didn't seem to care about the overflowing bars, the angry clumps of post-adolescent delinquents, the zombified drifters who held up cardboard signs on every intersection, offering everything from eternal salvation to work in exchange for food. Tonight, Mark's attention was focused on Tia. Feeling like Eva Peron, she sat in the passenger seat of the military-style vehicle and watched the streets get seedier, while the gorgeous man sitting beside her kept a proprietary hand on her knee.

'Ten years from now, none of this will be here,' Mark said with satisfaction. 'We'll get this area under control. Keep the bohemian flavour, just get rid of the scum.'

They were passing a bar that Tia used to frequent in the pre-Mark days, a Brazilian restaurant/jazz club where you could fuel up on icy beer and charred steaks before shaking what your mama gave you till sunrise. Tia had survived some manic nights at that place, grinding and undulating under a net of coloured lights, while sweaty, shirtless men pounded out a throbbing beat on Brazilian drums.

'Could we stop there later?' Tia asked, looking wistfully at the club's twinkling windows before Mark's urban assault vehicle swept her away. Mark's pronouncement gave her the feeling that she'd better enjoy the club while it was still standing, before it was razed to make room for art galleries or ultra-hip lofts.

'Not tonight,' Mark said. 'We won't have time. You're probably wondering where we're going, aren't you?'

'Um, yes. You might say that.'

'Well, wonder no more.'

Mark pulled the Hummer into an alley and parked. After switching off the motor, he turned to Tia, his arm draped over her seat, and gave her a level look. 'I'm going to ask you to do some things tonight that I know you've never done before,' he said. 'No matter what happens, I want you to go with it.'

'Is "it" legal?'

Mark grinned. 'Only because you won't be getting paid. Tonight it's going to be especially important that you follow your rules. Tell me what they are?'

'Rule number one: Don't say no,' Tia recited.

'And rule number two?'

'Don't even *think* no.'

'Good. Let's rock. Bring the shopping bag.'

He got out of the vehicle, then walked around to Tia's side to open her door. As he lifted her gently down, she met his eyes, and the look she saw there sent her heart into a trip-hammer beat.

He's in love with me, she thought, suddenly so high that she could have sailed out of his arms. He hadn't said the words yet, but the thought was as clear as daylight on his face.

Then Mark set her down on her feet, and he was leading her down the alley and out into the street. They rounded the corner and stopped in front of an establishment that Tia recognised from her days as a single girl. She'd never been inside but, after a night of drinking, she and her friends used to scream with laughter when they staggered past the place and saw its name written in ornate letters on the window: 'The Adult Booke Shoppe'. As if that weren't bad enough, the 'shoppe' advertised its merchandise as 'Beautiful Live Ladies (NUDE!) Behind Glass'!

'I'll never get over that "live" thing, if I live to be a hundred,' Tia used to tell her friends. 'What's the alternative to beautiful live ladies behind glass? Stunning cadavers in shrink-wrap?'

Now here she was, stepping through the front door of the joint, proving that mockery would eventually feed you your own words. In spite of its quaint name and the fancy script on the windows, the shop didn't look any different from any other hole-in-the-wall porn palace that Tia had ever seen. Racks of videotapes, packaged with all the scarlet glories of female anatomy, lined the walls. The shop's customers were a sombre-looking crowd, an assortment of men who might as well have been shopping for auto parts. Tia gave them a clandestine once-over, half expecting to see someone she knew, but in these surroundings, the customers became as featureless as day-old white bread.

'Can I help you?' asked the clerk, a multiply pierced kid who appeared to be working very hard at growing his first beard. He held a green highlighter in one hand and a dog-eared copy of *Steppenwolf* in the other. Tia missed those days sometimes. Going to college, reading the classics of youth for the first time, and having them kindle fires in your blood. Part-time bookstore jobs. Passionate, clumsy sex with boys who wore eyebrow rings and read Hesse.

'We're here to see Lola,' Mark said.

'Sure. Go on back,' said the kid, turning back to his book.

'Who's Lola?' Tia asked. She'd been relieved at first that the clerk didn't recognise her boyfriend. Now it appeared that Mark was on first-name terms with at least one of the shop's Beautiful Live Ladies.

'Lola is someone from my past,' Mark said fondly. 'From my *distant* past,' he added, noting Tia's sour expression. 'Don't worry. You'll like her.'

He guided Tia through the maze of videotapes, through a curtain of red plastic beads, and into a dark hallway that had the pungent odour of pine-scented Lysol layered with cigarette smoke and patchouli oil. The hall was lined with doors, whose shoddy frames pulsated with the sounds of disco music. Tia didn't want to think about what was going on behind them. Mark stopped at the last of the doors, opened it and took Tia's hand. She found herself balking.

'Don't say no,' he reminded her.

'I'm not saying no. My feet are.'

'Come on.'

Mark gave Tia's arm a tug, pulling her into the room. It was a smoky cave, dim except for a bank of lights that rimmed a mirror, where a woman sat painting black curlicues around her eyes. She turned around to see who'd entered her sanctum, then her face lit up when she saw Mark. A voluptuous blonde wrapped in a black kimono, she beamed at him and opened her arms.

'Markie! Come to Mama,' she said, in a smoky purr.

Great, Tia thought dryly. And I never thought he'd introduce me to his mother.

Lola engulfed Mark in the wings of her kimono and squeezed him tight, her breasts spreading across his chest with the force of her hug. Lola wasn't a lady; she was a broad, in the classic sense, her flesh so richly abundant that Tia felt like a teenage boy by comparison. When she finally let Mark go, his face was brick red, his cheek plastered with Lola's lipstick.

'Lola, I want you to meet Tia,' Mark said sheepishly. 'She's the love of my life.'

'Of course she is. What a doll! You finally met your one-and-only. Didn't I tell you it would happen?'

Lola stepped up to Tia in her three-inch heels, and then it was Tia's turn to be swallowed up by Lola's musky embrace. She was sure she could feel a few ribs giving way as Lola hugged her. That hug gave her proof positive that Lola's bountiful boobs were real, though the blonde's sincere affection soothed Tia's envy. The fact that Mark had called Tia the love of his life didn't hurt, either.

'So what are we doing tonight?' Lola asked. Her tone was brisk now, all business, as she scanned Tia's hair and makeup.

'Give her the works,' Mark instructed. 'Tia's going to wear what's in the bag, so I need her to be absolutely smooth. And I want her to be sexy enough to melt steel.'

Tia reluctantly let go of her prize from Delana's so that Lola could inspect the contents. When Lola's red acrylic fingernails touched the sea-green fabric, the blonde actually licked her lips. Now it was Lola's turn to be envious.

'Delana's. You really *are* serious about this girl.' Lola chuckled. 'No one's ever bought me anything from Delana's, in my whole career. Maybe it's time I separated my work from my love life.' She looked Tia up and down. 'Mark's right. You're going to have to be bald as a cue-ball to wear this.'

'Does that mean what I think it means?' Tia's eyes darted back and forth between Mark and Lola.

'Nothing less,' Mark said with a smug smile. He looked so out of place here, in his Italian suit and his leather shoes ... no wonder Lola had been so thrilled to see him.

'Couldn't you maybe leave one or two hairs down there?' Tia asked.

'We'll see. We might leave a little triangle in the middle, just to accentuate your goodies,' Lola said. 'Take off your jeans and have a seat in the corner.' She waved her hand at an old-fashioned salon chair that looked like it had come out of a beauty parlour in 1952.

'It might be better to do this where there's more light,' Tia suggested.

'Don't worry. I've been helping my girls fit into their thongs and string bikinis for fifteen years,' Lola said. 'I could do this with my eyes closed.'

'I'd rather you kept them open this time, if you don't mind.'

Mark watched Tia kick off her shoes and squirm out of her jeans. His face wore an expression of amusement mixed with lust.

'Panties too,' he said.

'Don't worry. It's just us girls,' Lola chimed in, when Tia hesitated. 'And one very sexy man. He's going to love this.' She batted her false eyelashes at Mark, who responded with a wink.

'At least one of us will,' Tia muttered.

The blonde was gathering an armful of supplies from the mess of bottles, brushes and paints that was spread across the counter. Tia saw her pick up a basin, a towel, a new razor wrapped in plastic, a can of shaving cream and a small flask of oil that gleamed golden under the fluorescent lights. Tia sat down in the high chair. The cracked vinyl seat dug into her bare bottom, but that was the least of her worries right now. Lola pulled up a stepstool and sat down on the floor between Tia's legs.

'This is going to sting,' she warned, squirting a pile of shaving cream into her palm. 'It's mentholated. I know they make special creams to shave the bikini area but, trust me, the mentholated men's cream works best. So do men's razors. I don't mess around with the fancy-schmancy stuff.'

'That's nice,' said Tia, feeling light-headed.

She still couldn't believe this was happening. Lola was spreading the cream across her pubes. The white foam burnt a bit, but the sensation wasn't unpleasant. In fact, as the foam touched her inner lips, the fiery tingle started to turn her on. Mark was standing right behind Lola, getting a bird's-eye view of the procedure. Tia could hear him breathing. Knowing that he was aroused heightened her pleasure even more.

'Ready?' Lola asked. 'I promise I won't leave a single nick.'

She spread Tia's thighs open wider, and made the first swathe with her razor. Tia squeezed her eyes shut, expecting it to hurt, but she barely felt the blade. Lola turned the razor skilfully, shaving every fold without leaving a scratch. Before Tia knew it, Lola was tapping off the excess shaving cream into the basin, and Tia was as bare down there as the day she was born.

'I thought you said you were going to leave a little,' Tia said, looking down at the naked pink shell between her legs.

'Sorry, honey. Smooth is my speciality.'

Lola didn't look sorry at all. She seemed downright proud as she wiped Tia clean with the damp towel.

'Won't it itch when it grows back in?'

'It won't grow back if you shave every day.'

'Every *day*?'

'A few twists and turns with the razor are all you need,' Lola reassured her. 'Once you get used to this, you'll love it. That gorgeous man of yours will give you touch-ups. Just look at yourself in the mirror.'

Tia looked. Her body was different, but somehow brand new. Instead of her familiar form, punctuated by a triangle of red hair, she saw a long swathe of skin, pearly and luminous. She had to admit, it would be a lot easier for her to wear the scantier pieces of lingerie in her collection.

'I could get used to this,' she said.

Lola spilt a puddle of oil into her palm and rubbed the warm lubricant into Tia's freshly shaven skin. Her nimble fingers coaxed a hum of pleasure from Tia's lips.

'She likes that,' Mark commented. 'Naughty girl.'

'Just getting her ready,' Lola said.

'Ready for what?' asked Tia.

'You'll see,' said Mark mysteriously.

Lola gave Tia one last rubdown with the cloth, then

picked up her tools and rose to her feet. 'Time for you to go,' she instructed Mark.

'Don't take too long. I'm ready for her right now,' Mark said, taking a last look at Tia as he opened the door.

'I bet you are.' Lola's laugh was lewd and throaty. The door closed. The two women were alone.

'What are you going to do to me now?' Tia said. She was almost afraid to ask.

'Turn you into a hoochie. Now take off your clothes.'

'Why?'

'Listen,' Lola said, planting her fists on the meaty shelves of her hips. 'We've got a lot of work to do, and not much time to do it. That man of yours is going places. He's not going to wait around all night.'

'OK,' Tia replied. It was easier to be meek and compliant than to try to fight with Lola. She stripped off her pink T-shirt, unhooked her bra and let her clothes fall to the floor, along with the rest of her identity. Here I am, just another live naked lady, she thought.

Strangely enough, the thought didn't bother her much at all.

The room wasn't big enough for a cat to throw a fit in, as Tia's grandmother would have said. But Tia's grandmother would never have set foot in the Adult Booke Shoppe, much less appeared live behind glass wearing nothing but a shimmering piece of cloth that clung to her curves like paint.

'Hope you're not scared of the dark,' Lola said. She gave Tia a nudge, pushing her inside. 'The lights go on as soon as the man puts his money in. Music, too. Soon as you hear it, start dancing. They only buy ten minutes at a shot, so you've got to put on a hot show in a short time, or they feel like they didn't get their money's worth.'

'Wait a second,' Tia said, balking in the doorway. 'You make it sound like some stranger's going to be sitting back there watching me. I thought it was going to be Mark.'

'It probably is.' Lola shrugged her broad shoulders. 'Mark didn't want you to know for sure.'

'Are you kidding?'

'Just following your man's orders. Listen, honey, dancing for strangers can be a turn-on, especially when you don't have to see them. This is an easy gig here. No eye contact, no touching, nothing. All you have to do is move your moneymaker until the music stops.'

Tia dug her nails into the doorway and refused to move.

'Go on,' Lola urged. 'Have an adventure. It's not like you have to do this every night. Ten minutes. Might be the most exciting ten minutes you'll ever have.'

'I sincerely hope not,' Tia said under her breath, but she let Lola push her into the room and close the door behind her. Her heart began to pound. She couldn't hear anything but the whisper of her own breath. Good thing she wasn't claustrophobic. She felt safe for the moment, the way she did when she was a child, playing hide-and-seek with the older kids in the neighbourhood. She was tucked away for the time being, but any second the closet lights could go on, and three or four bigger boys would pounce . . .

A wicked red glow filled the room. Tia froze, like a raccoon in headlights, staring at the pane of glass in front of her. She couldn't see anything but her own reflection. She looked hot – dangerously hot. Lola had teased her hair into a copper halo, and had applied twice as much makeup to Tia's face as she usually wore but, in this lighting, the dark lipstick and smudgy eyeliner turned Tia into a sultry siren. Then the music started. Campy disco beat, perfect for the kind of secret striptease Tia liked to do in front of her bedroom mirror when no one was home. The only difference was that now someone else was watching.

She just didn't know who it was.

Here we go, Tia said silently to her faceless audience. Hope you're the man I love but, if not, enjoy the show.

She didn't know what to do at first. Tia's hands flopped at her hips, which refused to kick into gear.

'Hello, world,' Tia whispered to her reflection. 'I'm live behind glass. We can start this performance any day now.'

Dead behind glass was more like it. A song from Tia's junior-high aerobics class kept running through her head: 'First you shake your hips, then you go like this.' The problem was, she couldn't remember what 'this' was. If she'd known back then that she'd end up half-naked in a box seventeen years later, suffering from severe performance anxiety as she tried to dance for a man who might or might not be her lover, Tia would have paid more attention to the song's instructions, and less to her envy of Cassie Platte's big boobs.

The first move was always a bitch, Tia reminded herself. She just had to close her eyes, hold her nose (figuratively, of course) and dive in. Tia remembered the way Mark had looked that night, when she saw him from the top of the stairs. The way he gazed at her as if he owned her, which he did, at least for twelve hours out of the day. She thought about the way his hands steered her body in bed, and she imagined his hard fingers latching on to her now, making her move exactly the way he wanted her to.

Tia danced. She closed her eyes and just moved, easing into the throb of the music a little at a time. No need to rush anything; if her audience wanted his money back, she'd be happy to pay him for his time.

But somehow she knew that it was Mark sitting on the other side of that glass. Even through that barrier, she could feel his eyes on her skin. When he watched Tia moving, dressing, making love, her skin responded as if she were being painted with an ice cube that was slowly melting: frigid at first, then warm, and finally hot as her nerves felt the contrast of temperatures. On the surface, Mark was cool and utterly controlled, but he had a centre of focused white heat that Tia had never found in any of her other lovers. She caught glimpses of that heat when he was tying her down to his bed, or when he was on top of her, thrusting into her. That heat never failed to melt her.

Tia was melting right now, in fact; she felt herself liquefying as her thighs brushed each other while she danced. She let her fingers trace the long diamond-shaped opening in the green garment, and the sensation of her own touch made her nipples harden. She lowered her head and let her bangs fall over her eyes, so that she was peeking out from under a seductive curtain of hair as she played with her body. Her pulse quickened, in synch with the music's electronic heartbeat. The more she danced, the hotter she got, and the easier it was to tease the man behind the glass.

What was he doing back there, in his dark cubicle? Was he touching himself, too? Mark would never touch himself in public but, then, this adult world wasn't really the same as public space. Here, you could be anyone you wanted; you could do whatever your impulses drove you to do, and no one would look twice.

The red-lit room became a fiery blur. Tia was really getting down now. Something had kicked in, a sensation that she hadn't felt for a long time. She was losing herself, and loving the ride. When the music stopped, she didn't even notice. She kept bumping and grinding, twisting her body, until it clicked. The room was dark now, and quiet.

She blinked. What happened to the music? she wondered. She was just getting started.

Then the door flew open. She recognised the smell and the feel of the man who grabbed her, but the intensity was all new. Mark had never been this hot or fast with Tia before. He always took his time, coaxing her into pleasure until she was shivering with expectation. Tonight, he didn't bother with any preliminaries.

He just unzipped his trousers, tore away the skimpy bodysuit and took her, rough and hard, against the wall. The only sounds in the room were the harsh rhythm of Mark's breath and the syncopated reply of Tia's moans. He rubbed his beard against her throat as he pushed into her, and nipped at her neck until she yelped. His hands squeezed her breasts, thumbs brushing her nipples, fingers kneading her flesh. Her newly shaven skin down below burnt from the abrasion of his body against hers. Every sensation he gave her made her wince and gasp with pleasure at the same time.

Was this really Mark? He'd never taken her like this before: up against the wall, with no romantic prelude, no complicated commands. Just animal sex, needy and raw. When he came, he bit her shoulder and groaned into her skin, pressing his full weight against her as he braced himself against the wall. Tia was still shuddering, still trying to figure out what had just happened, when Mark replaced his cock with his fingers and began to fondle the cling peach between her thighs. His forefinger skimmed expertly across the bead at the centre of the folds, while two other fingers worked their way into her channel. His mouth found her nipple, and he sucked in time to the motions of his hand. The nub puckered in his mouth, and Tia thought she was going to go crazy.

'Make me come,' she begged. 'You have to let me come.'

'Not until I want you to.' Mark slowed his tempo and pulled his fingers back.

Tia whimpered in frustration. 'You can't do that. It's not fair.'

'I can do anything. You're on my time,' Mark reminded her. 'I could tease you all night if I wanted to. I could play with you until you're dripping wet from head to toe, and never let you come.'

'You can't stop an orgasm!'

'Want to bet?'

Mark took his hand out of the crevice between Tia's legs. He cradled the back of her neck and kissed her deeply. She loved Mark's lips; they were warm and curvy, but not too mushy; never chapped, but never slippery. Just right, as Goldilocks would have said. With his tongue sweeping back and forth across hers, Tia thought she could come right now. If Mark wasn't going to touch her, she would have to touch herself.

'Don't even think about it, Tia.' Mark caught Tia's wrist as her hand was sneaking towards her pussy. In one swift move, he had her arms pinned to the wall above her head. 'You bad little girl. You were going to play with yourself, weren't you?'

'What's wrong with that? You love to watch me play with myself.'

'Not when you're being sneaky about it. I caught you with your hand in the cookie jar. You know what happens to bad girls who try to steal cookies, don't you?'

Tia yelped as Mark turned her around to face the wall. He pressed his hand into the small of her back, making her bottom jut out. He stroked her behind for a few moments, his palm gliding over its creamy contours, then he gave her cheeks a firm swat.

'Hey!' she cried. 'That hurt.'

'You're getting a spanking, Tia. Pain is to be expected,' said Mark, his hand landing smack in the centre of her ass.

Tears of surprise and shame stung the corners of Tia's eyes. Mark had never spanked her before. Up to now, she'd always been obedient, doing whatever he said when she was on his time. As her body adjusted to the sting of Mark's hand, the pain subsided into an exquisite tingle that spread from her bottom down to the warmer, more sensitive places below. The hum in her loins was building to a crescendo. She thrust her hips back and forth to meet Mark's hand, wordlessly urging him to spank her harder. When was he going to let her come?

Tia heard a weird noise – something between a squeal and a howl – coming from her own mouth. She'd been gnawing her lower lip as she tried to hold back the wave, but she wasn't going to be able to hold out much longer. If Mark didn't let her climax, that strange, primitive sound she was making was going to turn into the most embarrassing scream of her life.

'OK, bombshell. Punishment's over. You've suffered long enough.'

Mark let Tia go. She fell back against his chest, as limp and wet as he'd threatened she would be. But Mark wasn't done with her yet. He sank to his knees in front of her, oblivious to the fact that his expensive knife-creased trousers were making contact with a filthy floor, and kissed her. His lips made a tight seal against her shell. When he started to suck gently, and she heard the squishy music of his tongue against her folds, Tia went wild. She wasn't even embarrassed when she screamed like a banshee, clutching handfuls of Mark's hair and grinding her mound against him.

Time shifted into slow motion as the long-awaited orgasm took her. She and Mark might as well have been hovering in outer space, for all she was aware of the rest of the world. When she came to her senses, the first thing she saw was Mark's face looking up at her.

'Welcome back to earth,' he said and laughed.

Tia took a few seconds to catch her breath. She smoothed down Mark's hair, which she'd left in a total mess. She brushed her fingertips over his cheeks, his chin, his mouth. He was hers. This incredibly sexy, smart and successful man was actually hers.

Then she asked Mark the question that had been burning in her mind all night. 'That was you watching me dance, wasn't it?

Mark didn't answer.

'Come on,' she wheedled. 'You can tell me now. I mean, it had to be you. Otherwise you wouldn't have been so turned on. It *was* you. Right?'

Though she couldn't see Mark's features clearly in the gloom, she knew that he was smiling when he replied. 'You'll never know.'

Chapter Four

DSM-IV ME + U

When she was in grad school, starting on her Master's in art therapy, Tia had never thought she'd end up working in a public hospital, fighting an ongoing battle to justify her job. She'd imagined herself in an airy, sun-drenched studio, in a private institution that would be protected from the outer world by acres of impeccable lawn. The institution would pay her a generous salary and guarantee her full-time work, so that she could afford to buy a closetful of gauze dresses and accessorise them with bold scarves and funky jewellery. She'd sip cappuccino from a mug silk-screened with Van Gogh's sunflowers as she strolled around the room, studying her patients' work. Her patients would be sad, anxious, vaguely tormented, but, as she encouraged them to express their fears through art, they would reveal a hidden brilliance that would dazzle her.

Yet here she was, sitting in a windowless cinderblock room, across from a rumple-haired patient who not only wasn't displaying any signs of hidden brilliance, but wasn't showing any evidence that she could communicate at all. She clutched a yellow crayon in her clenched fist as she stared vacantly at a blank piece of butcher paper. Tia had planted that crayon in the girl's hand herself, in the desperate hope that she might be inspired to draw something. So far, 23 minutes had passed, and that pale hand hadn't budged. The yellow crayon stood up straight in her fist, as stubbornly cheerful as a sunflower.

'Where did you live before you came here?' Tia asked.

The question had a note of desperation. 'What kinds of things did you like to do? Do you have a family somewhere? A boyfriend?'

The girl didn't answer. Her china-blue eyes didn't move from the paper. Her face was as blank as a doll's. Tia was used to working with patients who were unresponsive, but this chick added a whole new dimension to the phrase 'flat affect'. She was pretty – so pretty, in fact, that a nurse with a sentimental mindset had named her 'Belle Doe'. But no one had come to claim her; no one knew where she'd come from or whether she was being missed.

'Believe it or not, I think I know how you feel,' Tia sighed. 'Blank paper has got to be the scariest thing on earth.'

She rested her chin on her hand. Seven more minutes, and she could call it a session. Her goal had been to spend half an hour with Belle, but she hadn't promised herself or anyone else that she could work a miracle. She'd pored over this patient's chart, but there wasn't much to see. The state police had found the girl wandering along the side of the highway, wearing a frilly white dress ('like the one I wore to my first communion', said her admitting psychiatrist), a pair of battered pink cowboy boots and six strings of Mardi Gras beads. Other than her clothes and the beads, she had no possessions, no identification, nothing but a clear blue stare and a tattoo of a rose on her right breast. The psychiatrist had estimated her age at somewhere between eighteen and 28.

So far, Belle hadn't said a word to anyone, including Tia. At least the girl's silence gave Tia some time to think, and today she was thinking about Jeremy. She was supposed to meet him later this afternoon, and she still hadn't figured out how she was going to handle the situation. She could be brisk and businesslike when she met with him, or she could be casual and friendly. Noelle wanted her to play the big-sister role, but Tia was thinking that it might be safer to play the mental-health professional. Maybe she could be a casual sisterly professional.

Working with Jeremy was going to be a challenge. Every time he crossed her mind, Tia felt a corresponding twinge deep in her belly, down in the dark and dirty part of herself that she didn't usually think about during the day. Had his eyes been blue or green, or an intoxicating mixture of both? Did he always go around without a shirt on, or would he be sociable enough to be more than half-clothed today? Would he be wearing those jeans that draped his lean hips just right, with the ripped back pocket that showed his boxer shorts underneath?

Tia glanced at her watch. Two more minutes, and she could escape to lunch. She was supposed to meet Noelle on the patio of DaVinci's, the restaurant attached to the art museum. Noelle, relentlessly punctual, would be sitting there already, comparing the time on the museum's ultra-modern wall clock with the time on her Rolex. When she wasn't clock-watching, Noelle would be sipping iced Evian with lime and scribbling down her goals for Tia's work with Jeremy.

None of those goals would have much to do with the thoughts that crossed Tia's mind when she remembered her first meeting with Noelle's little brother.

'OK, Belle. Let's call it a morning, shall we?'

Tia pushed her chair away from the table and surveyed the room to make sure all her supplies were put away. The countertop was stocked with glue and glitter tubes, scraps of felt and bags of sequins, lumps of clay in plastic bags and baskets of crayons. It didn't matter what Tia's diploma said, what her job title was, or how she thought of herself – she was helping her patients make crafts, not art.

Putting away the crayons, Tia heard a noise behind her. A small sound, no louder than a whisper, so faint that she couldn't identify what she was hearing. If anyone else but Belle Doe had made that noise, she never would have noticed.

Tia wheeled around. Too late, she'd missed it, but she could see the proof on the page that something had happened. Belle had made a mark. One waxy golden squiggle, just long enough to show that she had been here this morning. Tia held her breath, hoping for more, but Belle's hand was motionless again.

Trained in therapeutic communication, Tia knew that she shouldn't make value statements about her patients' work. She never made comments – good, bad or indifferent – about the things her patients created. Her purpose was to create a neutral refuge, where they could draw and paint and sculpt without pressure or judgement.

With Belle, the old rules didn't seem to apply.

'That's wonderful, Belle,' Tia said. 'Do you want to draw more?'

Belle looked up. Her eyes met Tia's for one quavering blue moment, then she looked down at the paper again. Her fist opened, and the yellow crayon rolled on to the table. Tia tugged the paper out from under Belle's forearms and held it up, studying the single yellow mark. The line was heavy enough to show deliberation, possibly determination. Maybe even hope.

'You know, I think that's the most beautiful drawing I've ever seen,' Tia said.

She could have sworn that she saw Belle's lips twitch up at the corners, forming a shadow of a smile. But Tia knew better than to confuse projection with reality, most of the time. Sometimes a smile was just a smile.

And sometimes it was more.

Noelle had landed the most visible table at DaVinci's, the one where she could get maximum exposure to the partners of law firms she hoped to join. Lunch al fresco with Noelle was always ripe with schmooze potential, but Noelle wasn't sniffing the air for contacts today. She huddled behind the tabloid-size menu, studying the lunch entrées for so long that Tia had to knock on the back of the thing to get her friend's attention. When Noelle put the menu down, Tia caught her nibbling her thumbnail. A bottle of Budweiser, almost empty, sat beside her plate.

'OK,' Tia said. 'What's up? You're obviously a wreck.'

'What do you mean? I'm fine.' Noelle increased the speed of her nail-biting.

'For one thing, you're chewing your nails like a woodchuck; I can see the chips flying. For another, you're drinking domestic beer, and swilling it straight out of the bottle.'

Noelle yanked her thumb out of her mouth. She grabbed the beer bottle instead, and began to pick at the label. 'I came *this* close to nailing Kevin last night,' she said.

'Kevin the future public defender? I thought he was too much of a leftie for you. Weren't you the one who was talking about buying liberal repellant the other day?'

'I want Kevin as a sex partner, Tia. Not as my political running mate. Liberal men are loaded with feminist guilt. That's a good thing; it makes them more creative in bed. He's passionate, he's smart and he's ripped. When a man's got a body like that, I don't care what he does in the ballot box.'

'So what happened last night?'

'We had good eye contact going during the study group. We even played footsie under the table ... well, OK, maybe it was more *me* playing footsie with *him*, but he knew what I was doing. Anyway, when we broke to order dinner, I made my move.'

The waiter interrupted to take their lunch order. Tia ordered rotelli with smoked salmon and a light tarragon sauce, a spinach salad and raspberry tea with two slices of lemon on the side. Noelle ordered another beer.

'What did you say?' Tia asked, as soon as the waiter

left. She was fascinated by Noelle's sexual techniques. Unlike most of the women Tia knew, Noelle never addressed men in the passive voice.

'What do you think I said?' Noelle asked irritably. 'I said, "Let's not fuck around here. Do you want to come home with me?"'

'And what did he say to that?' Tia laughed, picturing the horrified Kevin wilting under the intensity of Noelle's invitation.

'He looked at me with those idealistic, puppy-dog eyes of his and said, "Am I dreaming, or did the Land Shark just offer me casual sex?"'

'The Land Shark? Is that what they call you?'

Noelle made a dismissive chopping motion with her hand. 'That's beside the point. The point is, he was willing. More than willing. He put down his cashew chicken and kissed me. Not just one of those wimpy little pecks, either. This was a full-blown knee-knocker, with heavy tongue engagement. I haven't been kissed like that since I was seventeen. He's either been practising on his arm, or he's got a lot of experience. Either way, he could have had me right there.'

'But something stopped you.'

Noelle gave a deep sigh. '*Someone* stopped me. My pager went off. I made the mistake of answering the page.'

'And?'

'It was our landlady, calling to complain about Jeremy. He burnt a bag of popcorn in the microwave. The hall was filled with black smoke. I had to rush home and make sure our building wasn't a smoking pile of rubble.'

'But it wasn't.'

'Not this time,' Noelle said.

'Anyone can burn popcorn. That's why the bags are plastered with warnings about not abandoning the microwave while it's cooking. I mean, who keeps a vigil over the microwave while their popcorn's cooking?'

'Tia, you're doing it already, and you've only met him once.'

'Doing what?'

'Making excuses for my brother. Everyone's done that for him, his whole life, starting with our mom. First Mom, then me, then his teachers, then his friends. Especially his girlfriends. Females of all ages love Jeremy. Who wouldn't? He's adorable, he's angelic and, when he's on, he's brilliant.'

'And when he's off?' Tia prompted.

Noelle's smile was so brittle that Tia could have reached out and shattered those lips with a tap of her teaspoon.

'You tell me,' Noelle said. 'You're the one who had to memorise the DSM.'

'Oh, screw that. The DSM is just a guidebook to mental disorders. It's not the Holy Grail. Tell me what happened when Jeremy ran away.'

'Which time?'

'The last time.'

Noelle took a slug of her beer. 'We don't know what triggered this last episode. It might have been the pressure of college. It might have been love. Maybe he was feeling so good about life in general that he decided to stop taking his meds. Or it could have been the meds themselves. The side-effects could drive anyone insane. Anyway, one day he just vanished. Didn't show up for classes, didn't come back to his room at the dorm, skipped his appointments with his shrink. Six weeks later, we finally found him, in San Francisco. The cops caught him sleeping on top of an observatory in Golden Gate Park. They'd been after him ever since he got into town. He'd been painting crazy pictures all over public buildings.'

'Murals, you mean?'

Noelle gave an unpleasant laugh. 'If he'd been lucid enough to paint anything as organised as a mural, they wouldn't have put him on the locked unit of the state psych hospital. It took him about a month to float back down to earth again. I just want to make sure he stays anchored to the ground this time.'

'And I'm supposed to weigh him down to terra firma.'

'You could say that.'

'Great. I always wanted to be someone's ball and chain.'

'Listen, Tia, The point of this whole lunch today is to reinforce how important it is that you help me with my brother as soon as possible.'

Noelle took off her glasses, rubbed the pink bridge of her nose, then studied Tia with unfocused blue eyes that had an unsettling resemblance to Jeremy's. Though Tia hadn't seen Jeremy for over 24 hours, her memory of his eyes hadn't lost any of its power.

'All he's done so far is burn a bag of popcorn,' Tia reminded her.

'Oh, believe me, things could get much, much worse. There are a few warning signs I have to tell you about.'

'Such as?'

'One: he starts to climb things.' Noelle ticked off the first sign on her index finger. 'Jeremy loves heights when he's manic, and he's as fast as a greased chipmunk; he can shoot up to the top of a bridge in about fifteen seconds flat. If he starts scaling fire escapes or water towers, that's a good sign that he hasn't been compliant with his meds. Two: he starts painting freaky images. Scenes that are seriously strange, like something from a nightmare, or an Alice Cooper concert. Three: he falls in love. It's always dramatic, and it's always a disaster. Jeremy doesn't handle love well.'

'Maybe that's because love isn't something you handle,' Tia said.

'Thanks, Oprah.'

'No, seriously. If you handle love too much, it goes flat, like overkneaded bread dough. You have to give it room to rise and breathe.'

Noelle stabbed her glasses on to her face, so she could

fix Tia with one of her notorious glares. Now her eyes were all her own again: Windex blue and ferociously penetrating. 'Just remember to watch out if you see any signs of obsessive passion in my little brother. When he falls head over heels in love with someone, he might as well have flashing hazard lights on his shoulder blades.'

'I understand,' Tia said.

'I know you can help Jeremy. You'll be like another sister to him. The most important thing is that you keep an eye on what he's doing, make sure he doesn't destroy his surroundings. He can be a tornado when he gets swept up in one of his brilliant ideas.'

Tia had to blink away a flashback that had just overpowered her: Jeremy standing on the top rung of a ladder, pasting stars on the ceiling over his bed. *You'll be able to see stars in here any time you want*, he had said, so full of excitement that he hadn't seemed to hear the double entendre in his invitation. Tia had heard it. Boy, had she heard it. She only hoped Noelle couldn't see her squirming in her chair, as the echoing temptation of Jeremy's offer shimmered through her body.

'You've had a chance to meet Jeremy,' Noelle was saying. 'What's your assessment?'

Under Noelle's stare, Tia felt like a bug fixed by an extremely sharp pin.

'It's too soon to tell.' Tia hesitated. 'But I think he can make it. I think he could be a brilliant success, if he sticks with his treatment.'

Noelle sat back, smiling for the first time that afternoon. 'Good. That's just what I wanted to hear.'

That was what everyone wanted to hear, that the person they loved would stay stable, stay sane. For most people, people whose moods stayed below a certain amplitude, it would be hard to imagine a sweet kid like Jeremy turning into a wild-eyed rocket. Tia could imagine it all too well. She'd seen that transformation in her patients, the hypo-high that soared into mania, only to plunge back down into a trench so deep that the patient couldn't see the smallest wedge of sky. She'd seen the path of destruction that a manic episode could leave in someone's life: the wrack of debt from shopping sprees, the trail of nameless lovers, the shame of losing whole handfuls of memory.

But behind all that storm was a beautiful, sexy, sensitive young man, holding a handful of stars.

Tia had been fascinated by the *Diagnostic and Statistical Manual of Mental Disorders* since the first day she cracked it open but, in her experiences as an art therapist, she'd never found the book to be all that useful. Relying on the DSM-IV for all your interactions with patients would be like taking a roadmap on a rocket ship. Nothing laid out on paper by a human hand could prepare you for the wonders you'd see in distant galaxies, or the terror you'd feel when you stepped in a wormhole. As far as Tia was concerned, following the DSM-IV was the well-disguised equivalent of whistling in the dark. She'd rather let the patients guide her through their own version of space.

Which didn't explain why she was taking such a conventional approach to Jeremy. Later that afternoon, she found herself sitting with him in a coffee shop down the street from their apartment building, not the bustling, high-profile Starbuck's that Mark favoured, but a hole-in-the-wall place called the Java Dive, which was frequented by poets and novelists who were way too poor to own laptop computers. You always had to bus your own table at the Java Dive, and the staff looked like extras from an Italian zombie movie, but the Dive was Tia's favourite coffee shop in the city.

The owner, whose son had been one of Tia's patients, had invited her to paint a mural behind the bar last year. He had told her she could do anything she wanted, within the limits of public decency. Because the Dive was so dim and gloomy inside, Tia had let herself go nuts with colour, splashing the wall with gold and orange and lime, fuchsia and coral and violet. The result was a portrait of some of Tia's oddball neighbours: the exquisitely pretty ballet student who worked part-time as an escort; the jazz flutist who practised on the roof of his building; the pink-haired old lady who sat at the bus stop all day sucking mentholated cough drops. All of them were exotic or sexy or intriguing in their own way. So far, this mural was Tia's only piece of public work, and she was shyly proud of it. She kept meaning to bring Mark into the Java Dive to see the painting, but she always chickened out at the last minute, letting him lead her on to Starbuck's.

But she was sitting here with Jeremy this afternoon, the two of them perched on high chairs at a teetering wooden table, whose legs were stabilised by a matchbook. Two glasses and spoons danced on the tabletop as Jeremy rhythmically kicked at the table with his sneakers. A white sheet of paper sat in front of him, a copy of the Mini Mental Status Exam that was given to patients at Tia's hospital. Here she was, asking Jeremy to spill his soul on to the lines of an 8.5-by-11-inch form, when she'd promised herself she'd be different from the other 'mental-health professionals' who had been treating him.

'Why don't we start with a little test, just to get things rolling?' she suggested. Her voice sounded cheery and fake, but she couldn't get over the odd thrills and tingles that were buzzing up and down her nerves. Her hand trembled as she pulled a Number 2 pencil out of her purse.

'Sure.' Jeremy glanced at the form and yawned, a jaw-cracker that he didn't even bother to hide. 'I've taken a million of those.'

'Good. Then you'll be familiar with the questions. Can you tell me what day of the week it is?'

Jeremy wrinkled his nose. 'You've got to be kidding. It's Wednesday. I'm here at a coffee shop with a pretty redhead. We're in a state of grace, in the land of Oz, in the summer of love. How's that for being oriented to person, time and place?'

'Great.' Tia marked Jeremy's score on the form. 'I'm going to name three objects, and I want you to repeat their names after me. Ready?'

Jeremy sighed. 'Just give me the form. I'd rather finish it myself.'

'But you're not supposed to fill in the form yourself,' Tia said, as her reassuring prop was yanked out of her grasp. 'I'm supposed to ask you the questions.'

Tia looked at Jeremy. He gazed steadily back. The kid could win any staring contest with those eyes – blue-green flash, with flecks of precious metal floating in the pools like the flecks in a shot of Goldschlager.

'I've got my own way of doing these,' he said. 'Just trust me. OK?'

'OK,' said Tia. She sat back, helpless, and let her hands fall at her sides.

Jeremy pulled a battered pencil box out of his back-pack and, while Tia watched, he attacked the test with a handful of coloured pencils.

'No peeking till I'm done,' he said, making a wall in front of the paper with his right forearm. Jeremy was left-handed. That unexpected observation sent a tingle of surprise down Tia's spine. She'd never had a left-handed lover before. What would it be like to make love with someone who was a mirror of herself, someone who touched and stroked and rubbed her in directions that were the exact opposite of her own?

Stop, she reprimanded herself, pushing that thought back into its evil nook. Tia took a long, chilling gulp of her iced decaf – she was too jittery for caffeine – and hoped that Jeremy wasn't a mind-reader. If he could guess her bra size, who could tell what else he might be able to see?

'OK. I'm done,' Jeremy said. 'Check it out. What's my mental status?'

He pushed the test across the table, sat back and took

a slurp of his cappuccino. The drink left a foam moustache on his face, which he licked off his upper lip with one clean swipe.

Tia took the form. 'It's blank, except for the part I filled in.'

'Turn it over.'

Tia flipped the paper over and found herself face to face with a drawing of herself. It was a spare, fluid sketch, all colourful wavy lines, but she recognised herself immediately. He'd captured her sceptical lips, her cautious posture, but, under those defences, she could see a glimpse of her own spirit, the part of herself she thought of as entirely unique.

'How did you do that?' she asked.

'Pencils.' He gestured at the box of rainbow-hued sticks.

'I don't understand. Why?'

'This is my answer to the test. Every category of questions on the mental status exam can be found in that picture. Registration: I picked out the most beautiful thing in the room, and I drew what I saw. Attention: I noticed every detail about you, but I melted them all down into this one image. That takes attention. Recall: I drew you without looking up. Language-Naming: I can name every part of your body, if you want me to, but that wouldn't be polite with all these people sitting around. Repetition: That's not really here, but you know I can repeat things – I'm not in a coma. Three-stage command: I just followed the same one that artists have been following forever: Find a sexy woman, pick up your pencils and draw her picture. Reading and writing: I've been doing both of those things since I was four; I don't need to prove it to anybody. Construction/Copying: I think that speaks for itself, don't you?'

Tia couldn't say a word. Jeremy had a remarkable gift for leaving her speechless.

'So what do you think?' he asked. 'Am I cognitively impaired?'

'Um . . . doesn't look like it to me.'

Tia couldn't stop staring at the sketch he'd drawn. He'd somehow made a mass of multi-hued swirls that looked precisely the way she felt at that moment in time: awkward and guarded, kind of stiff, but expectant, too. Wanting something that she wasn't quite sure she was allowed to have.

'I had to draw that shirt you're wearing,' Jeremy said. 'It makes your eyes a mind-blowing green. It's intense.'

'Thanks,' Tia said, feeling warm. Her cheeks, from Jeremy's perspective, were probably a shade of red just as intense as the green of her eyes. Jeremy hadn't taken his eyes off her. He sat with his arms folded on the tabletop, swinging his legs back and forth, and humming under his breath as he stared.

'What's that music?' Tia asked. 'Sounds familiar.'

Actually, she'd never heard the tune in her life, but she would have said anything to deflect Jeremy's attention, even a little. Sitting so close to him, she could feel the warmth rising in waves from his sunburnt arms, like heat radiating from a furnace. She smelt the cinnamon gum he was popping as he hummed away.

'Something I was working on in my composition class at school,' Jeremy said. 'How do you feel about the harmonica?'

'Tell me about college,' Tia said.

Jeremy hunched his shoulders around his ears in the world's most overdone shrug. 'What can I say? College sucked. So I left.'

'What sucked about it?'

'What *didn't* suck about it? Too much structure. Too many boring professors. Too many women who wouldn't sleep with me.'

'That sounds a lot like my own college experience. If you substituted men for the women.'

'You had problems hooking up? Impossible.'

'I was shy and self-conscious and I didn't know the

first thing about sex. I tried to liven up my social persona with cheap beer, but that was a disaster. I didn't have a date all through my first three years of college. When I finally met someone, he was a lot older. A musician.' Tia sighed.

'A musician?' Jeremy perked up. 'What did he play? Tell me everything.'

'Maybe later.'

Tia took another sip of coffee, mostly to give herself an excuse to hide her face. She was revealing too much, but Jeremy seemed to do that to her. She wanted to tell him all kinds of things about herself, and she wanted to learn all about him, too. What was going on behind those dazzling eyes of his?

Jeremy leant forwards, squinting at something behind Tia's right shoulder. 'Check that out,' he said. 'That's cool.'

'What's cool?'

Jeremy pointed to the wall behind the coffee bar. 'That painting. I recognise those people! I've seen that old lady with the poodle hair, and the flute player. And that fuzzy guy with the notebook is sitting at the table by the window. Who painted that, anyway?'

Tia twisted a lock of hair around her index finger. 'I did.'

'You?' Jeremy stared at Tia. 'No way!'

'Way,' Tia said defensively. 'That's my work on the wall.'

'Unbelievable.' Jeremy hopped down from the table and bounded over to the bar. He spent several minutes scrutinising the painting, moving in close to squint at the colors and brushstrokes.

'Hey, everybody!' he called to the other patrons, pointing at Tia. 'The lady who painted this wall is sitting right over there. She'll sign your napkins for a dollar.'

'Jeremy. Get back here,' Tia implored.

'I'm serious,' Jeremy said. To Tia's relief, he came back to the table and climbed back into his seat. 'That rocks. You're a real artist. I don't care what Noelle says.'

'What does Noelle say, exactly?'

'She says you wanted to be an artist, but you gave up painting a while ago.'

'Gave it up? I never did!'

But Tia had to admit to herself that her creative well had been a bit parched over the past few months, except for two or three paintings that she'd devised while she was fast asleep and tied to Mark's bed.

'That's good, 'cause you're too talented to stop. You have any other murals like that around town?'

'I wish,' Tia said.

'Why don't you?'

Tia was aware that she should be the one asking Jeremy questions, not the other way around, but his intense attention was going to her head. It felt so strange, so intoxicating, to have a man not only asking her about her art, but also waiting to hear her answers.

'It's not that easy to get permission to paint a mural, especially on public structures.'

'Who said anything about getting permission?' Jeremy grinned. 'Come on. Let's go.'

'Where are we going? We're not running off to deface public property, are we?'

'Not yet. This is just a scouting expedition. There'll be plenty of time to deface stuff later.'

He jumped off his seat again and grabbed Tia's arm, pulling her off her chair. Even as they raced out of the coffee shop and into the street, Tia was aware of the warmth of Jeremy's fingers, each one of them, on the satin skin of her inner forearm. He was fast, much faster than she was ever inclined to be, and, as she raced down the street with him, the familiar storefronts and street signs turned into a blur of colour. Tia's blood thundered, her throat burnt, and she couldn't seem to get enough air into her lungs, but she felt happy, almost giddy, tearing after Jeremy, his energy carrying her like a chariot down the street.

By the time he slowed down, they had run all the way to the business district. Pink cheeked and sweaty and dishevelled, Tia tried to get her bearings among all the sleekly groomed men and women who were flowing in streams out of the skyscrapers.

'There should be some good surfaces around here, don't you think?' Jeremy was barely out of breath.

'Sure,' Tia gasped.

'Are you OK?' he asked Tia, who was panting like a steam engine.

'Will be. Can't ... breathe.'

'Sorry. I like to run. Let's go sit down.'

He lead Tia over to a bench beside a bus stop and sat down next to her, his elbows propped on his knees as he studied the planes of concrete and glass that rose all around them.

'This city's like a cage,' Jeremy commented. 'It's a spectacular cage, but it's still a cage. Just look at all these hamsters running around with their cell phones. These people need some outstandingly rude public art.'

'Where would you rather be instead?' Tia asked. Her lungs were finally doing their job again. Reminder to self, she thought: Get more aerobic conditioning. You're going to need it.

Jeremy turned his head and looked at her. The sunlight struck his face full on, turning his blue eyes incandescent. He grinned, and the crooked tooth sent an arrow of desire shooting from Tia's heart all the way down to the pit of her belly. She'd never had an erotic response to dentition before, but something about that jacked-up fang – sweet, slightly arrogant, out of line with the straight white teeth surrounding it – seemed to represent Jeremy himself. The tooth caught the edge of his upper lip when he smiled, tugging his mouth up at the corner and calling attention to the smooth fullness of his lips. He had the kind of mouth that invited hours of kissing, liquid kissing, like the never-ending plish-plash of rain on a summer afternoon, rain that made steam rise off the skin like mist off a hot sidewalk . . .

'Nowhere,' he said.

'Huh?' She'd forgotten her own question.

'I wouldn't rather be anywhere else. I like being where you are.'

Tia's heart performed an alarming stunt inside her chest, somersaulting in a wild way that couldn't possibly be healthy. How was she going to survive this blue-eyed wonder boy? He had a way of making her feel like she was skimming along the edge of the sky, the way she felt when she was dancing, or painting . . . or having an orgasm.

'OK,' she said brightly, leaping to her feet. 'Let's go look for those walls you were talking about.'

'This way,' Jeremy said, taking the lead again. 'I have a good feeling about this general direction.'

'That's nice. Because I have no idea where we're going.'

'We heading for that big ugly modern-looking thing over there.' Jeremy pointed at a staggeringly contemporary skyscraper that thrust against the sky like the world's biggest steel phallus.

'You mean World Bank? Painting on the World Bank isn't vandalism, Jeremy. That would be considered terrorism.'

'Just wait,' Jeremy said. 'You'll see what I'm talking about.'

They jaywalked across three major avenues, darted through a couple of alleys, and finally ended up in front of an abandoned six-storey building, circa 1890, that was wedged between a parking garage and the World Bank. The empty storefronts of the old building still sported the signs of its former tenants: a liquor store, a sandwich place and an art-supply shop.

'I remember this art store,' Tia exclaimed. 'I bought

my first Kolinsky brushes here, when I was in school! I thought they tore down this building a few years ago.'

'Nope. They just forgot about it. Look at the eastern wall over there. Nothing on it. It hasn't even been tagged.'

'Wow,' Tia said. 'This place brings back memories.'

The front of the building faced a narrow street, a strip of bohemian culture that had all but disappeared from the surrounding neighbourhood. There was a tiny Czechoslovakian bakery, a cobbler's shop, a used-book store and a tiny establishment that was somehow eking out an existence repairing typewriters.

'Memories of what?' Jeremy asked.

'I used to come here a lot when I was in college,' Tia said. Then she blushed, realising that she'd stepped in a big fat double entendre. 'Remember that musician I told you about? He lived across the street, in a one-room apartment over that bar.'

'Is he still there?' Jeremy asked expectantly. 'We could go over and see what he's doing.'

'God, no! I haven't talked to him in years. Besides, the apartment's probably been condemned.'

'I bet he still remembers you.'

'I doubt that very much.' Tia laughed. 'He had plenty of other girls to help him get over me.'

'But you're different.' Jeremy touched Tia's arm. 'I bet he thinks about you every day. I would, if it were me. I'd write songs about you and wish you were still around.' He paused for a second. 'No, wait. I wouldn't be that dumb. I'd go and find you and win you back.'

'What if I didn't want to come back?' Tia asked. 'Sometimes that happens with women. They grow up and move on.'

The window of the apartment where the musician used to live was curtained with dust. Tia doubted that anyone lived there now. What was that guy's name, anyway? Drake? No, Dirk. He had played lead guitar in a local band called Plunger, which broke up when the lead singer was miraculously offered a solo contract by a legitimate production company. When Plunger were still together, Tia used to follow them around from gig to gig. At the end of the night, Dirk would seek her out in the hordes of sweetly sweaty groupies. He would pluck her out of the crowd like a flower – she never got over the thrill of being the chosen one – and take her to the back room of the bar or nightclub and kiss her senseless. With her ears still ringing from the raucous music, she would feel like she was being swallowed by an ocean of sensations: the pounding of the amplifiers, the smell of Dirk's beat-up leather jacket, the texture of his fingertips, callused by guitar strings, against her inner thighs. His tongue used to taste of tobacco and booze, but even that sour flavour turned her on. She remembered that he used to like to french kiss her when she came, so that he could drink the sounds she made as she rocked back and forth against the palm of his hand. Dirk always claimed that Tia's moans tasted better than the finest malt whiskey but, since he never drank anything but the cheapest beer available, she wondered if he was qualified to use that metaphor.

Life was so much better now, with Mark. Mark was just as sexy as the bad boys Tia dated in art school, but he had a career, he didn't abuse any substances and he practised good hygiene. If anything, Tia sometimes wondered if she deserved so much stability. She used to be so wild, so hungry for new tastes and scents and colours, so easily intoxicated by pleasure. Mark knew that she hadn't exactly been a model of propriety in her twenties, but he probably didn't realise that she still felt those desires simmering under her skin.

'I don't mind the idea of growing up,' Jeremy said, rousing Tia out of her thoughts, 'but I don't see how you could just forget about someone you were in love with.'

'I wasn't in love with the musician,' Tia explained. 'And I didn't forget about him. I just wanted something else.'

'Like what? What do you want more than anything else in the world?'

Tia wished she could tell Jeremy not to cock his head at her like that; whenever he gave her that inquisitive stare, inviting her to open herself up, she felt something give way inside. For the moment, Tia had an effective defence system built up against Jeremy, but it wasn't going to last if he kept asking her the questions that men usually didn't ask – and acting as if he truly wanted to know the answer.

To make matters worse, Tia herself didn't know the answer to Jeremy's question. What did she want more than anything? The list could go on and on:

A relationship with a man who sets me on fire, but doesn't burn me out.

A life where I can have lots of adventures, while wearing sexy, overpriced lingerie.

A handful of sable paintbrushes, and a lover who wants to paint me with them.

One perfect work of art, splashed across an entire wall, where the whole city could see it.

'Can I get back to you on that?' Tia asked. 'I've got an appointment at six.'

The angle of the sun on the broken asphalt reminded her that the afternoon was ending; it was five thirty, only half an hour until her time became Mark's.

'Sure. You can tell me later,' Jeremy said, postponing the eternal puzzle of feminine desire as casually as if it were a pizza date. 'When do you want to get together?'

'I'll have to check my schedule. How about if I let you know later in the week?'

'Do we have to wait that long?'

'Tell you what,' Tia relented. 'Why don't you stop by my apartment tomorrow after lunch? I'll show you the art supplies I've got, and we can talk about what else we might need to do the mural.'

Jeremy beamed. The smile that spread across his face radiated enough energy to make the whole city glow.

Jeremy lunged forwards, arms outstretched as if he were going to hug her, but, when he saw Tia pull back, he shoved his hands in his pockets and bounced up and down on his heels.

'That would be incredibly cool,' he said.

'Good. It's a date.'

Cave away, old girl, Tia thought, as a whole section of her defence system crumbled. Good thing Noelle would be at home with her study group tomorrow afternoon. Nothing could dampen a young kid's passion like a roomful of law students bickering over torts. With his sister eavesdropping in the background, Jeremy wouldn't ask any probing questions, make any impulsive proposals or try to throw his arms around Tia and squeeze her against his chest until she could feel his heart knocking against her chest, asking her to let him in . . .

But part of Tia was starting to believe in the extravagant claim that Jeremy had made on the first day she met him, when he announced that he was capable of anything.

Chapter Five

Power Pumps

The courtroom was as quiet as a church after an announcement of Armageddon. The jury members sat open mouthed, held motionless by the spell that Noelle had cast with her closing argument. The echo of her voice, clear and assertive, rang through the vast elegant room, the same room where her mother and her grandfather had served as prosecutors. Noelle was wearing her faithful good-luck charm, her mother's Ferragamo pumps, the shoes that her mom had been wearing when she won the most controversial case of the decade, the trial of a gubernatorial candidate who had been accused of murdering a political opponent. No one had believed that a woman – a woman in devastatingly sexy footwear, no less – could win that case.

And, even after the intervening years of progress, no one believed that Noelle could win her case today. The defendant was a reputable community leader, on trial for statutory rape. The evidence against him was weak, but Noelle knew in her gut that the man was guilty. Her intuition went into overdrive whenever she looked at his sleazy brown suit. She knew that she could win, if the jury had any common sense.

The only obstacle to her victory was the defence attorney. Kevin Blake was hotter than a pistol these days; he had won his last three cases, and the word was that he was impossible to beat. All through the trial, tension had crackled between Noelle and Kevin – jagged streaks of electricity keeping them inseparable, yet opposed. Noelle hated to admit this, even to herself, but, when Kevin had presented his own passionate, heartfelt closing argument, she had got wet. Very wet. So warm and liquidy and loose jointed that, when she stood up, she'd almost lost her famous equilibrium.

But not quite. Noelle had still delivered a kick-ass close, and she knew that Kevin's eyes had never left her taut toned ass the entire time. She'd chosen a navy-blue skirt and blazer that clung to her curves like a scuba suit and, though not even the doddering judge could fault her wardrobe, any male with a pulse could see how fit she was in that number.

The judge's gavel fell; the jury was dismissed for deliberation. Noelle sat packing up the papers in her briefcase, when she felt a shiver of recognition. Someone very powerful and very male (if very liberal) was standing behind her.

'Counsellor, may I speak with you? Alone?'

'Certainly.'

Noelle straightened her notes by banging them on the table with a sharp thunk. Taking her time, she slid her pencils and pens into their appropriate slots in her attaché case. Then she rose, brushing invisible dust off her bottom with the palms of her hands. She topped off the show by giving her buns a brisk oh-so-suggestive smack.

'Damn the dust in these old buildings,' Noelle sighed. 'I can never keep my suits clean.'

'I'd never have noticed,' Kevin said. 'I wasn't exactly looking at your suit for the past four hours.'

Now that she was facing him, his gaze had shifted to her cleavage. Her breasts weren't her greatest asset, but with the help of her Wonder Bra, the mounds rose to valiant heights.

'What were you looking at, then?' Noelle asked, in the cool no-nonsense tone that she would have used with an impertinent mail boy.

'A magnificent prosecutor, with a body to match her mind.'

'Hah!' Noelle scoffed. 'Your flattery is as lame as your defence.'

'Look, Noelle, you're going to beat me on this case. We both know that. You're going to break my winning streak.'

'So? Does that threaten your ego?'

Noelle's mouth felt like it was packed with cotton, and all the soft, secret parts of her body were abuzz, but she still managed to come off like a hard ass. If Mom were here, she'd be glowing with pride.

'As a matter of fact, it does. But I have no intention of crawling out of here with my tail between my legs. Come on. Let's go.'

Kevin took Noelle by the arm. She gasped. He'd never touched her before, and this authoritative gesture literally left her breathless. As he hustled her through the almost empty courtroom, the few remaining stragglers looked up in surprise at the sight of the ball-busting prosecutor being dragged away by the handsome young defence attorney. They would have been even more shocked if they'd known where he was dragging her.

The judge's chambers were empty. The venerable judge was well known for having long multiple-martini lunches with his cronies, but the back of Noelle's neck still prickled when Kevin lead her inside and closed the door.

'I don't know about this –'

Before she could finish her sentence, Kevin had her bent over the judge's mahogany desk. She yelped as her elbows banged into the rich, lovingly waxed wood. Her right forearm sent a crystal paperweight flying across the room; her left knocked over a photograph of the judge standing next to his helmet-haired wife. A draft crossed Noelle's bottom, and she shivered. Up went the skirt, down went the panties and then Kevin's palm – hardened by a summer of volunteer labour building houses for the poor – made contact with her bare cheeks.

Too startled to shriek, Noelle stared at the judge's ink

blotter as Kevin delivered her punishment. She heard herself making a whimpering noise, but she refused to cry for this liberal, pervert-defending bastard. He must have had a lot of pent-up resentment against Noelle, because the spanking went on for what seemed like forever. At first it really hurt; then the pain took on a new identity, and her skin felt radiant, tingly. She actually arched her back, flattening her belly against the desk, giving Kevin access to the damp pink flesh between her legs.

Then Noelle made an amazing discovery, one that ought to rank right up there with the light bulb and the microwave oven. If she pressed her mound against the hard surface of the desk, and rocked her hips slightly to the rhythm of the spanking, she could produce a combination of sensations that was powerful enough to propel her into outer space.

'Never thought you'd enjoy being spanked by the defence, did you?' Kevin laughed.

If she'd been verbal, Noelle's answer would have been an emphatic *no*. No, she never would have believed that Kevin, the ultra-politically correct, avowed feminist, would be capable of spanking a female prosecutor, in anything but the figurative sense.

'I know what you're doing with those hips of yours, Noelle. You just keep on doing it, sweetheart. There's nothing I'd like more than to watch you satisfying your gorgeous self on Judge Pendleton's desk.'

But Noelle heard his words through a fog, because she was already having an orgasm – hard, shuddering spasms that made her rock back and forth against a piece of furniture that was probably over two hundred years old. She didn't care if Kevin taunted her; if humiliation felt this good, he could mock her all he wanted ...

A knock on the door brought Noelle crashing back to earth. She jumped away from the kitchen counter, where she'd been brewing a pot of coffee when she lapsed into her favourite courtroom fantasy, whose most recent star was Kevin Blake. Great, she thought, turning red as she realised that the climax of her fantasy had been all too real. Her sex life was at such an all-time low that she was making love to counter tops.

It wasn't an outraged judge standing at her door, but Kevin himself, looking a lot shaggier and more hippie-esque than he had in Noelle's fantasy. He was wearing a faded plaid flannel shirt, jeans and Birkenstock sandals. His fine brown hair was escaping from his ponytail in wild wisps, and he was in desperate need of a shave.

'What are you doing here?' Noelle asked.

He held up his overloaded backpack. 'Study group. Remember?'

'Oh. Right. I was just making a pot of coffee. Colombian rocket fuel. Would you like some?'

'No thanks. I brought tea.' Kevin unzipped his backpack and produced a plastic baggie filled with dried leaves and sticks.

'Isn't it a misdemeanour to carry that stuff around?'

'This isn't what you think. This is a special blend of herbs, packed with antioxidants. I make it myself. Once you try this, you'll never want coffee again.'

'I find that hard to believe.'

'Don't knock my brew till you've tried it. Where's your teapot?'

'On top of the stove,' Noelle sighed. 'Help yourself.'

As Kevin wandered off to the kitchen, his Birkenstocks slapping against the hardwood floor, Noelle tried to readjust to reality. What happened to the sexy clean-cut defence attorney who had administered corporal punishment in the judge's chambers? It wasn't Kevin's fault that he didn't measure up to her fantasies. Who could? Not even Noelle was the woman of her dreams.

'Hey, Sis!'

Noelle had left the door ajar, and a curly-haired, paint-splattered human projectile came hurtling through it. Jeremy, who never greeted Noelle with anything less than the enthusiasm of a prodigal child, flung himself at Noelle, throwing his arms around her neck. In spite of her irritation, Noelle hugged him back, taking the opportunity to sniff his skin. Jeremy had a distinctive odour when he was off his meds and starting to climb – sharp and citrusy, faintly dangerous. Noelle didn't know where the smell came from, or whether anyone else could have identified it, but she considered that scent her personal alarm system.

Jeremy didn't smell like anything today, except Ivory soap laced with turpentine. Somehow that made Noelle even more nervous.

'What are you doing down here?' Noelle asked. 'You're supposed to be seeing your psychiatrist this afternoon.'

'He cancelled on me. Some kind of golf-related emergency,' Jeremy said. 'I decided that the most therapeutic alternative would be for me to stay home and paint. Which I did. And now I'm here to meet Tia.'

'Oh, really?'

Jeremy nodded. His hair flew around his face with the motions of his head; Noelle couldn't resist calming the curls with her fingers. Her brother's hair, even when it looked like the wool of a hyperactive black sheep, was the softest thing Noelle had ever felt. Even softer than her own tresses, which were constrained in a French braid that ran from her forehead to the nape of her neck like a cod's backbone.

Jeremy stood still and let his sister groom him, but he couldn't stop smiling.

'So you and Tia must be getting along,' Noelle said, keeping her tone nonchalant.

'Slightly. She's only the coolest chick I ever met. We're going to do a project together. That's why we're meeting today, to talk about it.'

'What kind of project?'

'It's still in the planning phase. I'm not ready to discuss it with anyone else,' Jeremy said, with all the self-protective aplomb of a famous artist.

'OK. As long as you're happy.' And stable, Noelle added to herself. 'By the way, you need a haircut.'

'Tia likes my hair the way it is.'

'Hmm. What else does Tia like about you?'

'Everything. She thinks I'm a hot, brilliant genius. And a stud. She wants my body.'

'Hah. That's a good one,' Noelle snorted. 'Tia's thirty years old. I'm twenty-eight, and you think *I'm* as old as dirt.'

'Age is a state of mind. Tia doesn't think like an older woman. She thinks like an artist. She vibrates, like me.'

'Well, you'd better keep your vibrations above the waist. Tia has a mature, very sophisticated boyfriend. She's not in the market for sex with a young brat whose favourite mode of transportation is a skateboard.'

'Who said anything about sex?' Jeremy asked in a wounded tone. 'I wasn't even thinking about going there.'

He slipped out of Noelle's grasp, breaking eye contact.

How interesting, Noelle mused. Tia and Jeremy: a match made in hell. Taken separately, Noelle's roommate and her brother were delightfully idiosyncratic, enviably free. But together, they would be a disaster, neither of them organised enough to tie the other's shoelaces. She'd never intended for Jeremy to fall in love with Tia. A harmless crush would be plenty – just enough to throw Tia off balance, without putting Jeremy in any emotional danger.

'Listen, Jeremy,' Noelle said, taking hold of her brother's shoulders. He was hard to catch, and even harder to hold on to, when he wanted to avoid a confrontation, but Noelle wouldn't let him go. 'It's great that you're spending time with my roommate. That's what I wanted you to do. But more than that, I don't want you to get hurt. Do you understand what I'm saying?'

'Yeah,' Jeremy said, still avoiding his sister's eyes. 'I get it.'

'You've worked so hard to get back on your feet,' she said more kindly. 'I just don't want to see you go back to the way things were.'

'I know,' he mumbled.

'Hi there. What's going on? Is everything OK?'

Noelle had been so intent on Jeremy that she hadn't heard Tia walk into the room. The redhead was holding a distinctive pink bag and, from the pleased, slightly guilty look on her face, Noelle knew that she'd just spent too much money on some flimsy scrap of sheer sexiness.

'Everything's fine. I was just talking to Jeremy,' Noelle said. 'He says you two are working on a project.'

'That's right.' Tia and Jeremy exchanged a long inscrutable glance. Apparently, this project was somewhere on the level of a State Department secret. 'Jeremy came over so he could look at my materials.'

'Ah. Your materials.' Noelle crossed her arms over her chest. 'Should I leave you two alone, then?'

'Tia, can I talk to you? Outside?' Jeremy's face looked tense all of a sudden. His high-flown energy had plummeted to zero.

'Sure.'

Tia put down her shopping bags and followed Jeremy out of the apartment. Noelle tiptoed up to the door. She wouldn't stoop so low as to press her ear against the wood, but if she happened to be standing a foot or so away from Tia and Jeremy, and she happened to overhear their conversation, that wasn't her fault. After only a few seconds, the front door opened again, almost smacking her on the side of the head. Tia walked back in, without Jeremy.

'What happened?' Noelle asked. 'I thought you two were going to spend some time together today.'

'Jeremy's feeling run down. He thought he should go upstairs and rest,' Tia explained. 'That's a healthy sign, that he's aware of his limitations. I told him we could get together tomorrow.'

Tia picked up her bags and blithely walked to her room. Soon Noelle heard the sounds of tissue paper rustling, and Tia warbling a passage from *The Magic Flute*. Noelle was so relieved to hear her roommate singing opera that she went to the kitchen and treated herself to a handful of Oreos, stolen from Tia's stash. Tia was safely in love with Mark and, as ditzy as she could be at times, she wouldn't jeopardise the score of the century. Tia wasn't going to prey on Noelle's baby brother, as much as Jeremy might enjoy being preyed upon.

'Ready to hit the books?' Kevin asked.

Kevin had spread his legal texts across the kitchen table and was already making notes, a cup of herbal tea steaming at his side. Noelle had forgotten that he was here.

'Absolutely,' Noelle said. 'Let's get started. The others should be along soon.'

According to Noelle's calculations, Kevin wouldn't figure out that the rest of the study group wasn't coming – hadn't even been invited, in fact – until at least six o'clock. By that time, Tia would have flown off to meet her alpha-male lover, and the runway would be cleared for a seduction here in the kitchen. Maybe it wouldn't be the scene of Noelle's fantasies but, once she got Kevin out of his Summer of Love attire, she was reasonably sure that he'd be as appetising as she'd imagined.

Tia sang to herself as she unpacked the pink bag from Sassy, her favourite uptown boutique. She'd spent money she didn't have on a piece of cloth so sheer and small that it could be wadded up and pinched between her thumb and index finger. She held the panties in her hands and stretched them out, like a cat's cradle, to admire the way the afternoon sun turned the iridescent fibres into a gossamer rainbow. The garment was more absence than presence; when you bought crotchless panties, you were paying for something that wasn't there. The concept was staggeringly frivolous. As much as she would hate her credit card bill, she would love Mark's reaction to the sight of her newly bare lower lips, exposed in a web of silk.

Just this once, she had agreed to step out of her boundaries and meet Mark before six. He had a meeting with a group of architects and city council members at four, and he had unofficially added Tia to the agenda. She was going to slip in at about four-fifteen to make a surprise presentation. And Tia's show was going to be a heck of a lot better than whatever Mark was presenting with Power Point.

Tia rummaged through her closet, looking for the only business suit she owned. She'd kept the suit for luck; she'd worn it to her interview with the hospital, where she'd been hired as a therapist three years ago. The suit was inexpensive black gabardine, but the cut was stylish enough to make up for the cheap fabric.

So many hopes had been invested in that bargain-basement outfit, Tia thought, as she finally unearthed the blazer and skirt. The suit was crumpled, having been crammed behind last year's Halloween costume, but it would have to do. As soon as she bent over to reveal that she wasn't wearing a blouse with the blazer, no one would care about a few wrinkles. And a crease in the skirt didn't matter, when you were wearing thigh-high stockings and crotchless panties underneath.

At her interview, Tia had worn the suit with a bold purple scarf, an exclamation point of colour to make herself look like a creative risk-taker. Back then, her ideas about art therapy had been so high flown and ambitious. She'd imagined herself making stunning insights into her patients' minds, helping them accomplish miracles of healing with paints and clay. Not even her clinical experiences in school could have taught her how much dogged persistence she would need to coax self-revelation out of her patients. She couldn't help comparing her typical patients to Jeremy, who overflowed with the need to express himself.

Jeremy had sounded off-key when he told Tia that he needed to go upstairs and chill for a few hours. He'd seemed uneasy, distant, not like his usual self at all. Noelle must have been giving him a lecture when Tia walked in, one of her anti-pep talks about keeping his appointments and staying with 'the programme'. Noelle's programme, as well intentioned as it might be, probably didn't jibe with Jeremy's.

Right now, Tia didn't have time to contemplate the change in Jeremy's mood. She was running late, as always, and, if she didn't finish dressing and get her butt over to the courthouse, she would miss her moment. She stripped off her denim mini-skirt and baby T-shirt, then replaced them with the power suit, stockings and crotchless panties in a matter of seconds. A pair of black stilettos (an accessory from yet another costume party, where she'd dressed as a French maid) completed the outfit. She gave herself a quick once-over in the full-length mirror behind her closet door. Not bad, she thought. She looked like a woman with a real full-time job.

Tia foufed her hair, brushed on lipstick and spritzed her throat and cleavage with passionfruit body spray. The final touch to her costume was still waiting in her closet: her old faithful leather portfolio from her college days, as a studio art major. Today she was using it for an entirely different purpose.

'Good afternoon, gentlemen,' she rehearsed to her reflection, doing one last half-spin in front of the mirror. 'My name is Theodora McNair, architectural intern. I've got a little something to show you . . .'

The clickety-clack of Tia's heels rang through the halls of the courthouse. The stony faces of county judges of the past, reproduced in dark venerable oils, puckered in disapproval as she walked by. Amazing, how the staccato of a pair of pumps could turn men's heads, no matter what the woman wearing them looked like. Tia could have had an elephant's head sitting on her shoulders, and every man in the building still would have snapped to attention at the sound of her shoes.

But a glimpse of Tia was well worth a turn of the head. She'd put on a few pounds since she bought the gabardine suit, and the fabric fit snugly in all the right places. She'd worn a sheer lace pushup bra that made her cleavage rise like a loaf of shapely bread and, in the three-inch heels, her legs looked twice their normal length. Thankfully, the big portfolio added a professional flavour; otherwise, she wouldn't have looked much different than the tarted-up girlfriends of the thugs and petty thieves who were on trial at court today.

Tia couldn't help glancing at the defendants who shuffled along in pairs, handcuffed together at the wrists. Each couple was dressed in fluorescent orange jumpsuits and accompanied by an armed guard. The criminals looked sheepish; the guards looked bored. One twosome in particular caught Tia's eye. The only male-female couple she'd seen, they were both attractive, in a Bonnie-and-Clyde sort of way. His head was shaved, and he wore a goatee that reminded Tia of Mark's. Her dirty blonde hair was pulled back in a tight ponytail, but the style accentuated her pouty sex-kitten face. Tia found herself wondering what the two of them had done to end up here.

Suddenly, Tia had a vision of herself and Jeremy, cuffed together at the wrists, shuffling along in front of a jaded guard. Their crime: defacing public property. Their sentence: a big fat fine and three years in prison. Not together, of course. Two lovers could stand trial as a couple but, when it came to serving time, they'd have to do it alone. Tia was surprised at the sense of loss she felt when she imagined not being able to see Jeremy. She'd known him for less time than she'd owned the beloved French bra she was wearing; how could she already be attached?

Tia pushed the thought of Jeremy out of her mind as she rode the elevator up to the fourth floor, where Mark's meeting was being held. Meetings involving the city council were always stuffy affairs. Mark came out of them with his slate-blue oxford shirts stained with sweat – not because he was nervous, but because he had to work so hard to keep from breaking down with frustration at the passive-aggressive delay tactics of public officials. The council regarded Mark with a mixture of awe and suspicion; he was dangerous, an *enfant terrible* who had to be watched and regulated and ensnared in a web of contracts. But, when Mark's projects brought the city nationwide acclaim, there was always a council member scurrying into the foreground to take credit for nurturing Mark's vision.

Mark was in the process of expounding on that vision when Tia cracked the door open and peered into the room.

'All windows, no walls. That should be the motto for the way this city prioritises the renewal of downtown,' Mark was saying. He paced in front of a large screen, where the obligatory Power Point slides were illustrating his speech. 'We need to get past the grime, the blight, the decay – break down the old doors, replace the filthy brick with sparkling glass.'

'I doubt the homeless have much of an appreciation for sparkle,' remarked the deputy mayor. 'Who needs windows, when you don't even have a roof over your head?'

'That's where Nathan comes in,' said Mark, making a seamless segue into his buddy's presentation. 'Nathan? Why don't you tell us about that new relocation project you're working on?'

Nathan was the leader of the Housing and Development Committee. Mark's loyal friend, he acted as a buffer between Mark and anyone who accused him of being heartless to the homeless. As Mark sat down at the head of the long oak table, Tia slipped into the room and tiptoed along the wall. She found her seat in the corner, in the precise location where Mark had told her it would be. He still hadn't looked at her directly, but she knew he was watching every move she made. She lowered herself into the chair, sat up straight and waited to begin her performance.

The crowd wasn't very inspiring. The men who sat around the table looked more like church deacons than city officials. They wore shabby suits, scribbled notes with ballpoint pens and sipped water out of cloudy-looking glasses, which they filled periodically from a pitcher that sat in the middle of the table. At least two of the men were surreptitiously napping, and one kept jerking himself awake. At the far end of the table sat a mousy secretary, who had the honour of operating the laptop computer that held Mark's presentation.

Wow, Tia thought. This gang wouldn't turn a hair if I did a striptease and belted out a few verses of 'Yankee Doodle Dandy'. Mark hadn't even made eye contact with her. The lights had been dimmed, and Tia was starting to wonder if she could scuttle out and make her excuses later, when Mark met her gaze head on. He pulled off his glasses, gave her an exquisitely subtle wink and tapped the eraser of his mechanical pencil against his lower lip.

That was her signal. Tia's pulse speeded up, as she felt her body coming to life. She couldn't leave now, and with Mark giving her that taunting, predatory stare, she no longer wanted to.

'Fifteen years ago, we didn't think we'd ever find a solution to the homeless problem downtown,' Nathan was saying. 'Now we know we've got alternatives, and some of them are pretty damn exciting. Our ideas go way beyond the old solutions of shelters and motel vouchers.'

Nathan wasn't too hard on the eyes, himself; in fact,

if Mark weren't here, he could easily win the Hunk of the Room award. And the guy sitting catty-corner from Mark, the man with the salt-and-pepper hair who had taken off his jacket and rolled up his sleeves, wasn't too bad, either. He reminded Tia of a newscaster she'd had a crush on as a little girl. As she looked around the room, the men at the table came to life one by one, taking on attractive qualities that she hadn't seen at first glance.

Mark always had this effect on Tia; he sexualised her world, recasting ordinary objects and people in the glow of his erotic energy.

'Before you go any further, Nathan,' Mark interrupted, holding up his hand, 'let me introduce the lady who just walked into the room. This is Theodora McNair. She's a graduate student in architecture, an intern at the MacMillan Group. She's taking a course in public contracts, and I told her she could sit in on our meeting today. I trust no one objects?'

The way the faces around the table lit up at the sight of Tia, she was pretty sure that there weren't any objections. The secretary busily added Tia's pseudonym – a name that she and Mark had invented in bed a few nights ago – to the minutes. Then Nathan went on with his presentation and, as soon as the group's attention turned back to the speaker, Tia started her own show, replaying Mark's commands in her mind.

'Just before the meeting, I want you to buy the sexiest pair of crotchless panties that you can find, but leave some leeway for class,' he had said. 'After I introduce you to the group, you'll have to give them a minute or two to shove their eyeballs back in their heads. Once they've calmed down, you're going to do a performance, just for me. You're going to keep the portfolio flat in your lap at first, while you open your thighs. Not too fast, just an inch or so at a time. Keep it slow, keep it casual. While you're spreading your legs for me, I want you to lean back in the chair and open your shoulders.

Wriggle them a little, as if you were loosening up, stretching. Let your jacket fall open, so I can get a good view of the tops of your breasts.

'Next, I want you to work on your skirt. Inch it up, a little at a time. I'll be hard at this point. I might even let you see how hard I am, if you've been an obedient girl. If you've done everything I've told you to do, even the dirty, nasty things that make you blush . . .'

Tia followed Mark's directions, word for word. She never had a problem remembering the things he told her to do. When he took on the tone that she thought of as his Lord and Master voice, his orders burnt themselves into her consciousness. She threw her shoulders back, feeling the weight of her breasts shift and bob under her jacket. She even improvised – Mark loved it when she improvised – fingering the gabardine lapels and lightly stroking the satiny skin underneath. In her jacket pocket was a pencil, which she had no intention of using to take notes on this deadly dull meeting. She pulled out the pencil and flicked the tip of her tongue across the eraser. Just once. She was aiming for a suggestion, not a full-blown simulation.

That minuscule movement was rewarded by a glimpse of a considerable bulge in Mark's trousers. He leant back in his chair and let his thighs fall open, a gesture that was totally acceptable in dominant males. His hips were shielded by the table, so that no one but Tia could see his arousal. Tia smiled. Obsessive-compulsive that he was, Mark would have arranged the chairs at the perfect angle before the meeting. He'd probably been planning this out from the time the meeting was scheduled.

Seeing that bulge was like getting the go-ahead from an air-traffic controller. Tia licked the end of the pencil and ran it along the slope of her breast, letting the lead glide into the cleft between the mounds. Faking a yawn, she let the pencil sink deeper into her cleavage. Mark liked to use that tight soft space for his own pleasure when they were lying in his bed, sweaty and naked. The image of his firm hands squeezing her flesh around his shaft hit her like a grenade, igniting a liquid explosion in her pussy. When she closed her eyes, she could feel his warm weight hovering over her, hear the harsh groans he made as he thrust back and forth in the channel he'd made between her breasts.

Tia was plenty wet by now but, with her portfolio covering her lap, Mark had no chance of seeing how juicy she was. In one smooth move, she slid the portfolio on to the floor. But she hadn't been as discreet as she'd thought; when she started to sit up, she saw Nathan Broderick's eyes fixed on the apex between her thighs. Aware of how she must look, half bent over, with her twin assets spilling out of her jacket and her knees parted, she gave Nathan her best wouldn't-you-like-a-taste-of-this smirk.

'A lot of our stereotypes about poverty have been fucked – oh damn, I mean *fixed* – in the public imagination since the Great Depression,' Nathan said.

Mark, always a generous friend, gave Nathan a knowing grin. No one else seemed to have caught that Freudian plunge, except the secretary, whose face was almost as red as Nathan's. Sweet Nathan – from what Mark had told Tia, he had just been dumped by his girlfriend of three years, only days before Nathan had planned to ask her to marry him. If Nathan hadn't waited so long to make his move, he wouldn't be eating cold pizza most nights of the week, Mark claimed.

Feeling sorry for Nathan, Tia decided she should include him in the audience. From the lustful gleam in Mark's eye, she was sure he approved. She winked at Nathan to show that she'd heard his mistake, but thought it was sweet, then she tugged up the hem of her skirt far enough to show him the lacy tops of her stockings. The elastic dug into her upper thighs, just enough to create two small bulges of soft creamy flesh.

Nathan stared. Swallowed. His Adam's apple bobbed

as he tried to regain his composure. Tia wasn't ready to let him have it back. She let one hand dip into the shadows between her thighs, and moved her wrist languidly, as if she were doing nothing more risqué than propelling herself through a pond on a sultry summer's day.

'But if we're going to move forward as a city, we have to take all of our citizens with us, not just the wealthy,' Nathan went on. Tia had to give him credit; he'd only skipped a beat or two before ploughing ahead. But he hadn't taken his eyes off of Tia's hidden hand. If she had to guess what he was thinking, she'd bet it had to do with replacing that hand with his tongue ... or with something quite a bit firmer.

In the middle of Nathan's speech, Mark's cell phone went off. His personal ringer was the processional march from *Aïda*, suitably ponderous for this meeting. The operatic measures were a welcome break for the committee, most of whom had nodded off as soon as Nathan said the magic word 'poverty'.

Mark crossed one leg over the other, pulled his phone out of his pocket, and took the call. The exchange only lasted a couple of seconds. Mark slid the phone back into his pocket and pushed his chair back.

'Ms McNair, you've got an urgent call outside,' he said. 'Sounds like an emergency. Come with me, I'll show you where you can take the call in private.'

I just bet you will, Tia thought. With a few neat prim movements, she closed her legs, smoothed down her skirt and picked up her portfolio. Mark stood up and strode out of the room. Wrinkling her face into a worried expression, Tia hurried after him. They rushed through a drab little anteroom and into an interior hallway. Mark stopped in front of an unmarked door across from a copy machine, fumbled in his pocket and pulled out a key. Within seconds, he was pulling Tia inside a dark narrow room that smelt of paint and

Pinesol. Just before Mark slammed the door behind them, Tia caught a glimpse of a grove of mops and brooms standing in an industrial-size bucket.

'You know you've really made it when you have a key to the janitor's closet.' Mark laughed into the hollow of her neck. He had his arms around her, and he was pushing her against the wall, his chest a warm throbbing contrast to the cold concrete against her back. 'God, I thought I was going to explode back there. You were driving me crazy.'

'What about the rest of them? Do you think anyone else noticed?' Tia asked.

Half of her hoped that every man in the room had a hard-on right now; the other half prayed that she'd never see any of those people, including Nathan, again. Whose heart was that, hammering against her rib cage – her own or Mark's? She didn't have time to think about it; Mark was yanking up her skirt and plunging his fingers into the wetness she'd been dabbling in only a few minutes earlier. His touch wasn't anything like her own; his hand was rough and demanding.

'Crotchless panties,' he groaned. 'There should be a law that all women should wear them twenty-four hours a day. Except when they're stark naked.'

'You're delirious.' Tia laughed, but she was as giddy as he was. Outside the closet she could hear a couple of women chatting as they made photocopies across the hall.

'Are there rats in that closet again?' one of them was saying.

'No. That's just one of the custodians. They go in there to get sloshed.'

'Great. Your tax dollars at work,' remarked the first woman.

Tia stopped pumping her hips. She pressed her fingers against Mark's mouth. 'I think they heard us,' she whispered.

'Who cares? They're public employees; they could use a little excitement. I locked the door; let them listen all they want.'

Mark scooped up Tia's bottom and slid her a good two feet up the wall. He bracketed his body between her thighs, his hardness digging firmly into the softness between them.

'Reach down and unzip me. I have to get inside you.'

Her hands clumsy with lust, Tia obeyed, while Mark held her pinned to the wall. He was right; crotchless panties should be mandatory, at least for any woman who wanted to be ravished on a second's notice. His kiss – deep and hot and sloppy – went on and on as he pushed into her, moving back and forth at a near-frantic pace. In the dark dusty closet, with Mark's fingers digging into her flesh and his bulk driving her against the wall, Tia had never been so uncomfortable. She was also aroused beyond her wildest expectations. If this was what a woman got from teasing a man into a frenzy, then Tia had found a new calling.

Tia knew that she wasn't the only one enjoying Mark's sexual prowess. Those two women, probably lifelong employees of the public judicial system, were standing outside, slack jawed, as they eavesdropped on the ruckus coming from the custodian's closet. Tia tried to stifle the moans and grunts she was making, but there was only so much she could do, with Mark bearing down on her like a runaway train. All she could do was hang on for dear life and revel in the ride.

Mark's body tensed. He gave a long shudder, muttered a term of endearment – or was it an obscenity? – through clenched teeth, then came.

'Amazing,' he gasped, relaxing his grip on Tia and helping her sink back to the grimy floor. 'What have you done to me?'

'I'm the one who should be asking that question,' Tia retorted. 'Before you, I never would have had sex in a courthouse closet. Not in a million years.'

'Oh really? Then you probably wouldn't have put up with this, either.'

Mark began stroking her again through the gap in her panties, much more gently this time. It was incredible, how his state of arousal transformed his touch. Earlier he had been pawing her with all the finesse of a grizzly bear; now his fingers were exploring her folds as softly as a moth's wings. Good thing, too, because the treatment he'd given her had left her so sensitive that a more aggressive contact would have hurt.

'I want you to come,' he said. A guttural order.

'I can't. Not with those women outside listening . . .'

'That's why you have to come. Come so they know it. I can't disappoint my audience.'

He found the firm little button at the centre of Tia's wetness, and rolled it slowly between his thumb and forefinger. When she let out an involuntary moan, he picked up the pace, and added the extra stimulation of another finger. It wasn't long before she sensed a climax on the horizon, the climax that had been thundering towards her since the moment she sat down in Mark's meeting. The way he'd looked at Tia – wanting her so much, but confident that he already owned her – had turned her inhibitions into a handful of flimsy excuses.

The same thing was happening to her now. Mark was playing her like an instrument, strumming at her tenderest parts with a virtuosity that was driving her out of her mind. She heard herself making a harsh, growling noise, which crescendoed in a moan when Mark's fingers guided her over the edge. There could have been a whole crowd gathered outside the closet, from the cleaning staff to the governor, for all Tia cared. When Mark was orchestrating her senses like this, shaping her pleasure and bending her to his will, she didn't give a hoot about anyone else.

So how far are you willing to bend for this guy? asked a snide little voice in Tina's head. *And what's this about changing your shape? What are you made of – Play Doh?*

A sharp knock sent the voice scurrying away like a mouse.

'Is there someone in there?' asked one of the female voices.

'No!' Mark shouted. 'Go away!'

He held a limp and sweaty Tia in his arms, and they laughed together as they listened to two pairs of solid chunky heels clattering down the linoleum-covered hallway.

'We'd better get out of here before they come back with armed guards,' Tia warned.

'You're probably right,' Mark sighed. 'But I hate to leave. I could stay in here with you forever, doing one nasty thing after another to your gorgeous body.'

'We'd starve to death,' Tia reminded him.

'No, we wouldn't. We'd find ways to satisfy our hunger,' Mark said. And he got down on his knees to demonstrate to Tia exactly what he meant.

Noelle lay on her back on the kitchen table. The corner of her constitutional law book was digging into the soft spot between her ribs, but she wasn't about to ruin this moment by moving. Kevin was just where she wanted him: on top of her. He had unbuttoned her blouse and was working on removing her bra. Noelle was doing her best to resist the impulse to reach up and do it for him. There was a reason these bras were designed to unhook in the front. Kevin understood the rationale; he just couldn't work the latch.

'Your breasts are perfect,' he breathed, as her bra finally surrendered to his tireless efforts. 'They're exactly the right size. I adore them.'

And I adore *you*, Noelle thought, basking in his praise. She'd always considered her tits to be her weak point; they were too small, compared to her hips, and they'd never fill out an evening gown. Her nipples, however, were wide and dark and ultra-sensitive and, when she was excited, those buds took on a life of their own, blossoming like passionflowers. Kevin was just about to discover their exotic potential, when the front door of the apartment swung open with a bang.

'What are you doing? Why are you naked?' Jeremy asked. Incredulous, and apparently clueless, he stood in the kitchen gaping at his sister.

'I'm only half-naked, thank you very much,' Noelle snapped. Kevin leapt out of her way as she struggled into a sitting position. 'In case you haven't noticed, there's a man with me, who's also half-naked. If you weren't so naive, you might be able to read the subtle shades of meaning in this scenario.'

Jeremy blew away the shades of meaning with a wave of his hand. 'I don't care about that. I need to tell you something.'

'Fine. But make it quick.' Noelle crossed her arms over her chest and tapped her foot on the floor.

'I need you to stay out of my personal life. I'm going to fall in love with whoever I want to, and no one's going to stop me. Not you, not Dr Thernstrom, or anyone else.'

'Dr Thernstrom? What did he say? Does he think you're having another episode?'

The reference to Jeremy's psychiatrist had the effect of a bucket of cold water splashed over her libido; if Jeremy's surprise entrance hadn't dashed Noelle's hopes of getting laid that night, Dr Thernstrom definitely had.

'Naw. He just did this man-to-man thing, warning me about getting serious with a mature woman. But Tia's not "mature". She's almost as immature as I am.'

'Well, I'd have to agree with you on that point,' Noelle admitted.

'Just so you know, I'm going to seduce her,' Jeremy announced.

'Wait a second. *You* are going to seduce Tia? Have you forgotten who she's dating? Mark's the kind of guy who gets sold for thousands of dollars at high-society slave auctions in the name of charity. He's beyond desirable, Jeremy.'

'And I'm not?'

'Maybe to an eighteen-year-old cheerleader. Not to a woman like Tia.'

When she saw Jeremy's hurt reaction, Noelle wished she could take those words back and cram them into her mouth. Too late. Jeremy spun around and bounded up the stairs.

'Jeremy, come back! I'm sorry,' Noelle called up the stairs. 'I just don't want you to get hurt. How many times do I have to say that?'

Jeremy halted at the top of the stairs. He stood still, his back to his sister, panting. When he turned to look down at her, his eyes were on fire.

'You can say it half a million times. I won't listen. Don't you see that trying *not* to love someone is harder than anything else? If you don't, then I hope you never do. I hope your life is painless. But you know what? It probably won't be. Not if you let yourself feel anything.'

Jeremy flung open the door of his apartment and disappeared inside. Noelle waited for the inevitable slam, but her brother shut his door slowly and gently, making no sound at all.

At first Tia thought she was dreaming. The tapping on her door worked its way into her sleep, becoming part of a scene in which she was working with a group of elves on an inpatient unit. The elves were busy with minuscule hammers, building magical toys. Their enthusiasm made Tia wonder whether this ward really needed an art therapist. The lilliputian men dressed in green looked much more creative than Tia had been lately.

Tia realised that the noise was real when she opened her eyes to see her door opening. She lifted her head off her pillow and rubbed her eyes, then reached up and switched on the pink-shaded lamp on her night-stand.

'Jeremy?' she said in disbelief.

Noelle's brother was in her bedroom. Jeremy nodded and put his finger to his lips. He was wearing a dark hooded sweatshirt, like something you'd wear to commit a burglary. A black Oakland A's baseball cap was jammed down over his mass of hair, covering his eyes.

'Shh. My sister's still asleep.'

'So was I. How did you get in here?'

Jeremy held up a piece of plastic. 'A library card isn't just a pass to knowledge. I didn't think this would work on your door, but it did.'

'Great.'

Tia clutched the sheets to her chest. She'd been struck by the acute memory that she always slept naked, and that she'd probably been half-exposed when Jeremy opened her door. She also realised that today was Sunday, and that dawn hadn't even thought about breaking yet. She picked up the digital clock on her nightstand and squinted at the numbers.

'It's not even five o'clock. It's dark outside!'

'That's why it's perfect. Come on, we have to go.'

'Go where?'

'You'll find out. Just get dressed.'

Still trying to clear cobwebs out of her brain, Tia shook her head. 'I'm not going anywhere until you tell me what you're doing. Jeremy, this is so inappropriate –'

'I know. But I need you. I can't do this alone.'

'Do what alone?'

'Get out of bed, and I'll show you.'

He knelt beside her bed, his hands clasped on her mattress in what was almost a praying position. His face was a study in longing and, as furious as she was, Tia still thought he was the most beautiful thing she'd ever woken up to. There was a gleam of expectation in his eyes that would have made it impossible for Tia not to follow him, even if she'd been capable of saying no.

'Please,' he said. 'Please come with me.'

'I'm not moving unless you leave. Give me some time to get dressed.'

Tia wrapped the sheets tighter. She'd never been so conscious of being nude. Her heart was pounding from the surprise wake-up call and, with Jeremy so close to her, her pulse accelerated even more. Here she was with no makeup, her hair a disaster, and all she could think about was: why do I care so much what this kid thinks about the way I look?

'OK. I'm leaving,' he said. 'I'll be waiting for you downstairs.'

He stood up and backed out of the room. He dragged his feet, his eyes lingering on Tia's mummified curves, but finally he slipped out the door, and closed it behind him. When he was gone, Tia caught her breath. What had just happened? Her relationship with Jeremy seemed to be all about transference and countertransference, chasing each other like tigers running around a tree, until they blurred into a streak of butter.

After she'd pulled her clothes on and brushed her teeth and hair, Tia went downstairs. The sky was a glum, pre-caffeine shade of blue. Tia hadn't had her coffee fix, and she was feeling distinctly annoyed with the blue-eyed brat who was waiting for her on her front step. She was about to open her mouth to make a peevish comment about how nasty it felt to be out so early on a weekend, when she saw what he held in his hand.

'Double soy latte with Sweet 'n Low,' he said, flashing his crooked tooth as he grinned. He held on to the sleeved paper cup for a few seconds too long, and Tia's fingers brushed his hand.

'Where did you get a soy latte at this hour?'

'Java Dive. They don't open till six, but there was someone in there grinding beans and stuff. I knocked on the door, and she let me in.'

She. But of course. Tia didn't have to work very hard

to imagine how Jeremy had charmed the barista into making him a drink at five o'clock in the morning.

'She wasn't real happy about me being there at first. Then I told her I was in desperate need of coffee so that I could get the most beautiful woman in the world to come out and watch the sunrise with me. That softened her up a lot.'

'I bet it did.' Tia took a long drink of her coffee, turning her head so that Jeremy couldn't see her cheeks flaming. In all her thirty years, no man had ever made her blush so early in the day. She didn't know if that was a promising sign, or an ominous one. 'So is that where we're going? To watch the sunrise?'

'Yep. But we have something else to do first. We have to hurry, or it'll be too late.'

After the swig of caffeine, Tia felt much more alive – almost alive enough to keep up with Jeremy as he set off down the street, his overloaded backpack bouncing between his shoulder blades. Tia followed him at a semi-trot. Except for a couple of joggers, a homeless man and a little old lady walking her terrier, the streets of her neighbourhood were deserted. Jeremy was heading towards the golden-domed Capitol building, which was only a few blocks from Tia's apartment. Tia had walked this route in her stiletto heels and tight skirt when she went to the courthouse to do her erotic performance for Mark. Today she was making the same journey in flip-flops and jeans. The discovery that she felt happier today, in flip-flops and no makeup, caught her off guard.

Without the weekday crowd of attorneys, clerks, secretaries and jurors, the courthouse, with its marble pillars and engraved Latin inscriptions, looked as lonely as an overdressed woman who's shown up too early for a party. Noelle probably knew what all those inscriptions meant. This was her territory, not Tia's.

Jeremy, who had already bounded up the steps, looked back over his shoulder. 'Come on, Tia!'

She was still hesitating, her head filled with memories of that sexy doomed couple she'd seen walking down the hallway, cuffed at the wrists and escorted by an armed guard. 'What are we doing here?'

'We're going to make art. Right here, right now.'

'I was afraid of that,' Tia muttered to herself as she climbed the stairs.

Jeremy had already disappeared around the side of the building. When Tia caught up with him, he was crouching on the ground in front of a sandstone wall, unpacking an assortment of colourful jars from his backpack. The only reassuring thing about this scene was the fact that the paint was in small bottles, not spray cans.

Tia took another gulp of coffee to steel her nerves. 'Care to tell me what you're planning to do?'

Jeremy peered up at her from under the brim of his baseball cap. Her heart did a double-beat at the sight of his smile. 'I'm not going to do anything. You are. I'm just going to watch. And help.'

He held out a paintbrush. Nothing overwhelming, just a size-12 nylon sash brush, the kind you'd use to paint a window trim or do other quick touch-ups around the house. But Tia didn't dare to take it. She could paint on the walls of coffeehouses, but she wasn't enough of a rebel to paint on courthouses.

'You're not serious about this, are you?'

Jeremy nodded.

'We could get caught!'

'So? That's half the fun. Go on. Pick a colour,' Jeremy said. 'You can paint anything you want. It doesn't have to be huge. It doesn't have to be beautiful. It just has to be *there*.'

'But we haven't planned this. We don't have permission –'

'You don't need an invitation to make art,' Jeremy said. He opened a jar of purple acrylic paint, stood up and placed the jar in Tia's hand. 'Sometimes art just happens. Here, if you won't pick a colour, I'll pick one for you.'

'What's Noelle going to say?' Tia moaned.

'Who cares? Noelle's not my superego. She's my sister. And she never has to find out about this. I won't tell her, if you won't.'

'I don't know what to paint,' Tia said.

'Look at the colour. Let it tell you what it wants to be. This is just a dry run, Tia. You don't have to be so nervous.'

'A dry run for what?'

'For the mural. The one we're going to paint together. Remember?'

Jeremy took the cup of coffee out of Tia's hand and replaced it with the paintbrush. He held her hand for a long time, much longer than the time it took to wrap her fingers around the brush handle. Then he took her other hand, the one that held the paint, and guided the brush into the jar.

'Brush into paint,' he said. 'It's instinctive. Kind of like sex, don't you think?'

'Kind of,' Tia echoed faintly.

She felt light-headed, not because she was about to violate several city ordinances, but because Jeremy was standing so close to her that she could hear the jagged rhythm of his breath. When he finally let go of her hand, he took hold of Tia's hips. For a second, she was so sure he was going to kiss her that her lips tingled. Instead, he turned her around to face the stone.

'You can do it,' Jeremy urged her on. 'I'm with you.'

With her was an understatement; Jeremy was holding Tia so close that his body was all but melting into hers. He stood behind her with his palms cradling her hips, his mouth nuzzling the curve of her neck as she worked up the courage to commit her first act of vandalism. The blank wall of the county courthouse stared her in the face. She held a paintbrush dipped in violet acrylic, but she couldn't make herself daub the colour on the wall.

'Just close your eyes and paint,' Jeremy said. 'Every work of art has to start somewhere, right?'

Jeremy's hands slid up to the bend in Tia's waist. His grip was warm and firm. Tia was supposed to be keeping this kid under control, but he was the one guiding her body as she made her first brushstroke on the stone. He was the one making her feel like she'd start acting like a wild thing as soon as he let her go.

But Jeremy didn't let Tia go. His hands never left her body as she painted the petals of a purple iris on the courthouse wall, except when he broke away to get her another shade of paint. Tia forgot that she was out in public. She forgot that she was breaking laws with every stroke of her brush. Under her brushes, something new was taking shape, and she no longer cared about anything but her creation. It felt just like painting in her dreams, only she'd never dreamt that she'd have someone like Jeremy with her, a kindred spirit who also happened to be sexy as hell.

By the time she was done, a flower was unfurling on the wall, lush and wide open. The sun had risen and was gracing the iris with light. Without thinking about it, Tia had painted a calyx that was a botanical version of her own labia.

'You know what that flower makes me think of?' Jeremy said.

Tia was afraid to ask. Her hands weren't very steady as she screwed the tops on to the paint jars; the bottles kept slipping and knocking against each other as she stuffed them into Jeremy's backpack. Now that she'd felt the rush of public vandalism, she was starting to feel the more practical fear of being arrested.

Jeremy got down on the ground beside Tia. 'I want to paint you,' he said. 'Would you model for me?'

'I don't want to be painted,' Tia said.

'You're lying. You've always wanted someone to paint you. But no one's asked you yet.'

Jeremy was right on target. In the months she'd lived with Steffen, he'd never shown any interest in having Tia model for him, though he'd had plenty of other models draped on the furniture, the floor and on Tia's bed. She actually used to lose sleep trying to figure out what those other women had that she lacked. Were her legs too stubby? Hips too bovine? Freckles too freakish?

Finally, Tia had forced herself to face the truth. Steffen didn't find her beautiful. Never had, never would. Sexy, yes. Convenient, absolutely. But not captivating enough to fill one of the canvases that she bought for him.

'Oh, shit. We gotta get out of here. Cops!'

Quick as a streak of lightning, Jeremy sprang to his feet and set off running down the portico, his backpack banging crazily against his shoulders. He was gone before Tia got her first glimpse of the police car that was rounding the long drive in front of the courthouse. She leapt up and ran after Jeremy, but he was so much faster that she couldn't find him at all. She ran two blocks, just far enough to feel comfortably far from the wall she'd just defaced, then she stopped, panting. She was way, way too old for this.

'Hey, Tia! Where'd you go?'

A pair of male arms swept her halfway off her feet. Jeremy had flown into her like a missile.

'Where did *I* go? You're the one who took off running,' she said laughing. 'You're just going to have to accept the fact that I'm older and slower than you.'

'Older is sexier. And everyone's slower than me,' Jeremy said, his eyes dancing.

That cocky grin was really getting to Tia this morning. Every time he smiled, she wanted to mash her lips against his and make out for an hour. But it wouldn't happen. Couldn't happen. If Tia repeated those words to herself, maybe she could get used to the sense of loss that she felt when she thought about keeping her relationship with Jeremy on professional – well, semi-professional – level.

'I'm going to paint you, Tia,' Jeremy said, picking up where he'd left off before the mad escape. 'Whether you like it or not.'

'Let it go, Jeremy. It's never going to happen.'

'I don't let things go,' Jeremy said cheerfully. 'You're going to get painted. No way you'll get out of it.'

Can't-happen-won't-happen-can't-happen-won't-happen. Tia repeated the words to herself as she and Jeremy walked back to their building but, with the memory of Jeremy's touch so fresh and vivid in her mind, the mantra wasn't working. Not even close.

Chapter Six

Random Acts of Kissing

'Rothko was bipolar. Van Gogh was most likely bipolar. The condition seems to be characterised by an odour of artistic genius,' Leo said, tapping a precise measure of Sweet 'n Low into his iced coffee. His nose wrinkled, as it always did when he spoke of anything artsy.

'So what are you saying?' Tia asked. 'That Jeremy's creativity is just a symptom of his disorder? I know you wouldn't say that to *me*, Leo. Not unless you're in one of your fighting moods. Jeremy's talent is part of who he is.'

'But, as an art therapist, you should be willing to accept the possibility that your wonder boy's gifts are fuelled by the ups and downs of his brain chemistry: gloriously high, miserably low. If he were a patient on your unit, you'd be all over his work looking for signs and symptoms of his mood and mental status.'

'Jeremy's not a patient on my unit. That's the whole point. I'm trying to understand him as a person, not as a therapeutic subject.'

Tia and Leo were sitting at the Java Dive, at the same table where they always sat, half in the sun, half in the shade. Tia preferred light, while Leo preferred the seclusion of shadows, and this table offered the perfect compromise.

Leo gave his friend a sidelong look. 'No need to jump down my throat, sweetpea. You're awfully defensive of this kid. Are you sure this relationship is strictly professional?'

'It is so far,' Tia mumbled.

'I see.' Leo sat back in his chair. 'If that's the best you can do, I suggest you forget working with Boy Wonder therapeutically.'

'I never wanted to work with him therapeutically in the first place. Noelle manipulated me into taking on this assignment. She basically wants me to babysit her brother. To help rein him in, bring him under control.'

'If she wants him controlled, she should consult your friend Mark,' Leo suggested snidely. 'He's the control meister, not you. What's going on with Mark, by the way? Does he know about Jeremy?'

Tia twirled her long spoon. 'Not exactly. Well, he knows Noelle's brother is living in our building. And he knows I'm going to be working with Jeremy . . .'

'But he doesn't know you're having lecherous thoughts about a younger man,' Leo finished for her.

'Mark's a younger man, too. He's two whole years younger than I am.'

'Don't try to change the subject, Tia. Your face is a most revealing shade of fire-engine red. Are you in love, or is this just a sexual infatuation?'

'Leo, for crying out loud!' Tia wailed. 'I hardly know Jeremy. We just seem to connect. I don't know where this is going, if anywhere. As you've so kindly pointed out, he's younger than I am. He's too cute not to have girlfriends his own age.'

'If there's a twenty-two-year-old heterosexual male on this planet who can't appreciate the allure of a thirty-year-old woman, I'd like to check him for a pulse.'

'So what are you implying? That Jeremy needs a check-up?'

'No, I'm implying that you should be careful. Use your judgement, especially if you want to maintain a relationship with Mark. A man with an ego like that won't appreciate having a punk like Jeremy infringing on his territory.'

'I'm not Mark's territory, Leo.'

Leo narrowed his eyes. 'Aren't you?'

'Well, only for twelve hours out of the day.'

'And which twelve hours make you happier? His, or yours?'

'His, of course,' said Tia hotly. 'Or else we wouldn't be together.'

'But something's bothering you, isn't it? Something's tearing at a corner of your mind, the way you're shredding at that napkin.' Leo nodded at the pile of confetti Tia had made on the table. 'You might as well tell me. I'll find out sooner or later.'

Tia hated it when Leo tried to crawl around inside her head, but he was right. And he was the only person she trusted enough to confide in.

'Mark has a thing about closets,' Tia blurted.

'Closets? As in cleaning them? Hiding in them? Coming out of them?'

'As in fooling around in them,' Tia said, lowering her voice. 'Mark likes to take me into small dark enclosed spaces, and have sex with me. Forcefully. Preferably when other people are listening.'

'Small dark spaces. Could it be that he wants to return to the womb?'

'Maybe. But I don't think that's it. I think he associates me with surroundings like that. Cramped, stuffy, hidden rooms, the kind of places where you'd seduce the maid, or your secretary.'

'I wouldn't know. I've never had a maid or a secretary at my disposal,' Leo said wistfully.

'But you know what I mean. I think he thinks of me as his personal tart. He's never introduced me to his parents.'

'Wait. Time out. You told me you were terrified of his parents,' Leo reminded her. 'You said they were out of your league, socially.'

'They are. Maybe that's the problem with Mark, too. He's out of my league socially. And no matter how many times he takes me to Le Cerf d'Or, or to the opera or the ballet, I'll still be the tramp he wants to grope in the closet.'

'Fair enough.' Leo stirred his coffee. 'So how does Boy Wonder make you feel?'

Tia wracked her brain, but she didn't have the vocabulary to describe her reaction to Jeremy. All that came to mind was an image of flying, of soaring over the city, looking for clean spaces that could be splashed with brilliant colours.

'I have no idea,' said Tia, raising her hands in an I-give-up gesture.

Leo gave her a tight mandarin smile. 'Don't worry. You will.'

The week had passed without any more interference from Jeremy. No exuberant announcements, no dramatic confessions, no forced attendance at impromptu exhibitions of his art. He met with his case manager, went to his groups, kept his appointments with Dr Thernstrom, his shrink. In fact, Noelle hardly heard from her baby brother at all.

Sheer bliss. Things were going so smoothly that Noelle probably should have been worried, but she wasn't in the mood for stressing, not when she was getting ready for a leisurely afternoon run. Noelle braced herself against the back of a park bench as she stretched her quads, luxuriating in the sensation. She set off down the trail at a warm-up pace, feeling her legs loosen with the motions of her body. Her muscles had been as tight as armour lately. She ought to treat herself to a massage.

Better yet, she should lure Kevin into giving her a massage. Before Jeremy had interrupted their kitchen-table encounter the other night, she'd taken careful note of Kevin's hands. They were broad and firm, with long sensitive-looking fingers. The thought of those fingers kneading the aching muscles of her back into warm, compliant dough made Noelle start to tingle as she jogged along the trail. She picked up her pace, intensifying the friction between her thighs. She was wearing a pair of faded running shorts that dated way back to high school, so they were a size too small. The shorts were riding high right now, the cloth scooting upwards at a snug angle. Noelle ran faster. Her panting added a nice sound effect to her massage fantasy. In her overheated brain, Kevin's fingers were now working their way down her lower back, squeezing the taut curves of her bottom, and gliding into the warm, moist crease between her thighs.

A happy-looking couple was jogging by Noelle in the opposite direction. They said hello as they passed, and Noelle waved at them, wondering if they could tell that she was hot and bothered by something more than her run. She was feeling very juicy down below, and her thighs were so hot at their apex that she could have lit kindling right about now. Meanwhile, the imaginary Kevin was now easing his way on to her, parting her thighs with his knee so that he could ease into her crevice with something a lot more substantial than his fingers . . .

'Hey. Noelle?'

Noelle turned. A man had come jogging up alongside her. Lost in her fantasy, she had to take a moment to identify the blond male with the sexy slate-blue eyes.

'Mark!'

The surprise of seeing Tia's lover sent a shockwave down Noelle's spine. The sensation blossomed into a soft explosion at her core, and Noelle realised, to her infinite embarrassment, that she'd been shocked into orgasm by Tia's perfect boyfriend. Noelle had always thought Mark was a prize, but this reaction was a bit extreme.

'Are you OK?' he asked. 'You look winded. Maybe you should stop and stretch.'

'I think you're right.'

Noelle stopped and bent over, her hands on her knees. She breathed deeply. Of all the mortifying things that had ever happened to her – feeling the gush of her first period in the middle of her sixth-grade piano recital; leaving her sticky panties in her high-school sweetheart's car and having his father find them; slipping naked under the covers with the man she thought was her boyfriend, only to rub up against his horny roommate – this had to be the worst. Other women might lose control of their sexual responses, then write about the incident in letters to *Cosmo*, but Noelle wasn't one of those intrepid girls.

If Mark had noticed her overeager response to his appearance, he wasn't letting on. He rested his hand on her lumbar curve and studied her face with a look of genuine concern.

'You look flushed. You shouldn't jog in this heat. I usually go out in the morning, but I had an early meeting today.'

'I didn't know you were a runner.' Noelle stood up. She willed her face to settle into a pleasant, sociable expression, but she knew that the patches of flaming heat in her cheeks hadn't disappeared.

'I wouldn't call what I do running.' Mark laughed. 'But I like it. If you're feeling better, I'll join you.'

'No problem.'

They started off down the trail again. They were heading into Noelle's favourite part of the park, where the trees were so thick and the foliage so dense that you could almost pretend you were out in the wilderness somewhere. The noise of traffic disappeared, and the asphalt trail gave way to dirt. There was a secret clearing up ahead, a stretch of loamy earth sheltered by the overhanging branches of an evergreen tree, where Noelle and one of her dates had once made out all afternoon. The possibility of being caught by hikers, or one of the park's security guards, had been so arousing that Noelle had actually come twice – something that never, ever happened to her.

She wondered if Mark knew about that clearing. If he jogged here as often as Noelle, he'd probably seen the place. No man with a healthy libido could look at that inviting, dark tunnel without conjuring up scenes of torrid, semi-public sex.

Of course, Mark would be imagining sex with Tia, and that put Noelle out of the picture. She shouldn't be thinking about Mark like that, anyway. Sure, he had a great body, lean and tight and streamlined: not too bulky, not too thin. His hair was just long enough to give him an edgy look, without making him look like a reject from a heavy-metal garage band, and his sleek blond goatee was too sexy for words.

Mark was successful enough that he didn't have to broadcast his achievements, but Noelle knew how accomplished he was. She had read an interview with him in *Urban Pace* magazine, published six months after he won an award for being the most sought-after urban planner in the American West. The article had appeared with a photo inset of Mark, wearing faded jeans and a white T-shirt over his muscular chest, his arms folded in a gesture of casual, precocious confidence.

Noelle had a dark, dirty secret about that article. After she had read the interview with Mark, especially the paragraph where he talked about 'mastering the sprawl of the American city', Noelle had played with herself while looking at that picture. She hadn't done anything of the kind since she was fourteen years old, drooling over photos of her favourite bubblegum pop stars in *Teenbeat*. But Mark's knifelike form against the navy-blue evening sky, the contours of his hips and pelvis in the skintight denim and the cocky thrust of his jaw had merged together in a formula that always had the same result: Noelle got wet. Smart, aggressive young men who designed huge phallic skyscrapers had a tendency to do that to her.

Now, with Mark running along beside her, Noelle felt the ghost of her fourteen-year-old self tickling her imagination. She wouldn't have admitted this to Tia in a thousand years, but Noelle had a serious crush on her best friend's man. Tia had confided in Noelle that Mark had a taste for kink, that he had inspired Tia to do things that pushed her limits to the edge. When Noelle listened to Tia's tales of self-exposure and public sex, she would purse her lips and shake her head and remind Tia that women hadn't spent hundreds of years resisting male patriarchy so that they could wear dog collars at the ballet and nibble peanuts out of their boyfriends' hands.

But, in the sweaty depths of the night, when Noelle was lying awake trying to cram one last case study into her overworked brain, she would let her fantasies wander Mark-ward. If he were to ask Noelle to do some of the things that Tia had done, how would she respond? If he ordered Noelle to slide down between his legs and go down on him during the processional march in the opera *Aïda*, would she pull out her pepper spray and blast him in the face?

Or would she squeeze her tall body into the cramped dusty space between the seats, kneel between his legs, unzip his trousers and do exactly what he wanted?

'We should do this more often,' Mark was saying.

'What?' Noelle almost tripped over a rock, but she caught herself before she could hurtle into her second humiliating moment of the day.

'I was just saying that we should run together more often. We have the same stride, and we run at about the same pace.'

He was right, Noelle noticed. Running beside him was challenging, but she was keeping up. If she were in better shape, she could probably kick his ass now and then. Noelle had stopped running with boys long ago, after her brother had left her in the dust one too many times. In high school, when she was trying out for the track team, Jeremy had begged to go with her on her solo practice runs. Because she'd never been able to say no to her little brother, she'd let him come along, even though she knew the workout would leave her feeling as fast as a tortoise on Valium. Her clearest memory of those days was watching the back of Jeremy's red T-shirt as he flew away into the morning sun.

Two years later, Jeremy had become the star of the track team, winning state championship in three different events. Noelle hadn't even made the first cut at the try-outs. She still loved to jog, with her ipod cranked up, playing her favourite rock songs, but she always ran alone. Running with other people had always brought back humiliating memories of being dusted by Jeremy.

But running with Mark was making her feel good. Too good. They were sailing along on a mellow, even keel, neither one of them acknowledging that the park was emptying and the shadows were lengthening. By the time they finally stopped at a drinking fountain, it was almost seven o'clock.

'Wow,' Mark said, barely winded. 'I haven't run that long in ages.' He gave Noelle a long admiring look. 'I never knew you were such an athlete.'

'Me neither.' Noelle knew that she was beaming like an idiot, but for once she couldn't stop her face from broadcasting her feelings.

Mark glanced at his watch and frowned. Great, Noelle thought. Here's where my fantasy comes to a screaming halt. He's got to rush off to meet Tia.

'Do you want to go get a drink?' he asked Noelle.

Noelle made a sputtering sound. 'Drink?'

'Yes. As in beverage. I'm in the mood for a beer, but you could have water, if you like. Tia says you're a raving health freak.'

'Tia said that?'

'I believe those were her words, yes.'

Noelle stopped for a second, stung. 'Well, I do have a lot of self-control. But anything goes after dark.'

Noelle let her voice curl like smoke around the words. Her seduction techniques were rusty, but she thought Mark got the hint. Tia deserved it, for calling Noelle a freak. There was nothing wrong with exerting a little self-discipline now and then.

'Let's go, then. I can't wait to see what happens to you after dark,' Mark said. 'There's a bar called Racine's about a mile from here. The crowd is always drunk and sweaty; no one will notice a little clean healthy perspiration.'

This is just a friendly drink, Noelle reminded herself, as they strolled to the parking lot, but her knees were shaking and her stomach felt like a jarful of moths. They agreed to take Mark's Hummer, since Mark never liked to be parted from his car, and Noelle had never had a ride in an urban assault vehicle. When he opened the front door for her, he held her arm as she climbed into the passenger seat. He let his fingers clasp her skin for a fraction of a second longer than they needed to.

Mark was just being polite. Just being a gentleman. Just being all the things that Tia said he was. He undoubtedly thought he was doing a favour for Tia's old-maid roommate by taking Noelle out for a cocktail. Later, he would tell Tia all about the altruistic act he performed that evening, and Tia would rub his shoulders and kiss the strong curves of his neck and tell him how kind and generous he was.

What the hell, Noelle thought. She wasn't too proud to accept a mercy drink from one of the city's most gorgeous up-and-coming young designers. Mark was a success story in the making and, at the very least, he'd be a great career contact for Noelle.

And, at the most, he was still eligible. Tia wasn't wearing any sparklers on her left hand. The verdict wasn't in yet on Mark and Tia's relationship, which meant that Noelle had a chance to sway the jury in her favour.

If she were so inclined.

Mark didn't call that night at his usual time. Tia was relieved; she'd been late getting home, and her spirit was still coasting on the currents of Jeremy's enthusiasm. She made a mental note to grill Noelle about her brother's meds. What was he taking, exactly? Was he being compliant? Was he keeping his appointments with his psychiatrist? Tia had worked with enough manic patients to recognise that second-hand high that came from being around them when they were on the upswing. Maybe Jeremy was hypomanic, the bipolar equivalent of being on a low boil.

As Tia got ready for Mark, she noticed that she was looking off-kilter, herself. Her hair looked like she'd done cartwheels through a wind tunnel; her clothes were a wrinkly disaster and her cheeks were a hue that definitely earned her the nickname Mark had chosen for her: Cherry Bomb. Her eyes danced with a half-crazed light, as if they were reflecting the glow of a hundred birthday candles.

Thinking about the mural, Tia felt a promising tingle spread through her hands and arms. She always got that buzz in her hands when she was planning a big project, something that would burst the skin of her ordinary dreams, leaving something absolutely new behind.

By six thirty, Tia's relief about Mark's silence had turned into worry. By six forty-five, she was working her way into a state of panic. Mark was never late, especially when he was claiming his time with Tia. Noelle hadn't come home, either, but that was no surprise. She was probably out studying with Calvin or Kelvin, whatever his name was, waiting for her chance to pounce. Tia already felt sorry for the guy. Once Noelle had her sites set on someone, the poor male didn't have a prayer of escape.

Seven o'clock came and went. Tia gave up. Mark wasn't a vital organ; she could get by without him for one night. Starving, she went to the kitchen to make herself something to eat. As she browsed through the cupboards, she realised that she'd forgotten what she liked. Since she met Mark, she'd been eating the kinds of foods that he favoured. He liked healthy, power foods, not the kind of junk she'd been accustomed to since college, when the base of her food pyramid consisted of the dried noodles group (macaroni and ramen), topped by the cheap proteins group (tuna and peanut butter), crowned by the instant caffeine group (Nescafé and No-Doz).

Lo and behold, at the back of Tia's cupboard, behind Noelle's array of vitamins and herbal supplements, Tia's hand made contact with a dusty package of chicken-flavoured Top Ramen. She boiled a pot of water, added the block of coiled noodles and packet of bouillon, *et voilà*, instant nostalgia. She carried the steaming bowl into the living room, where she curled up on her futon and grabbed the remote control.

Within half an hour, Tia was engrossed in reality television. Winding masses of noodles around her fork, she watched the misadventures of a woman who was trying to find a husband. Tia thought the title of the show, *Never Too Late*, was grossly unfair, considering that the woman was only three years older than she was.

'I feel like a turkey in the oven, whose buzzer went off about an hour ago,' complained the woman, a bleached-blonde cocktail waitress from Daytona Beach. 'I really want to settle down before it gets too late, but the fish aren't biting like they used to. I blew a few chances back in my twenties. Some of those guys are probably married and divorced by now – I might have a chance, if I could hook up with one of them again.'

Tia snuggled into the futon, curling her body around the warm bowl. Good thing I don't have to worry about finding a mate any more, she thought, feeling safe and smug and cosy. Mark was already dropping hints about having her move in with him and, though she hated the thought of leaving her charming 1920s building, she could get used to Mark's ultra-modern loft. Most of all, she loved the man who had marked that loft with all the passions and achievements of his life, from his design and architecture awards to his collection of opera CDs to his trophies from the high-school swimming team.

She was letting her thoughts wander from Mark's apartment to Mark himself, thinking about how strong and powerful he felt when he came up behind her in his kitchen and pulled her away from whatever she was doing, scooped her off her feet and carried her to his bed, which was so enormous that it seemed to float in the centre of the loft like an island. And, once she was with him on that island, Tia could give herself up, surrendering to whatever Mark wanted. He was as gifted at sex as he was at design – maybe more so, because his desire for Tia stoked his imagination. Every experience was like a fabulous building that he constructed for her, complete with walls and windows, skylights and doors, and ceilings that opened straight into the sky. And, inside these structures, she was extravagantly naked, free to do whatever Mark ordered her to do, no matter how wild, kinky or downright dirty it might be.

Tia set her soup bowl on the coffee table and glanced at her watch. Quarter past eight. Where *was* Mark? It wasn't like him not to phone. Not like him at all. Suddenly she heard footsteps outside the front door and she bolted off the futon, her heart tripping with anticipation. But her spirits plummeted back into place when the footsteps went away.

Someone had slid a folded piece of paper under the door. Tia walked over, picked up the paper and opened it.

Tia didn't have to study the handwriting for very long to recognise the curves and back-loops of a left-handed writer. And she didn't have to read all the content to realise that the writer was Jeremy.

'My Mini Mental Status Examination,' read the left-handed squiggles across the top of the page. 'Best taken while drunk or high, preferably while thinking about me.'

A smile spread across Tia's face, matching the slow warm pleasure that was unfurling inside her chest. She wasn't drunk or high (not on any artificial substances, anyway), but what the hell. Jeremy had been willing to take her test; the least she could do was take his.

Tia curled up on the futon with Jeremy's test and a freshly sharpened Number 2 pencil. Using a coffee-table book of pictures of Greece as her lapdesk, she began to read his questions:

Orientation (Choose your favourite)
- Bach or Elvis?
- Green Goblin or Spiderman?
- Crack or chocolate-covered espresso beans?

Self-concept (The questions get more personal)
- What do you dream about when you're sleeping alone?
- What do you dream about when you're sleeping with someone else?
- What's the first Halloween costume you ever wore?
- Would you wear that costume now?
- What's the most important thing you could teach another person, if the two of you were stranded together on a desert island?

Ethical Index (Squirm on it, Tia!)
- If you were the last person alive on earth, would you stop your car at a stoplight?

- If you were the last person alive on earth, would you dance naked in the street?
- If you kissed a stranger blindfolded and it was the best kiss you ever had, would you want to know who kissed you?
- Would you tell your boyfriend you'd been kissed by someone else?

Tia laughed in spite of herself. She shouldn't put up with this; Wonder Brat was melting a path through her boundaries and, the way she felt now, those walls might as well be made of butter. But how had he guessed that chocolate-covered espresso beans were her personal version of crack? And who had ever asked her whether she'd dance naked in the street if she were the last person on earth? The answer was a loud ecstatic YES!, but that wasn't any of Jeremy's business. If that hypothetical scenario ever happened, he wouldn't be around to spy on Tia's naked dance, anyway.

When she got to the questions about blindfolded kissing, Tia's mouth started to go dry. When she read the very last question, her hands began to shake. She had to clutch the paper tight, or it would have flown straight out of her fingers and through the window.

The last line of Jeremy's exam was: *Would you ever think about kissing me?*

Now there was a question.

Would she do it?

Absolutely.

Not.

Without giving herself time to think calmly about how to handle this situation, Tia marched out of the door of her apartment. She should have known, after three years of working with psychiatric patients, that it was dangerous to let your barriers slide. You couldn't let yourself be manipulated, or seduced. You had to be honest, first and foremost, with yourself.

Jeremy must have been lurking behind his front door,

because she only had to rap once. She was raising her fist for the second knock when he threw the door open. He wore a black T-shirt, stained with paint, over his low-slung jeans. His bare feet were paint spattered, too, and there was a bright-blue smear across his right cheek. His tousled hair fell over his forehead in a way that was both sexy and endearing.

Why did he have to be so damn cute? She could have killed Noelle at this moment for pushing Jeremy into her life. Just when Tia was learning the adult pleasures of sophistication and control, here was some ridiculously adorable, paint-stained punk making her run around the city like a fool and wanting her to answer questions that were too intimate and bizarre for words.

'What do you think?' Jeremy asked. He beamed with such utter joy, such childlike pride in the work that Tia held in her hands, that the scolding she'd planned to deliver stuck in her throat.

'How is this supposed to reflect my mental status?' Tia asked. Her strict admonishment came out in a helpless squawk.

Jeremy had the decency to look embarrassed. He stared at the ground and scuffed the floor with his bare toes. Tia couldn't help noticing that he had beautiful feet: alabaster white, laced with blue veins, flawlessly shaped. If Michelangelo had seen those feet, he would have begged Jeremy to let him sculpt them, without the multicoloured paint splatters, of course.

'It's not really about your mental status,' Jeremy said.

'So it's a joke?'

'No.' Scuff, scuff.

'What is it then?' Tia pressed.

'It's ... um ...'

'Look, if there's anything you want to know about me, you should just come out and ask. From now on, I want us to be up-front about everything. No more tricks. Here. Take this back.'

Tia handed the piece of paper to Jeremy. He took it

without a word. She reached out and closed Jeremy's door, making enough of a bang to emphasise her point. Then she walked briskly back to her apartment, brushing off her jeans as if she'd just cleaned up a troublesome mess. She stopped for a moment in front of her own door, took a deep breath and let it out again.

There. Much better. Tia placed her hand on her doorknob and turned it. The knob rattled, but didn't give. She'd locked herself out.

'Shit!' Tia cried. 'Shit-shit-shit!'

She pounded on the wood with both fists. All the emotions she'd just tried so hard to squelch – happiness, joy, confusion, anger – came rushing back with a vengeance. She shook the doorknob with all her might, but it wouldn't give way. It was late; she was tired and she couldn't even get back to her safe nest.

'Tia?'

She spun around, wiping a tear of frustration off her cheek. Jeremy stood there, pale and miserable. There was a cast of pain on his face that made him look suddenly older, more like a man than a boy. Tia saw the accumulation of his experiences in that face, all the wounds and uncertainties, the shame and fear.

'There was only one question on that quiz that mattered,' Jeremy said. 'I'm sorry that I couldn't come right out and ask it. I was too afraid you'd say no. And it was important to me – really important – that you say yes, because I like you. I think I more than like you. I'm not totally sure about this, but I think I'm falling in love with you.'

'You ... what?' Tia stammered. 'You ... why?'

'Because you're everything. You're sexy, you're talented, you're sweet, you're smart. And most of all because you *get* me. You're not scared of me. Are you?'

'No,' Tia said. She had to wrap her arms around her body because she was shaking and she couldn't make herself stop.

Jeremy moved closer, reaching carefully for Tia, as if

she were a stray kitten. Something happened then, a curtain seemed to fall over Tia's conscience, as Jeremy's arms opened for her. She was falling into him, and he was kissing her, and her consciousness dwindled to that single point, the point where their lips met, because that warm soft place was the beginning of a world. They could have spent three minutes in liplock, or three hours; Tia had no idea how much time she spent in the eye of that tornado. She only knew that she was high – soaring, spinning and then dancing leaflike to solid ground again when Jeremy finally let her go.

'He's here,' Jeremy whispered. His fingers skimmed the surface of Tia's hair, her cheeks, her throat, her shoulders, as if he were trying to put her back together after blowing her to pieces with that kiss.

'Who?'

'Your boyfriend. You'll be able to get back into your apartment now.'

Jeremy nodded in the direction of the stairwell. The whole foyer of the building had filled with light from the headlights of Mark's Hummer. Muffled strains of *Die Valkyrie* echoed from the vehicle. Some drivers blasted rap music when they were behind the wheel; Mark blasted the Ring Cycle.

The lights went off. The music stopped. The roar of the engine died away, and then Tia heard Jeremy's front door slam. She looked around for the boy who had just given her the most mind-altering kiss of her life, but he had disappeared.

Noelle and Mark sat in the front seat of Mark's car. He'd switched the headlights off. A promising electricity filled the vehicle's interior, that good old first-date anticipation that Noelle hadn't experienced since high school. As a grown woman, she'd worked hard to streamline her pursuits so that she'd reach the goal she desired: efficiently orgasmic sex with men who were as driven and career obsessed as she was. That hopeful

uncertainty of her teenage years, the kind of expectation that left her nerves abuzz and her stomach in
turmoil, was long gone. She hadn't realised how much
she missed being out of control.

'I had fun tonight,' Mark said. 'Even if I had to let you
win at darts.'

'Let me win?' Noelle snorted. 'I kicked your butt, fair
and square.'

They had started out ordering a couple of draft beers,
then the two beers had turned into a pitcher and a few
shots of Jack Daniels, topped off with two baskets of
tabasco-drenched chicken wings. Noelle could already
feel the first sinister rumblings of heartburn, but it had
been worth it. God, she had needed a night like tonight,
laughing and flirting with a sexy man, sparring with
him the way she could only spar with men who were
as smart as she was.

'Everything's a competition for you, isn't it?' Mark
asked.

Noelle jerked back in the seat, as if his words were a
physical blow. What an idiot she'd been, to imagine
that there was some kind of cheesy romantic build-up
going on in this macho vehicle. The tension she was
feeling was probably emanating from Mark's wounded
ego. The guy couldn't even lose at darts without biting
back.

'You're the one who's being competitive. Why do men
always have to ruin everything by being superior?'

Noelle's eyes burnt. Tears. How fucking humiliating.
She fumbled for the door handle, but her hands were
trembling so much that she couldn't get a grip on
anything.

Then Mark's arm was reaching across her, his hand
catching hers, keeping her from shattering.

'You misunderstood me,' he said. 'I only meant that
you're a lot like me. Not that I'm superior. We both have
to win, even when we're supposedly out to have fun.'

'Is there something wrong with that?' Noelle bristled.

'I don't know. Is there?'

Of course there was something wrong with having to win *all* the time. Noelle knew that better than anyone. She was the one who had to live with her inner drill sergeant, the voice that drove her to push herself harder and harder, in the hopes of being the first to tear through that ribbon at the end of the finish line. The problem was, no matter how hard she ran, the ribbon slipped out of reach; victory was a promise that always eluded her. Noelle did get tired of that race, and she got tired of the headaches and heartburn that went along with having to be the best, every single time.

'I'd like to take a break once in a while,' she admitted cautiously.

'What would you do, if you could take a break?'

Check into a cheap motel with you and spend an entire week learning the way every inch of your body tastes, Noelle thought.

'Find a hobby,' she said. 'Something creative and soothing, like knitting. The problem is, I've never been a creative person. I'm not artsy at all. I could never paint like Tia, or my brother. I see everything in monotones.'

'That can't be true. Everyone has creative potential.'

'Actually, I was being very literal. I'm colour blind. Maybe that's an advantage for an attorney, but it can make life as dull as dirt. When I was growing up, my brother was always the crazy, brilliant genius. I was the solid, grounded plodder. Do you know how infuriating that gets?'

'I can imagine.'

'I've never admitted this to anyone, but I tried to kill Jeremy when he was eight years old. I sat on his head in a swimming pool and wouldn't let him come up to breathe.'

'But you didn't kill him, obviously.'

'I couldn't go through with it,' Noelle sighed. 'I only held him down for a few seconds, but those were the most intense seconds of my life. I honestly thought I was going to murder the little bastard. I was so mad at him that day.'

'Why?'

'He did a flawless dive off the highest board at the pool. That board had always scared the bejeezus out of me. I used to have nightmares about it. Because it scared me so much, my dad insisted that I confront the fear, but I couldn't make myself climb that ladder to the board. I'd freeze up, start blubbering like a baby. Then Jeremy came along, scrambled up to the top, and did the most fabulous dive you've ever seen. It was heartbreaking. No lessons, no practice; he just made a perfect arc sailing through the air. He was so beautiful that I started to cry. And then, before he could get back up to the surface, I tried to kill him.'

Mark laughed. 'Ten minutes ago you refused to admit that you're competitive.'

'I'm *not* competitive. And I don't always win.'

'But you manage to get what you want most of the time. How do you do it?'

'Here. I'll show you.'

The next few moments unfolded in slow motion. Noelle watched her hands floating towards Mark, reaching for his face as if it were a shiny toy sitting on the highest shelf at a shop she'd never dared to enter. She saw her fingertips making contact with his cheekbones, gliding downwards, taking hold, and using his square jaws to pull his mouth closer to hers. Closer and closer, her eyes taking in every detail of those lips that were framed by his beard, until his lips were the only things in Noelle's universe. She was still disembodied but, at the same time, she was nothing but body – need, drive, hunger.

If she'd known that kissing her best friend's boyfriend would feel so good, Noelle would have done this weeks ago. Mark's lips tasted like beer and tabasco, with the aftertaste of salt from the sweat that had dried in his beard. Smooth, firm lips – not too thin, not too full. She was so busy devouring Mark's mouth that she didn't even notice if he was kissing her back. It didn't matter. Noelle had grabbed what she wanted, and she wasn't going to let go until she'd had her fill.

When she finally let him come up for air, Noelle knew there was only one thing she could do.

Run like hell.

She grabbed the door handle that had eluded her earlier, flung the massive door open with the adrenalised force of a woman who's just kissed a man she's wanted for months, ran up the stairs to her building and pushed the door open. She never even saw Mark's face after she kissed him. She'd been too scared to look. Now she'd never be able to face him again, but no one could ever accuse her of hesitating when the brass ring sailed by.

'Hi, Noelle. I locked myself out. Isn't that Mark's car outside?'

Tia stood on the landing. She looked pale and small, confused and forlorn. Noelle's big kissing thrill suddenly soured into shame.

'Um, yes. He gave me a ride home tonight. I guess he was working late. We sort of ran into each other downtown.'

'That was nice of him.'

When Tia glanced away, Noelle surreptitiously smoothed her curls. She'd unleashed her hair at the pub, and now the black strands were flying all over the place, corkscrews gone mad. She reeked of second-hand cigarette smoke, and so would Mark. Hopefully Tia wouldn't notice. She had an odd expression on her face – dazed, preoccupied, possibly even guilty. Noelle was usually good at reading faces, but she couldn't interpret Tia's look.

'Is everything OK?' Noelle asked. 'Jeremy didn't cause any problems, did he?'

'No! Not at all. I'm just an absent-minded twit. I went outside to take out the trash and forgot my key.' Tia's laugh was tinny, like a marble bouncing in an empty can.

Noelle pulled her key out of her pocket and set about unlocking the door with brisk overly efficient motions. Behind that door, reality was waiting, in the form of a stack of legal texts and a brief that was due tomorrow. She should have been at home working on the assignment five hours ago.

'Hey, Cherry Bomb. Sorry I'm so late. Go get ready. Let's spend the night at my place.'

'I'm ready,' Tia said. 'I've been ready for hours.'

'Then let's go.'

Mark stood at the foot of the stairs, waiting for his lover. Noelle darted inside to her safe little nest. She'd never known that romantic love could be so exhausting. No wonder Tia could never seem to get ahead in her career.

'Night, Noelle! Sweet dreams,' Mark called.

'Bye! Thanks for the ride!' Noelle hollered back, before she slammed the door shut and collapsed in relief. There was weird juju in the air tonight. Noelle wasn't the only one who'd been up to something.

Eerie noises were seeping through the old plaster walls. Human, but not really human, a wail that turned into a husky, throbbing moan, then sailed back up to a near squeal. Noelle sprang to her feet, grabbed a broom out of the closet and pounded on the ceiling.

'Jeremy, cut that out!' she shouted. 'It's too late to be playing the harmonica. Put the thing away!'

As far as Noelle was concerned, it was always too late for the harmonica, except when it was too early. The mouth harp was probably her least favourite instrument in the world. When Jeremy played, she had visions of him sitting in a rail yard somewhere, taking lessons from a hobo. That was exactly the kind of thing Jeremy would do in a manic state – go out seeking instruction in the blues, as if his own blue periods hadn't been hard enough.

The caterwauling stopped. Noelle took a deep breath. Then she remembered something, and forgot to let the breath go.

Of all the instruments Jeremy had ever played (piano, flute, xylophone, drums, bass guitar, aluminium cake pan with rubber bands stretched over it), the harmonica was the only one that he saved for a unique state of being. Jeremy only played the harmonica when he was in love.

Noelle exhaled. She looked up at the ceiling, her eyes scanning the plaster as if she could read a message on that blank white expanse. Jeremy's bed was right above her living room. His apartment was unnaturally quiet now. If Noelle knew Jeremy – and she did, better than anyone else in the world – that stillness upstairs was about as permanent as the moment of quivering calm just before a riot erupts.

'I've got my eye on you, little brother,' she said aloud. 'If you mess up anything for me, I'm going to cash in on all those death threats I never carried out.'

Through the ceiling, Noelle thought she could hear the light growl of Jeremy snoring.

Chapter Seven

Colourlingus

Mark was unusually quiet on the drive to his place. He kept one hand on the steering wheel, and the other parked on Tia's thigh as he guided the Hummer into the heart of downtown. Mark lived in an old saddle factory that had recently been restored and converted into luxury lofts. Tia thought the phrase 'luxury lofts' was an oxymoron, especially when those lofts were situated in what used to be a blue-collar manufacturing facility. She had once cracked a joke about the ghosts of lonely cowboys and resentful minimum-wage leather workers roaming through the vast expanses of modernised architecture, but Mark didn't think it was funny.

'I paid half a million for this place,' he had said. 'At that price, there'd better not be any negative supernatural energy in the building, or I'll have my realtor's head on a platter.'

Mark didn't get Tia's sense of humour, but she was used to that. Most people didn't laugh at her jokes; why should he?

'So what were you doing this evening?' Tia asked, when they stopped at a traffic light.

'Why do you ask?'

'Just making conversation.'

'There must be more interesting things to talk about.'

'Look, I'm not being the jealous girlfriend, if that's what you're thinking.'

'I never implied that you were.'

'Good. I'm glad. Because that would really piss me off.'

Silence. Mark drummed out the seconds, hammering the steering wheel with his thumbs. As soon as the light turned green, he stepped on the gas and sped through the intersection.

'I got called to an emergency meeting,' he said when they came to the next light. 'The library annex again. One of the architects freaked about a potential coding violation, and we had to work through all the hairy details with the contractors before we could move forward.' Mark turned to look at Tia. 'What did you do tonight?'

Tia shrugged. She kept her shoulders hunched around her ears for a bit longer than necessary. 'Not much. Watched TV. Television sucks these days.'

'I agree,' Mark said. There was a note of relief in his voice. 'That's why I don't own one. If I want drama, I'll go to the opera or the ballet. Which reminds me, I have tickets to *Coppélia* on Thursday. I already have your accessories picked out – you can choose your dress. Make sure it's elegant, and very, very sexy.'

Mark's palm swept along Tia's thigh, making a suggestive trajectory from her knee all the way to the pocket of softness near her crotch. The weight of his hand so close to her pussy, combined with his reference to the ballet, made her shudder with anticipation. Last time they'd attended a ballet together, Tia had barely seen the performance. She'd been too busy carrying out a solo act for Mark, in the dark cramped confines of his balcony seat.

Those dark cramped spaces again. What was it about Mark and his need to get Tia into the smallest, tightest places imaginable? It wasn't the kind of thing you could confront your boyfriend with, not unless you were in the mood for an hour-long argument. Which Tia wasn't.

When they pulled into the high-security underground parking lot of Mark's building, he was taken by a surge of sexual energy. He scooped Tia out of the passenger seat, slammed the door shut with his foot, and carried her upstairs to his loft, tongue-kissing her in time to the creaks and squeaks of the old freight elevator.

'What's up with you all of a sudden?' Tia laughed, when he let her come up for air.

'What isn't?' Mark grinned.

He carried Tia across the threshold, then set her down, took her hand and guided it to his crotch. Her fingers made contact with a bold ridge of flesh that jutted away from his pelvis. Through the light cotton of his running shorts, Tia could feel every twitch, every throb. The erect penis was a paradox that never stopped surprising her; she loved the way the organ could feel steely and supple at the same time, resilient in its outer layers, while rock firm underneath. She let her fingers explore the warm shaft, squeezing and teasing and tantalising, while she watched Mark's tense features relax.

'Great touch,' he moaned. 'Wrap your fingers around the base – that's good. Tighter. There. Keep stroking me, just like that.'

'You mean it? You'd rather have a quick and dirty hand-job than a nice lazy screw on the bed?'

'Who says I can't have both?' Mark asked, but he picked Tia up, Neanderthal style, and carried her bedwards.

Mark's loft had so much sheer square footage that it took forever to reach that oasis. The loft, spare and elegant, all track lights and geometric furniture, reminded Tia of a gallery in a high-tech museum. Mark had a cleaning lady who came in twice a week, so his dwelling had none of the typical masculine clutter that Tia was used to. With its sprawling view of the skyline, whose lights twinkled like a forest of gigantic Christmas trees, the apartment was the perfect setting for a hip successful professional.

So where did a therapist-slash-painter with a taste for Top Ramen and dreams of defacing public buildings fit into this vision of urbane sophistication? When Mark brought her here, Tia felt like a contemporary Cinderella, with about five minutes to go before her coach and ballgown turned into a pumpkin and rags.

Tia's doubts faded as soon as Mark threw her on to his bed. She squealed like a kid on a trampoline as she sailed through the air, landing flat on her back on the blankets. Having tossed her where he wanted her, Mark stripped off his shorts and T-shirt and threw them on the floor. Tia was too aroused by the sight of his tawny body, prowling across the mattress, to wonder why he'd been wearing his running clothes to a late meeting of the library planning committee.

'You are way too dressed,' he said, nipping at Tia's earlobe. 'Let me correct that for you.'

Mark skilfully relieved Tia of her T-shirt and jeans, panties and bra.

'You're good at that,' Tia remarked. 'You have a subtle way with women's clothing.'

'Comes from years of monotonous training and gruelling practice. Let me show you some of my other subtle qualities.'

Mark pressed the length of his cock against Tia's belly. He rubbed the shaft against her skin, in an insistent rhythm that promised much deeper, harder penetration.

'That's subtle, all right. I think the words "freight train" come to mind,' Tia said.

Her laughter dissolved into a moan when Mark took her wrists, pinned them above her head and began to cover her breasts with kisses. Her nipples tightened under his mouth, peaking into rosy buds in their bid for attention.

'Don't tie me up tonight,' Tia begged. 'I want to be able to touch you.'

'You won't be using your hands tonight, sweetheart. Not in this position.'

With one effortless motion, Mark flipped Tia's body so that she was lying underneath him on her belly. Tia felt something primal stir into life as he scooped up her hips and spread her thighs with his knee. Here she was, an independent creature of the twenty-first century, caught in the world's oldest mating position – ass up, high and vulnerable, her face pressed against the mattress. Gripping her hips, Mark entered Tia in one long stroke, all the way in, hitting the base of her channel without apology. He took her in a blur, a series of thrusts that rocked her relentlessly, blows that were painful and pleasurable at the same time. No verbal segue to this episode, no excruciating foreplay. Just a fast, furious, animalistic fuck.

Tia loved it.

'Harder,' she moaned. 'Give it to me harder!'

She sounded like an actress in the world's cheesiest porn video, but that was part of the fun. Pinned under Mark, his cock lodged deep, Tia was totally prone and submissive; she had no choice but to unleash her inner slut. She'd never felt so powerless and, when he began to spank her, with blows that rained in rough syncopation with his thrusts, Tia's pleasure was heightened by a burst of humiliation. At the same time, the stinging pain came as a relief, letting her forget her guilt about what she'd done earlier that night.

But she couldn't forget the kiss itself, not even with Mark driving her into a state of carnal nirvana. Nothing could pound away the lingering halo left by Jeremy's mouth, or the overwhelming gentleness of the way he'd touched her. Jeremy had held Tia as if she were something precious that he'd been allowed to hold for a moment, a gift that wasn't truly a gift at all, because he'd have to hand the treasure back to the person who owned her.

Wait a second, Tia thought. Who *did* own her nowadays? In the game Tia played with Mark, she belonged to him, at least from dusk until dawn. Up until now, that thought alone could send a cascade of spasms through Tia's loins, leaving her dizzy and damp. With

Mark's muscular physique bearing down on her, the thought was still wildly arousing. But, through her pleasure, Tia glimpsed a future when she'd lose her taste for being a possession – clutched, tossed and passed back and forth like a football.

'Stop thinking, Tia. You're tensing up. We're making love, remember?'

At first Tia thought she was hearing the voice of her conscience, but it was Mark; he had lowered himself on to the mattress, forming a warm cage around her body, and was speaking into her ear. 'You didn't even feel me come, did you? What were you thinking about?'

Mark pulled away from Tia, his sweaty skin clinging to hers with tiny, kissing noises. He rolled Tia on to her back, held her face in his hands and gazed down at her.

'Oh, you know me. I'm always thinking too much.'

Mark smiled. 'That's the therapist in you. Always analysing. I can cure you of that tendency, you know.'

Tia could tell that he'd already climaxed; after sex, his grey-blue eyes always darkened a few shades. Her gorgeous man had had an orgasm, and she'd missed it.

'Go ahead. Cure me.'

Tia spread her legs for him, her body posing its own challenge. Mark was as good as his word. He moved into the space between Tia's thighs and got busy, first kissing her mound, then parting the ruffled petals with his tongue. Tia had been surprised – and more than a little annoyed – at how much work it took to maintain her nude smoothness, but suddenly all her efforts seemed worthwhile. With the most sensitive skin on her body fully exposed, lips pouting like an orchid for Mark's mouth, she was aware of a hundred gradients of sensation, merging into one ecstatic spectrum.

Tia experienced oral sex in colour – 'colourlingus', she called it. The first time a boy had crouched down between her knees, parted her legs, pushed her panties aside and touched his tongue to her clit, she'd seen red. Vibrant, bright red, like the Chinese red that signified good luck. That first brave lover brought her good luck, all right. She had her first orgasm (the first one that she didn't give to herself) under his exploratory tongue. But, before he brought her to that shattering climax, Tia saw a marshmallow pink when he lapped at the outer whorls of her labia, and a throbbing violet blue when his tongue wandered into her vagina. In between those bolder strokes of colour came the softer hues: pale lemon yellow, grass green, a fleeting ribbon of cyan.

Ever since then, Tia had had the same experience when a lover was licking her. Sometimes the rainbow was more intense than others, depending on her partner's technique and level of enthusiasm, but the colours always made themselves known.

'You don't drop acid before you have sex, do you?' Mark had asked, his eyes narrowing sceptically, when Tia tried to explain the phenomenon.

'Of course not! I don't need drugs to have psychedelic experiences,' she had replied in a hurt tone.

She'd never brought up the topic with Mark again, but he did make her see colour. Lots and lots of rich vivid colour. Mark's tongue seemed to generate a lot of greens, possibly because he was the only lover she'd had whose income was above the federal poverty level. But, tonight, the overriding colours were crimson, purple and orange. Lovely. Mark was outdoing himself tonight, performing tricks with his lips and tongue that Tia had never imagined, much less experienced.

Unlike some of the other lovers she'd had, Mark never rushed this special act, or complained about it afterwards. He took his time, so deeply engaged in pleasing Tia that he might as well have been holding a private meeting with her pussy. She never would have guessed that such an ambitious driven man would be so slow and languorous in that area, but, as Mark explained, expert cunnilingus was the best way to control a woman.

At this moment, Mark had absolute control over Tia.

Every muscle, every nerve, was awakening to the drum-beat of his tongue against the bud between her lower lips. When Tia's thighs began to quiver, Mark bent her legs at the knee, tilting her bottom upwards so that he could dive deeper into her secrets. When he reached up to rub her breasts, and pinched her tender nipples, the unexpected twinge sent her skywards. Tia arched off the bed, her fingers clutching at Mark's bedspread, in a wave that unfurled in her centre and spread from her toes all the way to the top of her head. It started with an electric tingle and culminated in a power surge that left her stunned, weak and giggling with joy.

'Are you all right, Tia? *Tia!*' Mark was peering up from between her legs. He looked proud of himself, but slightly worried.

'Red. Red, purple, red,' Tia babbled. 'And gold this time ... that's the first time I saw gold.'

'Should I take that as a compliment?' Mark asked.

Tia, who was floating into unconsciousness on a sky-blue carpet threaded with silver, never heard his question.

After that orgasm, Tia slept like a sunken ship. She didn't wake up when Mark's alarm went off. She woke up much later, alone in his bed, twenty minutes before she was supposed to be at the hospital to meet with Belle Doe for their second session.

'Damn! Why didn't he wake me up?' she moaned.

Mark had left a mug of coffee, now cold, on the night table, with a note underneath it, written in his sharp, angular draughtsman's handwriting.

You looked so beautiful I couldn't wake you up, the note read. *Don't be mad at me – I made you see gold last night.*

Tia smiled. Her irritation had vanished, like the heat from the mug of coffee. She drank the black brew anyway, in hasty gulps, then took a three-minute shower and put on the jeans and blouse she'd worn the day before. She felt gross, but she didn't have a choice. With her hours already cut down to 28 a week, she couldn't afford to be late. She had had to beg the charge nurse to let her have another meeting with Belle so soon after the first one. The nurse thought that too many sessions so close together would be overstimulating. Tia had to convince her that the single mark Belle had made on the page didn't just mean something, it meant something important.

Besides, Belle wouldn't notice. Belle, clad in a queasy-green hospital gown, wouldn't be inclined to critique Tia's attire, even if she could peek out of her inner world long enough to see that Tia was in the same room.

When Tia arrived at the locked unit, the nurse who buzzed her in told her that Belle hadn't left her bed since her last art-therapy session.

'What did you do to her?' the nurse asked, an accusatory glint in her eye.

'I helped her make contact,' Tia snapped. 'Let me talk to Belle.'

'I don't know if that's a good idea,' the nurse said. 'Any overstimulation –'

Tia cut her off. 'If I hear the word "overstimulation" one more time, I'm going to lose it. Belle needs to try to communicate. She *needs* positive stimulation. Let me talk to her. If she doesn't want to draw today, that should be her choice.'

'Fine,' the nurse said, rolling her eyes.

Tia stalked past the nurse's station. She ignored the whispers and snickers that followed in her wake. No one on this unit believed in what she was doing. Most of the nurses thought she was fluff, a shallow distraction. They only tolerated her because she gave them a break from watching some of the needier patients.

The door to Belle's room stood halfway open. Belle had a roommate, another woman who was Belle's polar opposite in affect and behaviour. While Belle lay on her bed, an inert lump covered by a threadbare public-hospital blanket, her roommate was pacing around the room, making whistling noises and scooping at the air.

'Oh, thank goodness. Help me catch my parrot!' the woman cried when Tia appeared.

'I'm sorry, but I don't see your parrot,' Tia said.

'You don't? Why not?' The woman stood stock still and stared at Tia, her eyes huge with disbelief. Her hair was a frizzy grey crown on top of her head.

'Because I don't,' Tia said, trying to be gentle but firm. Maybe this was how Mark felt when Tia rambled on about seeing colours during sex. 'I need to talk to your roommate, Belle.'

'She is whacko,' the woman said in a confidential sotto voce. 'Be careful.'

To Tia's relief, the roommate side-stepped out of the room, leaving Tia with the lump that was Belle. Tia tiptoed towards the bed. 'Belle? Are you awake?'

The lump didn't move. At the top of Belle's bed, draped along the pillow, were loops of blonde hair. From the rhythmic stirring of the blanket, Tia could tell that Belle was breathing. Breathing was good, Tia reminded herself. Breathing was the beginning of everything else.

'Belle, it's Tia. We were drawing together the other day. Remember? You were holding the yellow crayon, and you made a mark on the paper.'

Silence.

'How would you like to come back to the art room with me? We'll draw again. You can use the yellow crayon, or blue, or pink, or any other colour that you like. You can use more than one colour, if you want to. Would you like to do that?'

The blanket inched up even further as Belle curled deeper into herself, blocking Tia out of her private world.

Tia straightened her spine and willed herself not to

sound desperate. 'Belle, I need to talk to you. Can you turn around and look at me?'

More silence. The blanket didn't even move this time. The charge nurse had been right – that single yellow mark hadn't meant anything. Belle had been catatonic then, and she was catatonic now. She wouldn't respond until she was ready, and nothing Tia could do was going to change that. At times like this, Tia wished she had any other job but this one. Driving an ice-cream truck, selling beer at rock concerts, dancing nude behind glass: preferably something where the customers would come rushing to her, instead of her having to beg them to respond.

'Give up already?' asked the nurse, glancing up from her magazine as Tia left the unit, carrying the brand-new sketchbook and 64-pack of crayons that she'd purchased for Belle.

Tia held her chin up. 'I never give up on my patients,' she said. 'But I can't force her to do anything she's not ready to do. I'll be back.'

Whistle on, Tia, she said to herself. Keep on whistling in the pitch-black dark. She was getting tired of waiting for someone – anyone – to whistle back. Mark was always urging her to give up this job for something better. She could work for a private hospital, eventually go into practice for herself. Better yet, she could drop the whole therapy gig and become a design consultant. Mark had lots of connections in the city; he could get her a cushy position selecting art for corporate lobbies and restrooms. Companies took that kind of thing seriously these days. Studies showed that art affected employees' moods and, more importantly, clients' buying decisions. So in a way, she'd still be working with art therapeutically. The only difference would be two or three extra digits on her yearly income.

'Forget it. I'd rather starve to death,' Tia muttered,

slamming quarters into the coffee machine. The automated spout poured frothy amaretto straight through the drain, without dispensing the paper cup. Tia wanted to cry.

'Hey! Tia!'

Tia looked around for the source of the exuberant shout.

'Up here!'

She glanced up. Jeremy stood on the open level above her, leaning over the railing and waving. Her reaction stunned her: soaring heart, buckling knees, a near swoon on to the hospital floor. Then Jeremy was racing down the stairs, bounding like a deer, somehow avoiding his own untied shoelaces.

Kiss me again, Jeremy, Tia prayed. *Give me a big transfusion of energy and colour. I need that right now.*

'What are you doing here?' Tia asked. She might have thought that Jeremy was a beautiful hallucination, if he hadn't thrown himself at her neck, half-choking her in a hug that left her gasping.

'Bipolar support group. I promised Noelle I'd go.' Jeremy wrinkled his nose.

Tia had never noticed that the bridge of that nose was dusted with faint cinnamon freckles. She found herself wondering where else he had freckles. Shoulders, maybe? Chest? That's where Tia had her own constellations of spots. If she and Jeremy were lying naked together, they could make their freckles touch . . .

'So how was the group?' Tia asked, with a bright smile. Playing the supportive big sister to Jeremy was probably the hardest thing she'd ever had to do. It felt fake; it felt wrong and, with Jeremy giving her that melting blue stare, it was starting to feel very temporary.

'Well, it didn't totally suck. We talked about a lot of different stuff. Meds. Jobs. Relationships. I told them about me and you.'

Tia gulped. 'Me and you?'

'Yeah. You know. Us.' Jeremy did a half-spin, scanning

the room. 'Is there any coffee in this hospital, besides the crap in that machine? I need an espresso.'

Tia thought Jeremy was probably the last person on earth who needed espresso, but she lead him outside to the coffee cart and bought him an overpriced cup of black rocket fuel.

'So what did you tell the group about us?' Tia asked.

Jeremy swirled his cardboard cup, staring intently into the ink. 'I told them there was a woman I liked a lot, but that she was already with some older guy who made a lot of money and drove a pseudo-military vehicle. I asked the girls in the group what they'd think if a guy with no job and no car asked them out on a date, and they had to walk there, or take the bus, when they already had a boyfriend who could drive her around in a Hummer.'

Tia hid her smile. 'What did they say?'

'Well . . . one chick flat out admitted she'd rather date the Hummer guy. The other one said that it shouldn't matter what kind of car a guy drives, if he really likes you. And he has a classic physique like mine.'

This time Tia laughed, and didn't bother to hide it.

'That wasn't supposed to be funny,' Jeremy said.

'Were any of the girls close to your age?' Tia asked.

Jeremy stopped in his tracks. He blew air through his lips, and pitched his empty coffee cup into a trash can. 'Yeah, they were. So?'

'So . . . was there anyone you might be interested in?'

'Look, Tia, I know where you're going with this. You want me to hook up with some hot little hoochie and take her out to MacDonald's for a ninety-nine-cent hamburger. So think about this – how would you feel if I fell in love with her? How would you feel if I took her out to the city to look for places to paint? How would you feel if I took her back to my apartment and fucked her brains out?'

A couple of medical students, following their attending physician like ducklings, paused at the phrase 'fucked her brains out'. Tia recognised the doctor; she was a psychiatrist who often consulted on the acute inpatient unit. The students probably figured Jeremy was a patient, out with his nurse on a cigarette break. One of the residents actually pulled a mini-notebook and pencil out of his pocket.

'Jeremy, stop,' Tia whispered. 'People are watching us.'

'No. I won't stop. One thing you have to know about me is that I don't care what strangers think any more. With all the things I've done, and all the memories I've blacked out, I'd go crazy if I worried about people I don't know. The only people whose opinions matter are the people I love. Noelle, my parents, you. That's my whole list of people I care about right now. And one more thing, Tia. I may be eight years younger than you, but I am not some "kid". When you go through the kind of stuff I've been through – when you've been in psych units, and on the streets, and in jail – you are done with being a kid, no matter how many candles you've got on your birthday cake.'

Tia stared at Jeremy. He stared back. She'd never known that fire could be green and blue, and radiant with gold.

'I'm sorry,' she said. 'I was stupid. I don't know what else to say.'

Jeremy took her hand and squeezed it hard. He was smiling again, his eyes suddenly illuminated with excitement instead of anger. 'Say you'll come look at my paintings. You're an art therapist, and you haven't even seen my art.'

Tia steadied herself. She was about to take a step over a precipice. Was she ready? She didn't know. The only thing she knew for certain was that she couldn't be Jeremy's therapist. Not now. No way.

'Jeremy, I want to see your paintings, but I can't analyse your work professionally, because that would put us in a professional relationship. And we're already past the point where that would be ethical. When you kissed me –'

'Did you like that? I haven't kissed anyone in a long time. I didn't really know what I was doing. I just jumped in.'

'I liked it, yes. I liked it a lot. But if we're going to be ... intimate enough to kiss, or even if we were going to be close friends, then I can't be your therapist. It wouldn't be right.'

Jeremy's face was so radiant that it made the world around him look like a grainy black-and-white movie. Childhood might be lost to him, but innocence wasn't. His smile was the purest expression of happiness that Tia had ever seen.

'I never wanted you for a therapist,' he said. 'If I thought I could never kiss you again, I'd give up therapy of any kind. I'd give up everything. I'd stop breathing.'

'OK, Jeremy,' Tia sighed. 'Don't stop breathing. You don't have to do anything that dramatic.'

'I know, but if I did –'

'You will *not* stop breathing. Your respiration will continue as usual.'

'What about kissing?'

'We'll see. Let's take this slowly, OK?'

'Slowly?'

'Yes. You know. As in one step at a time. Not rushing. Considering the consequences.'

'I can deal with that,' Jeremy said, with a carefree shrug.

Tia gave him a long look. 'I hope so,' she said.

Tia hadn't seen the inside of Jeremy's apartment since the day he moved in. When he opened the door for her, she had to stop for a few seconds, steadying herself with both hands on the doorframe, otherwise the sheer profusion of colours and shapes would have blown her away.

'What do you think?' Jeremy asked, hovering behind her. 'I like vibrant. Does the room seem to vibrate?'

Tia nodded. 'The whole *world* seems to vibrate. Has Noelle seen what you've done here?'

He'd painted the walls of his living room a bright clear blue, painted with cumulus clouds, like a Magritte painting. The ceiling, with its dignified crown mouldings, was a purple so profound that it was almost black, like a midnight sky. An eccentric assortment of chairs, end tables and bookcases had been arranged around the room. Each piece of furniture had been painted a different hue, and Tia would have been willing to bet that none of those colours represented the object's original state. At least Jeremy had left the hardwood floors untouched; the antique oak gleamed under a fresh coating of wax. A flock of carpet remnants, in eclectic patterns, served as area rugs. Taken separately, the mismatched elements of the room would have been overwhelming but, together, everything worked. Tia couldn't figure out why, but the colours formed a harmony that was absolutely unique.

'Noelle hasn't seen it,' Jeremy admitted, ruffling his mass of black hair. 'Neither has the landlady. But she said it was OK for me to do some painting.'

Poor Mrs Crouch, Tia thought, thinking of the elderly widow who had owned this building since 1962. When she said that Jeremy could 'paint', she had probably meant that he could apply a fresh coat of eggshell.

Tia's vision of Mrs Crouch's reaction to Jeremy's décor made her giggle. The giggle deepened into a belly laugh.

'Does that mean you like it?' Jeremy asked.

'I love it.'

'How does it make you feel when you first step into the room? Be honest.'

Tia thought for a moment, considered a polite lie, then decided that Jeremy deserved the truth. Even if she wasn't going to be his therapist, she should be as honest with him about his creations as she was with her patients.

'Well ... it feels like the way I feel when I walk into a new milieu on a psychiatric unit. Like I don't know what to expect, but I can't wait to find out what I'm going to discover. It feels like an imaginary jungle, full of strange things – disturbing and beautiful at the same time. And, in a very bizarre way, it feels like home.'

'It does?' Jeremy's shy pleasure was a marvel to behold. He seemed to glow with light, the reflection of all the colours inside and outside of his mind.

'Yes. It does,' Tia said. 'I don't know how else to put it. I feel comfortable. Like I belong.'

'You do. You were my inspiration for all this.'

'Really?' Tia looked around at the glorious explosion of colours. 'I'm flattered, I think.'

Jeremy edged up behind Tia, who'd been blocking his doorway. He wrapped his arms around her waist, tentatively, the way he'd done the night before, as if she might disappear if he held her too tight. He pulled her against his chest and touched her hair, and spoke into her ear as he rocked her back and forth.

'I know you're not like me, Tia. I mean, you don't go up and down like a roller coaster if you're not on medication. You don't ever get so sad that you feel like you're trapped in a box at the bottom of the ocean, and you'll never see the surface again. You don't run away to places you've never been, or do things you don't remember. But there's one way that you are like me. You see how intense life really is, how things can light up all around you, if you let them. And it doesn't make you scared, or wear you out. That's why you belong in this room, with me.'

Tia knew that Jeremy was going to kiss her again, but she never expected him to have improved his technique since their last encounter. His hands were more confident; his mouth pressed more assertively on her own. He didn't hesitate to open her lips with his tongue, or to tilt her chin so he could french kiss her more deeply. Tia was different this time, too. Without the element of surprise, she was softer and looser. She could respond to him like a lover, melding with him from hips to shoulders, letting her curves find their place against his torso. This time, their kiss wasn't an accident; it was a dance, long and sinuous and graced by reciprocity.

'I have to spin you,' he said, breaking his lock on her lips.

Without waiting for her to consent, Jeremy pulled Tia into the room and pushed the door shut with one hand. As he kissed her, he began to spin her, first slowly, then faster, until her peripheral vision was a whirl of blue, broken by the occasional slash of green or red. Tia hadn't been spun since she was a little girl. The first time was at a birthday party; she was five or six years old, blindfolded, broomstick in her hand, ready to whack a piñata. She'd been so giddy from the spinning that she let the stick fall from her hands and kept twirling, twirling by herself, oblivious to the cries of the other children.

Forget the piñata. Who needed to crawl around in the dirt grabbing penny candy when you could be spinning in mid-air? Tia had found a delicious delirium that she could recreate for herself, any time – all alone, the ecstasy of vertigo. It wasn't till she discovered masturbation that she found anything to rival that sensation. But, like masturbation, spinning had always been a solitary pleasure ... until now.

Kissing and spinning, why hadn't Tia thought of this before? Why hadn't she ever found a man who would whirl her around like this, his strong hands keeping her from falling, his mouth giving her everything that she needed to breathe? As if the ecstasy of spinning weren't enough, there was the reminder of desire in the pressure of insistent flesh against her pelvis, the ragged sound of Jeremy's breathing and the quivering of his arms as he held her against him.

The only bad thing about spinning was that it couldn't last forever. Tia had forgotten the falling part. When Jeremy lost his balance, she went down, too; they both landed hard, knocking over one of the straight-backed chairs, the one that Jeremy had painted black with red and white spots. Or were those spots floating across Tia's field of vision?

'Wow,' Jeremy said, clutching his skull. 'That rocked!'

'You know it's a good spin when you pass out,' Tia agreed. 'I haven't done that in years. Now I remember why.'

She was feeling woozy, too faint to stand up. Another chair toppled as she tried to pull herself into a sitting position, but her legs were still tangled around Jeremy's, and she fell to the floor again.

That was how Noelle found them.

'What's all the banging and crashing up here? Sounds like mating season for elephants.'

Tia looked up to see Noelle standing in the doorway. Jeremy had closed the door, but he hadn't locked it, and now Noelle was towering over them in a Lara Croft stance, legs spread, fists planted on her hips. All she needed to complete the Tomb Raider look was an ammo belt. Behind her hovered a serious-looking man wearing a ponytail and a Greenpeace T-shirt. Tia guessed that he was the current object of Noelle's sexual agenda, the tender liberal beefsteak who went by the name of Kevin.

'Oh, no. Oh, Jeremy. What have you done?'

Noelle's gaze had turned away from the tangle of arms and legs on the floor, as she saw the condition of the room. Her arms flopped at her sides. Her shoulders sank. Her face fell, in an expression of despair so pitiful that Tia wanted to jump up and hug her. At the same time, she wanted to protect Jeremy from the volcano that was about to erupt.

'It's only paint, Noelle,' Tia said, in the calm steady voice that she'd learnt to use with agitated patients.

'Yes. I can see that. Did you *throw* the paint at the walls, Jeremy, or did you actually use a brush?'

Tia could tell that Noelle was escalating: her fingers opening and closing, her breath coming in short pants. A high-pitched, strangled moan was coming from her throat.

Jeremy scrambled to his feet. 'Help me, Tia! My sister's losing it!'

Tia got up and hurried to help Jeremy stabilise Noelle, who was swaying back and forth.

'I co-signed the lease on this place. My deposit is not going to cover this,' Noelle said. Her eyes stared straight ahead, unfocused. 'We will *not* tell Mrs Crouch. She'll have a stroke.'

'Shhh. You're the one who's going to have a stroke.' Jeremy rubbed Noelle's arm in long soothing motions. 'It's going to be OK.'

'How? Tell me how this is going to be OK,' Noelle said through clenched teeth.

'Simple. I'm never going to move,' Jeremy said. 'I'll just stay here forever, and change my locks so Mrs Crouch can't get in. Will that make it better?'

I knew this was going to happen, Jeremy mouthed to Tia behind Noelle's head.

Me too, she mouthed back.

'That might work,' Noelle squeaked. 'Then no one would have to find out.'

'That's right, Sis. No one will know except the four of us. My paint job will be our dark dirty secret,' Jeremy said, rubbing the small of Noelle's back.

'I kinda like it,' Kevin remarked. 'You know, if you wanted to paint the walls white again, all you'd have to do is strip the colour.'

'Great. A voice of reason,' Tia groaned.

Jeremy and Tia guided Noelle out the door. Her arms

and legs stuck out stiffly, like a human billboard. With Kevin's help, the three of them managed to get her down the stairs and into the apartment she and Tia shared. They manoeuvred her through the living room and past the kitchen, where three other law students were studying at the kitchen table, too focused on their legal tomes to see that their classmate was in shock. When they laid Noelle on her bed, she stared up at the ceiling, muttering reassurances to herself.

'It's not that bad. No one has to know. Jeremy. Jeremy did it,' Noelle said under her breath.

'Would you mind sitting with her till she comes to her senses?' Tia asked Kevin. 'I think she'll be fine. Just give her some time to recover, and make sure she doesn't choke on her tongue or anything.'

'Sure,' Kevin said. He sat on the bed next to Noelle and began to stroke the damp curls off her forehead. He pulled off her glasses, folded them and set them on the table. 'I've never seen her like this,' the law student whispered. 'She's always sooo in control.'

'Not when I'm around,' Jeremy said cheerfully, covering his sister with a crocheted afghan that lay folded at the foot of the bed. 'I do this to her at least once every six weeks. I think she needs a little excitement once in a while.'

'A little excitement might do her good, but you don't need to send her into cardiac arrest,' Tia scolded.

'She'll survive. Just be gentle with her.' Jeremy gave Kevin a manly pat on the shoulder.

'Come on. Let's give her some peace and quiet.' Tia took Jeremy's hand and led him out of the room. He followed contritely as they made their way through the apartment, but, as soon as they were outside in the hallway, he moved Tia against the wall, planted his hands on either side of her shoulders, and landed her with a kiss that turned her insides to strawberry jam.

'Now you've seen what my world is like,' Jeremy said,

when he finally pulled away. 'That scene upstairs was just a taste of how normal people react to me. Do you still want to be part of my life?'

How could Tia say no? At the moment, she couldn't say anything at all. All she could do was nod her head: yes, yes, yes. When she saw Jeremy's eyes light up like a fireworks display, she knew that she'd made the right decision.

'Come upstairs with me. You still haven't seen my paintings,' Jeremy said, pulling her close and sliding his hands along her back. Now that he knew she could be his, his touch was so assured. He was growing as a lover – in more ways than one, Tia noted, feeling the evidence of his arousal against her pelvis – in leaps and bounds.

'I can't. Not yet. I need to hang out here and make sure Noelle's OK.'

'She'll be fine. She gets over things fast.'

'Listen, Jeremy.' Tia stroked his cheek. 'Your sister's a strong woman, but you can't take her for granted. She seems superhuman but, in some ways, she's brittle. She's also my friend. I have a responsibility to look after her.'

Jeremy pulled away, pouting. He stared at his feet, doing his scuffing routine. 'You have a responsibility to me, too. Noelle wanted you to keep an eye on me.'

'I know. And I couldn't have done a worse job if I tried. When she comes to her senses, she's going to kill me.'

'No, she's not. She'll know that I did most of that painting in the middle of the night. That's how I work. If you'd been around to watch me twenty-four hours a day, you would have had to sleep in my apartment.' Jeremy's pout turned into an evil grin. 'I guess this means that you'll have to move in with me.'

'Hah! I guess it doesn't,' Tia retorted. 'We've kissed three times; that doesn't make us live-in material.'

Live-in material. The words reminded her, with a jolt, of Mark. He was getting more aggressive in his efforts to get Tia to move in with him. Three months ago, he had fallen in love with Tia's independence, her sexy idiosyncrasies, her bohemian habits. Now he was trying to claim her, tame her and rope her into his high-tech corral: the loft that still didn't feel like home, no matter how many nights Tia spent in his bed.

Still, Mark's perfection was as undeniable as the panoramic view of the Rocky Mountains outside his window. He was brilliant, gorgeous and the best lover Tia had ever had, certainly the most inventive. After ten-plus years of dating men who couldn't commit to anything more permanent than a choice of sexual positions, Tia had met someone fabulous who wanted to keep her.

So why was she falling for a kid who had no job, had dropped out of college and measured his stability from one round of medication to the next?

'You've been counting,' Jeremy said, his voice soft with delight.

'What? I'm sorry, I didn't hear you.'

'You counted the times we've kissed. That means I matter to you.'

'It's easy to count kisses, when you've only had three,' Tia reminded him. But Jeremy was right. Her counting did signify something. She just wasn't sure what it was.

'I need to go check on Noelle,' Tia said. She gave Jeremy a peck on the cheek – too cursory to count as Kiss #4 – then withdrew into her apartment.

'Don't forget about my paintings,' Jeremy reminded her, as the door was closing. 'I've got something to show you. Something incredible.'

'I won't forget,' Tia said. She was starting to realise that, for Jeremy, the incredible was an everyday occurrence.

When Tia went back inside, she found Noelle's classmates still poring over their books, furiously scrawling on the pages with pencils and highlighter pens. Nice friends, Tia thought. So concerned about Noelle. Or maybe they were like Jeremy, assuming that the Land Shark would always be OK, no matter how life shocked or bruised or buffeted her about.

'Noelle?' Tia called, knocking lightly on her roommate's door. 'Are you still resting?'

No answer. A muffled groan came from the room. Tia peered around the open door, to see that Noelle was doing anything but resting. Her response to Tia's query had been swallowed by Kevin, whose mouth was devouring Noelle's, while his hands kneaded her breasts. He had pushed up her Stanford sweatshirt and bra to gain access to her small firm tits. Noelle was squirming under his touch, moaning and writhing with more abandon than Tia had ever thought her capable of. Her jeans were tangled around her knees, and her panties had been pulled down to reveal a curly black bush that glistened with dew.

Talk about resuscitation! Kevin had not only helped Noelle recover from shock, he was also relieving her of weeks' worth of sexual frustration. Tia knew she should give Noelle her privacy, but she was mesmerised by her roommate's sudden display of sensuality.

Noelle's beauty made Tia catch her breath. Nude, Noelle's frame was long and lithe, her silken skin the colour of honey whipped with butter, her nipples a shade of sun-baked brick atop her small firm breasts. Kevin pulled the band out of Noelle's hair, then roughly combed out her curls with his fingers, giving her a mane worthy of a raging Jezebel. Luckily for Tia, Noelle's glasses had already been discarded, leaving those striking blue eyes in a state of blissful myopia. Kevin couldn't even wait to undress before he entered her; he unbuttoned his jeans, hastily slid on a condom and mounted, easing himself between Noelle's bare tanned legs. If Tia had considered her roommate inflexible before, she changed her mind when she saw Noelle wrap her calves around Kevin's upper back and cross her ankles gracefully between his shoulder blades.

'Harder! Faster!' barked the she-beast to her lover. 'Listen, I need you to go deeper, *now*. And shunt it up a bit ... good. That's it. Ahhhh.'

Tia smiled. Same old Noelle. Sex might transform her physically, but her personality hadn't changed. As Noelle's moans crescendoed, Tia stepped back behind the door. Spying on her roommate during foreplay was one thing, but watching Noelle achieve nirvana went a bit too far. She could hear Noelle's teeth gnashing, Kevin's groans escalating. Noelle had been right about her new lover; he was politically correct to the very end, letting Noelle cross the finish line first. He held back until she had reached a noisy climax, then took his own pleasure at a more subdued volume. Unlike Noelle, he was probably still aware of his classmates studying in the next room.

With the show over, Tia scurried to her own bedroom. Her heart was doing a crazy dance against her sternum; her palms were sweaty and her panties felt sticky. Maybe the charge nurse on the psych unit had been right when she warned Tia about the dangers of overstimulation.

Never mind, Tia thought, remembering the way her soul had soared when Jeremy kissed her. The alternative to overstimulation was much, much worse.

Strains of Wagner blasted Tia back to reality. She patted herself all over, but couldn't find the familiar oblong bump. Mark wanted her to keep the phone on her body at all times, but suddenly it was gone. Finally, she found it, buried at the bottom of the wicker basket where she kept her dirty lingerie.

How on earth did the phone end up there? she wondered, frantically pressing buttons on the tiny menace.

'Hello? Mark?'

'Hey, Cherry Bomb. What are you wearing?'

Tia looked down. 'The same clothes I was wearing when you saw me last night. I never had time to change.'

'No problem. Listen, I'm on my way over. We're having cocktails with my parents.'

'What? Mark, you can't do this to me!' Tia checked her watch. 'Besides, it's not six o'clock yet. You can't tell me what to do for another three hours.'

'I know, sweetheart, but my dad starts mixing martinis in fifteen minutes. Can't we change the rules? We've done it before.'

'No. We can't,' Tia panicked. 'You can't spring this on me; I'm not ready. Mentally or otherwise. I'm sweaty, tired and rumpled. I look like hell.'

And I was kissing another man less than half an hour ago, she added inwardly.

'Look, Tia, we've been dating for months. I've told them all about you. Now I need to give them concrete proof that you exist. And, if I didn't ambush you, you'd never agree to go,' Mark said.

He was right. The mere thought of meeting Mark's parents was enough to make Tia hyperventilate. His mother Beth was a renowned art dealer, a patroness of the performing arts, a socialite renowned for her poise and beauty. His father was a famous nature photographer who had climbed Mount Everest, and had the award-winning shots to prove it. Meeting a couple like that would require at least a week's preparation, with trips to her hairdresser (or better yet, a more glamorous woman's hairdresser), manicurist, day spa and the mall. Tia couldn't even picture herself crossing the threshold of their high-rise penthouse unless she'd lost five pounds.

'Please,' Tia whimpered. 'I'll do anything. I'll come over to your office and give you a blowjob. I'll come over to your office and give you two blowjobs. I'll have that threesome you wanted with your bisexual ex-girlfriend; I'll wax your Hummer every day for a year; I'll –'

'OK. Calm down. You're starting to wheeze. If it makes you that nervous, I'll reschedule. Let's see . . . I'm off to

San Francisco on Tuesday for that Envisioning America conference, back in town on Thursday morning. Mom and Dad are flying to Tokyo on Friday; they'll be gone for about a week. Let's plan to meet them on the weekend they come back.'

'On the weekend?' Tia said weakly, her mind boggling at the idea of parents who flew to Asia as casually as her own mother and father would have driven to Boise. 'Won't they have to go to a fundraiser or an opera or something?'

'They're my parents. I think they can pencil me in,' Mark said dryly. 'Really, Tia, there's no need to be so intimidated.'

'Oh, of course not. Just because your father's work has been all over *National Geographic* and *Time*, and your mother looks like Faye Dunaway and owns half the artists west of the Rocky Mountains doesn't mean I need to be intimidated.'

'They're *people*, sweetheart. They're accomplished, but they're not snobs. They'll love you. Especially my mother.'

'Swear?'

'I swear.' Mark lowered his voice. He must be calling from the office. 'But that doesn't mean you're off the hook. Saturday evening – put it in your Palm Pilot.'

'Palm Pilot? I don't even know what that is.'

'Seriously? We'll have to get you one. I couldn't survive without mine. Speaking of which, I've got a meeting with the money guys for the new telecom tower in fifteen minutes. I've got to jet.'

'Call me at six?'

'Mmm. I'll try, sweetheart. But it's a money meeting. You know how that goes. We'll probably end up working till ten and ordering takeout. I'll call you on a break. Love you.'

He signed off before Tia could reply. She stared at the phone, tucked in the palm of her hand. The device looked smug, as if it knew it wielded all the power in this relationship. Mark wouldn't be calling back for several hours, if at all, and Tia was staring at the digital display as if it might broadcast an order for her at any second.

Tia set the phone down in front of her mirror. She picked it up again and slid it back into the pocket of her jeans. The phone felt heavy all of a sudden. Bricklike. She pulled it out of her pocket and set it back on the dresser.

She'd never carried a cell phone before Mark. She'd never kept a calendar. If she wanted to talk to her friends, she knew she'd see them around the neighbourhood. And her life had never been so complex that she couldn't keep track of it with a few coloured felt-tips and a pad of sticky notes. Today, for example, she knew that she had a coffee date with Leo Baines at four. It was written down in pink highlighter on a lavender sticky, hanging on the mirror right at the level of her forehead.

Tia's watch informed her that it was four o'clock right now, which meant that Leo would be sitting at their regular table at the Java Dive, checking the old Rolex he'd inherited from his grandfather and tapping his pencil impatiently against his chin. Tia picked up her handbag and hurried out of the room.

Mark's cell phone stayed behind.

Kevin's handsome face, dreamy in post-coital bliss, loomed over Noelle's as he moved in for a kiss. With his light-brown hair hanging loose around his sculpted shoulders, he looked like a nearsighted angel. Noelle was happy to open her mouth for him, to let his tongue slip and slide across hers as he massaged her breasts in preparation for Round 2, but she couldn't concentrate. She was too busy trying to eavesdrop on Tia's phone conversation in the next room.

Noelle could have sworn she turned off the ringer on that cell phone before dropping it discreetly into Tia's laundry basket. Noelle was an ethical woman, an honest competitor. She didn't need to resort to dirty tricks to get a man. Tia had left the phone on her dresser last night and, when Noelle found the device, she'd decided to put it in a safer place, where its operatic ringtone wouldn't disturb her study group.

Yeah, right, sneered the voice of Noelle's conscience. *Like you weren't aware that Tia only does her laundry once a month.*

Kevin was swimming down her torso now, his mouth planting worshipful kisses along the planes of her abdominal muscles. Only a few days ago, she would have been lying here like Cleopatra on her barge, basking in the adoration of her latest conquest, leftwing slaveboy. Instead, she felt like batting him away so she could get up and plant her ear against the wall. She could swear she heard Tia having another anxiety attack over Mark's parents.

Tia would never be brave enough to meet the illustrious couple. Mark had been trying to drag her to his parents' penthouse for weeks, but she kept making excuses, inventing emergency meetings. Chickening out, in other words. Noelle would have met Mark's family in a red-hot minute. If you didn't run the gauntlet, you'd never grab the prize.

'Does any other man know how incredibly sexy you are?' Kevin was saying. He was rubbing his cheeks along Noelle's inner thighs, moving closer each time, approaching the fleecy temple in between, but always drawing back before he reached it.

'I don't think so. I try not to let the world know what a slut I am.'

'Well, the world's ignorance is my good luck. Can I kiss you here?' He shyly set his palm on Noelle's mound.

She wondered why he was asking permission to lick her in the same place he'd claimed with his cock only a few minutes earlier, but she played along. 'You may,' she said, regally patting his head.

Kevin slid downwards and set about licking her with all the passion that she would have expected, as if her sex were a brand-new idea that he was exploring. Noelle laid her head on the pillow and closed her eyes. Kevin made for an entertaining afternoon, but he wouldn't last. Noelle didn't want a man who requested permission; she wanted a man who staked claims. As his tongue wended its way in and out of her lower lips, she imagined that Mark was the one between her legs.

Mark wouldn't ask; Mark would just take. First, he would blindfold Noelle and tie her wrists over her head, stripping away that power that she took for granted. Then he would grab her thighs with his strong hands, push her knees back against her chest and devour her. He would go much further than Kevin was going now, down past the juiciest part of her cleft to the tight pink bud below. Mark would do things to her there that she'd only seen in those videos that she'd ordered off the internet. He would take possession of every opening, especially the ones that she was ashamed to offer to most of her lovers.

After only a few minutes under Kevin's tongue, Noelle could already feel herself cresting. Her mind felt floaty; her inner lips tingled and her hips were making those involuntary belly-dancer motions that meant her orgasm was going to be a big one. But there was one more thing she craved, one thing that would make her climax as special as a big fat pink-and-blue birthday cake . . .

'Spank me,' she whispered.

Kevin lifted his head and stared at her. 'Did you just say what I thought you said?'

'Yes. Turn me over and spank me. Please. I know it's not PC, but I need it. I've been a very, very bad girl, and I need discipline.'

'Geez, Noelle, I don't know –'

Noelle rolled out from under him, crawled on to all

fours and presented Kevin with her ass. If Kevin could ignore those taut buns, he didn't have a pulse.

'Spank me. Now! Or you'll never see paradise again.'

Kevin obeyed. He gave Noelle a hesitant swat on her right cheek, then another on her left.

'Please, Kevin,' Noelle implored. 'I need a real spanking. Smack me harder; I'm not going to break.'

Kevin picked up the pace. He wasn't delivering the masterful correction that Noelle had read about in Victorian erotica, but his spanking was enough to give her orgasm wings. Up, up, up, and Noelle was going where she wanted to go, way above the land of control, above the law school and the library, the county building and the courtroom, winging along on sheer pleasure with a mild afterburn of pain.

The spanking also made Noelle feel a teeny bit less guilty about burying Tia's cell phone in a basket of dirty underwear.

Chapter Eight

Paint Job

On Tuesday morning, Mark left town for Eviscerating America or Vaporising America or whatever his conference was called. Though Tia had a vague understanding of what Mark did, she couldn't grasp the scope of his career, which seemed to involve everything from adding new wings to the public library to rearranging the city's skylines as if the buildings were his own personal Lego set.

Meanwhile, Tia was back at the hospital as usual, working with people who could barely cope with the demands of holding down part-time jobs and subsidised apartments. She had taken over a therapy group on the adolescent ward, and was spending her afternoons poring over paintings of human sacrifices and fiery apocalypses, created by teenagers who were so angst ridden that they made her feel like a singing ant in a Pixar movie.

Mark's cell phone sat like a grenade on her dresser. Every once in a while, when she was on her way in or out of the bedroom, the little monster would catch her eye and she'd feel a tickle of guilt. A dedicated girlfriend would carry the phone with her everywhere, would probably sleep with it under her pillow at night when her boyfriend was out of town. No matter how hard she tried, Tia couldn't bring herself to carry the thing while Mark was gone. She even picked it up at one point, her hand poised to slip it into her pocket, then she set it carefully back down.

If Mark wanted to call, he could always reach her on

her favourite archaeological relic, the old princess phone that sat on the nightstand by her bed. Tia loved that phone, which she'd got as a gift on her fourteenth birthday. She'd discussed all of her teenage love affairs through its receiver, and had carried it with her like a security blanket into the twenty-first century. As much as she hated to admit it, Tia wasn't a digital girl. She didn't like being at the subservient end of an electronic leash, not even when the hand holding the leash was attached to the man of her dreams. But, lately, she was starting to wonder whether Mark held that title any more.

Tia made herself wait before she went back upstairs to Jeremy's apartment. She needed to test herself, to see how it felt to be away from him. Instead of getting easier, the distance between them got harder to take, especially since she knew he was only a few breaths away. She held out as long as she could, and on the third day, after an unproductive afternoon at City General, with patients who didn't seem to care about anything but getting done with their therapy so they could race outside for a cigarette break, Tia couldn't wait a second longer to see Jeremy again.

As soon as she saw his blue eyes, his sweet down-turned mouth, she realised that those days could easily qualify as the longest 72 hours of her life.

'I thought you'd forgotten about me,' Jeremy said. 'You never came back to see my work.'

'I'm here now, aren't I?'

'You were supposed to come a lot sooner. I got all my paintings set out for you, and I waited.' Jeremy kicked at the doorframe with the toe of his red Converse sneaker. On his other foot, he wore a battered blue running shoe with a lightning bolt on it. Both shoes were untied. His jeans were rumpled and his chest, bare under a ragged flannel shirt, was stained with paint.

'I had things to do, Jeremy,' she said lamely.

'For three whole days?'

'Yes. I have a life, you know.'

'I thought I was part of your life. A *big* part.' Jeremy was chewing his thumbnail, exactly the way his sister did when she was anxious or upset.

'You are,' Tia said, feeling her heart fall apart. 'It's just that other parts kept me too busy to come back here. Can't you forgive me?'

Jeremy sighed. He gave Tia a wary look through the fences of his long black eyelashes. 'Well, I guess so. As long as you're never that busy again. Being busy kills people. It's worse than smoking.'

They stood there for a moment, awkward after being apart for so long, then Jeremy made a grab for Tia and pulled her into his arms. He nuzzled her neck with his lips and rubbed her cheek with his soft curls. Smelling his skin brought back memories of his kisses, sensory impressions so vivid that they left her reeling. With Jeremy squeezing the breath out of her, Tia was starting to see pink clouds in front of her eyes. When he let her go, she almost fainted. Then she saw how he'd rearranged his living room, and she was too startled to fall.

Jeremy's apartment looked like an art-clearance warehouse, except that the art wasn't anything like what you'd find in a discount barn. He had propped his canvases against the walls of his living room, where they formed a spectacle of colour. Jeremy's paintings were stormy abstractions of lines and shapes, squiggles and splatters, but each canvas had a magnetic sense of unity that was all its own. With Jeremy shadowing her every move, Tia walked from one painting to the next, taking deep visual drinks of colour.

'What do you think?' Jeremy asked. He was rubbing his head, making his curls stand up even more than they were naturally inclined to do. 'If you didn't know me and you saw these, would you think I was insane?'

'No. I wouldn't say this was the work of a disorganised mind. There's a sense of direction in all of them, a kind of guiding vision. They're spontaneous and unconstrained, but it's clear that the artist is in control. They're awesome, Jeremy.'

Jeremy smiled and gave a relieved sigh. 'I was hoping you'd think that. Some people don't get my work at all. They take one look at it and think I'm nuts.'

'Well, that's true of any abstract artist. Some people can't appreciate anything but pure realism. They don't want to be challenged by art; they want to be entertained.'

'I used to paint in a way that people thought was realistic. Ask Noelle. I did everything an artist is supposed to do when they're learning: studied anatomy, did a billion charcoal sketches of body parts, got out my paintbox and painted fruit and flowers like a good boy. I got to the point where I was good enough to paint live nude models, and that was outstanding. But I still wasn't painting what I saw.'

'And these are what you see?'

'Sure. They just need some explanation. Like that one.' Jeremy pointed to a canvas that was a mass of blacks, blues and greens, spattered with yellow and red. 'That's two boats on the ocean at midnight. They're about to crash into each other, but the sailors don't know it yet. And that one, with the red and orange streaks, that's me when I was a kid, winning the fifty-yard dash. And the one that looks like an exploding frog is actually an anguished dinosaur.'

'What's he anguished about?'

'Extinction. You'd be anguished, too.'

'What about that one?' Tia was standing in front of a rainbow ribbon of violet, blue and yellow, arching over a sea of swirling red.

Jeremy's cheeks turned pink. He shuffled his feet. 'I call that one "Bridge to a Heart",' he said. 'I painted it after the first time I kissed you.'

Now it was Tia's turn to blush. 'I like it.'

Jeremy stepped closer to Tia. He reached out and

brushed back a lock of hair that had fallen across her forehead.

'I want to paint you, too. That's why I wanted you to come up here.'

'Really?' Tia touched her hair and smoothed her wrinkled slacks. 'I'm a mess.'

Jeremy grinned. 'You think you're a mess now? Wait till I'm done. Come on.'

He took Tia's hand and led her into his bedroom, which he'd obviously been using as his studio. Every inch of flat space, including his unmade bed, was occupied by canvases, rags, sketches, brushes or flattened tubes of acrylic paint. Tia remembered her lover Steffen's apartment; were all artists this messy, or was it only the men she fell in love with? While she watched, Jeremy unrolled a big drop cloth and spread it over the floor.

'What are you doing?'

'Getting ready to paint you.' Jeremy produced a jar of remarkably clean brushes and handed the jar to Tia. 'What do you think about these? Do they look familiar?'

Tia examined the brushes. There were dozens of them, in all shapes and sizes: classic round brushes and dainty riggers, flat one-strokes, slant-shaders, fans and stipplers. Some of the tips were unbelievably soft, as soft as a goodnight kiss, made for painting delicate lines. Others were thick and firm, designed for painting bold streaks and washes.

Steffen had been a jerk, but he had known how – and where – to use a paintbrush. It was Steffen who had gifted Tia with an obsession with the texture of sable on skin. The cat's tongue brushes had always been her favourites; their flat oval heads tapered to a point, making them useful for delivering wide sensual strokes along an inner thigh, or excruciatingly dainty circles around a nipple.

'They're Kolinskies,' Jeremy said proudly. 'All of them. Maybe it's just me, but I don't like synthetic brushes.'

He ran his palm across the tips of the forest of brushes. 'After copping a feel of these beauties, who'd want to use anything else?'

Kolinsky. The name had a sensual impact of its own. Brushes made of red Russian sable, beautifully crafted, expensive. As an art student, she'd spent obscene amounts of money on Kolinskies. Somewhere in Russia, entire populations of the red sables were mourning the loss of their tail hairs because of Tia.

'Where did you get all these supplies?' Tia asked. 'The brushes alone must have cost a fortune.'

'My mom gives me an unlimited allowance to buy art supplies. She knows what keeps me sane,' Jeremy said. 'But I didn't tell her what I bought these brushes for. I've been saving them to paint you with.'

All of a sudden, as her eyes made contact with Jeremy's, Tia saw exactly what he had in mind. 'Were you planning to use a canvas for this painting?' she asked.

Jeremy shook his head. A smile, sweet and slow as a molasses spill, spread across his face. 'No canvas. Just skin.'

'Whose skin?'

'Whose do you think?'

Tia's skin came alive with head-to-toe goosebumps. 'Am I going to have to take my clothes off?'

'Yeah. Unless you want me to paint those, too.'

Tia's fingers fumbled with the top button on her blouse. She hoped that Jeremy couldn't hear the sound of her blood thundering through her veins. She had a sense of déjà vu, remembering the first time she'd met this wonder boy, and how she'd gone through these same motions according to Mark's instructions. This time, she wasn't going to stop at two buttons. And Mark's cell phone was far, far away.

'Does it make you nervous when I watch you undress?' Jeremy asked.

'No,' Tia lied.

'How come you're shaking?'

He took hold of Tia's hands and lowered them to her sides. Then he took over the task of unbuttoning the row of tiny pearls.

'Your fine motor co-ordination must be better than mine,' Tia said. Her voice wasn't any better than her hands; her words had a tremor, too.

'Nah. I'm just used to undressing girls,' Jeremy said softly.

'I didn't know you were so experienced.'

'Like I said, I've painted nude women before. They've even let me be alone with them. Does that surprise you?'

'I don't think anything would surprise me about you.'

What startled her was her own reaction. Tia ached to ask him how he'd painted those girls: on a canvas, or as the canvas. She pictured those other models as a parade of nubile beauties stepping gazelle-like through Jeremy's past. College co-eds, much younger than Tia, not yet frustrated with the way their lives had turned out.

Having undone the last of the buttons, Jeremy pushed the blouse off Tia's shoulders and helped her untangle the sleeves from her arms. He brushed the back of his hand from her cheek down to her throat, across her clavicle and over her shoulder, then all the way down to her forearm, where the coppery hairs were as erect as the tips of his paintbrushes. With his other hand, he made the same journey along her left side, and then he brought his hands back to her collarbones and pushed the straps of her black lace bra over her shoulders. Instead of unfastening the latch between the satin cups, he stopped and let the straps dangle in loops along her arms while he gazed at her.

'This is the first time,' he said.

'First for what?' Tia panicked. He couldn't be a virgin. What they were doing now was almost more than her nerves – or her heart, for that matter – could handle. If she had to teach Jeremy how to make love, she'd be the first person in history to die of stage fright.

'The first time I've painted a woman as gorgeous as you.'

When Jeremy leant in to kiss her throat, and unhooked her bra in the same practised motion, she knew he had all the experience he needed. Her bra slipped off of its own accord, falling away like an unsolicited opinion, leaving her nipples exposed. The buds rose against Jeremy's chest, then against his palm, as he cradled her breasts in his hands.

'You're really shaky now.' He laughed, pressing his hips against hers and grinding at such a subtle pace that she almost wasn't aware of it. 'If I plugged you with quarters, we could both have fun all night.'

'I'm only shaking 'cause I'm cold.'

'Really? Not because I'm making you nervous with my manliness?' Jeremy flexed his biceps.

'No.' Tia laughed.

'If you're not nervous, you should be. I'm a legendary lover.'

'Wow. And to think you've reached those heights at twenty-two.'

'Age has nothing to do with it. Being a great lover is all about appreciating a woman's beauty. And I'm real good at that.'

Jeremy ran the back of his hand from Tia's throat along her clavicle again. That one smooth motion brought out a layer of gooseflesh over her whole body.

'Jeremy, you were going to paint me. Remember?'

'I remember. I was just prepping the canvas.'

Jeremy winked at Tia – long black lashes, turquoise blue flash – and then he backed away, his fingertips trailing along her waist. As soon as his body separated from hers, she felt a twinge of regret. She should have let him lead. Tia knew, just from the way he'd moved against her, that he could discover secrets under her skin, the way an art restorer uncovers hidden treasures through the careful, persistent removal of layers.

While Jeremy busied himself choosing tubes of paint from a wooden box, Tia kicked off her shoes, then pulled off her slacks. She felt gawky standing around in nothing but her panties; she hadn't felt so open to scrutiny since the school nurse did a scoliosis check on all the students in fifth grade. She crossed her arms over her chest and hugged herself.

'You can go ahead and lie down,' Jeremy said. 'Don't worry. I won't look till you're ready. Like I said, I've worked with a lot of models.'

'I'd hardly qualify as a model. Victim, maybe.'

'Not victim. Subject. You're going to be the subject of my masterpiece.'

Tia got down on the floor and lay face up on the canvas. Staring at the ceiling, she could see the faint outlines of Jeremy's stars. Thinking about those constellations, and how it would feel to navigate through them in Jeremy's arms, almost made up for the discomfort of lying naked (well, naked except for a scrap of ivory satin and lace between her thighs) on a hardwood floor. She wriggled, adjusted her weight, but she couldn't get comfortable. Even through the canvas, Tia could feel every splinter in the floorboards, every speck of grit.

'Could I have a pillow or something?' Tia piped up. 'This floor is kind of –'

'Hard?'

Jeremy was crouching on the floor beside her, lifting her head, already propping it on the pillow, and from this perspective she could see that, when he'd said 'hard', he wasn't referring to the floor. His faded jeans weren't fitting very well; a very visible swelling strained at the buttons on his fly, distorting the waistband.

'Princess and the pea,' he murmured, stroking the undersides of her breasts. 'That was my sister's favourite story. You feel every bump, don't you, Tia? But you don't show it. You always look like you're sailing along in life, like nothing bothers you, but you feel things more than other people.'

'Sounds like you're the one who should be the therapist, not me.'

Jeremy shook his head. 'Couldn't do it. My other patients would be pissed off – I'd want to spend all my time talking to you. And doing things to you ... like this.'

He straddled Tia's legs and hovered over her for a moment, just drinking in the sight of her body, before he began to peel off her panties. She was so aroused that the fabric clung to the folds between her thighs. She was ashamed to let Jeremy see how excited she was. Jeremy made Tia feel wet and ripe and lewd; he was so much younger and, in some ways, innocent – with all he'd been through, he still painted dinosaurs and compared the world around him to fairytales.

'You don't have to be embarrassed,' he said, his voice husky.

'What makes you think I'm embarrassed? This isn't exactly the first time a guy's taken my panties off.'

'Maybe. But this time, you're pink everywhere. Seriously. From your forehead all the way down to your ... wow. You're naked! I mean, you're *all* naked. I've never seen that before, not in real life. Wow,' he echoed, his hand rubbing his forehead. 'I'm in love.'

'With me? Or with the work of my Lady Bic?' Tia laughed.

Jeremy didn't seem to hear. He was mesmerised by the sight of her bare lower lips. Tia couldn't blame him. She'd fallen in love with shaving, herself. She'd even become vain about her grooming down there, spending way too much time with a hand mirror propped between her thighs, gazing at the orchid in between. She'd studied her sex when the lips were pale and sealed, and when they were swollen and aroused; she'd opened the shell and admired the ruby-red door to the labyrinth inside. Now Jeremy was staring at her with the same rapt fascination, and his attention was intoxicating.

'I can't paint that. It's already perfect.'

'Why don't you start somewhere else, and see where you end up?' Tia suggested.

'Right.' Jeremy raked his hands through his hair. 'Right. Good idea.'

He pulled her panties down the length of her legs, peeling them over her feet, stroking the arches as he went. He took his time with each foot, examining her toes, then running the back of his hand along the soles, before pressing his thumb into the bones of her arches.

'When I was in college, I spent a whole month drawing feet,' he said. 'I kind of got obsessed with them. I mean, feet are amazing. We just walk around on them all day, taking them for granted, but they're so miraculously complex. Just try to draw one some day. And they're sensitive, too. Wait. Don't go anywhere.'

'I wasn't planning on it.'

Jeremy jumped up and grabbed the jar of brushes and a handful of tubes of paint. He sat down tailor-fashion between Tia's legs and squirted red paint on to a square of cardboard. Then he took one of her feet and held it on his lap. As if by instinct, he chose her favourite brush, the cat's tongue, and dipped it into the paint.

'Jeremy, don't! I'm ticklish there!' she shrieked.

He ignored her. The first strokes of the brush against the sole of her foot felt like torture. But, as she gave in to the feathery sensation, her muscles loosened and her reflexes slowed. The brush really felt like a tongue, laving her soles with long rhythmic strokes. Up and down, up and down on one foot, then the other, back and forth between the two, until she was shuddering uncontrollably. Then Jeremy applied the pointed tip of the brush to the spaces between her toes, and Tia went crazy. Those tiny crevices might as well have been attached to her pussy with rippling ribbons; she experienced every twist of the sable brush as if it were winding along the folds between her thighs. She'd never felt anything like it, not even with Mark.

Jeremy was so focused on his work that he didn't seem to notice Tia's reaction. When he decided that he'd applied enough paint, he picked up a piece of white paper from his collection of supplies and pressed it against her right foot, then against her left. Then he held up the result for Tia to look at.

'What do you think?' he asked. 'I'm going to hang this over my bed.'

Her own red footprints floated in the air above Tia's head, like a gigantic version of the ink prints that had been made on the day she was born. But Tia had passed the point of thoughtful consideration of Jeremy's art; all she wanted was to feel the kiss of that sable again.

'Don't stop painting,' she said.

'Oh, I won't. I'm going to keep painting until the day I die. Art is my life, Tia –'

'No, Jeremy! Don't stop painting on *me*.'

He dropped the footprints and looked down at his human canvas. He stared at her, his eyes widening, all blue astonishment.

'You're turned on,' he said. 'Your nipples look like pink gumballs. What if I painted them purple? Would you like that?'

'Please,' Tia begged.

He hovered over her, using a brush with a flat oval tip. Jeremy didn't paint her nipples, as he'd promised, not until he had painted the valley between her breasts and the creases underneath, and the soft expanses of skin that lead up to the areolae. With every gliding, silken stroke, Tia could feel her skin puckering. The paint was thick and warm, viscous, creamy. As if he hadn't tortured her enough, Jeremy stopped his brush only centimetres away from the dark wrinkly skin that rose into pink buds, so that he could turn his attention back to his work. With maddening deliberation, he chose a new set of colours – blue and yellow – to paint her belly. Using two brushes this time, he painted her abdomen in swirls, which lead to her thighs, all the way down to her knees. Her thighs he painted in black and gold stripes.

'Now you're Tia the Tiger,' he said, sitting back to admire his work. 'My sex kitten. My wild animal. My furless feline –'

'You said you were going to paint my nipples,' Tia reminded him.

She had trouble getting the words out; it was hard to talk when you couldn't breathe. Her whole being ached for a huge starry release; she felt like she was standing on tiptoe on the head of a pin, poised so precariously that a breath could have knocked her into a freefall. Her fingers kneaded at the canvas underneath her, and her hips were already starting to go into that old familiar bump and grind.

'Wait a minute,' Jeremy said. 'There's just one more thing I have to do.'

'*What?*'

Jeremy got up and rummaged around in the pile of supplies on his dresser, until he found what he was looking for. With a sly smile, he held up his digital camera. 'I have to capture my masterpiece. This is by far the most excellent work I've ever done.'

While Tia squirmed on the canvas, Jeremy took her picture. She did everything he asked her to do: raising her arms over her head, lifting one leg to her chest, assuming every cheesecake pose she could think of. She forgot everything else but the connection between her body and Jeremy's eyes; for the moment, she was his painted woman.

'Photo shoot's over,' he said.

Jeremy put down the camera and stood looking down

at Tia. She couldn't tell if he was admiring her as a piece of art, or as a hot female body, or both. The silence between them held a gleaming promise.

'What are you going to do now?' Tia asked.

The few beats that followed felt more like hours, as she waited for his response. Finally, when she didn't think she could take any more, Jeremy shrugged off his shirt. An invisible fist clutched Tia's heart as she saw again how beautiful he was, all quivering anticipation and taut energy, his abdominal muscles twitching as he breathed. Then he began to unbutton his fly, or to try to unbutton it. His fingers fumbled, taking forever, and then he finally shoved his pants down, and there was his cock, so young and straight and hard, quivering like a divining rod. Tia opened herself up for him, and he was moving down on to her, lowering himself with a degree of control that she wouldn't have thought possible, so that he could paint her nipples with his tongue.

She knew that she was going to come when she felt her heels digging into the floor, getting ready for take-off. As her thighs and bottom rose off the ground, Jeremy lifted himself on to his hands and sank into her, their bodies meeting in a slippery collision of skin and paint. He only thrust a few times before she climaxed, but her body was so exquisitely self-aware that the friction seemed to go on and on, when in reality she was so wet that he pushed into her within a fraction of a second. She closed her eyes tight and held on to his ass for dear life, making him go deeper, because all the way in still wasn't enough.

'Oh, Tia,' he whispered, just before he came.

She'd never heard her own name sound so sweet – like a plea, like a prayer. It made her feel like a different woman, beloved and powerful. She wanted to pull him into her, so that she could melt around him. And when she opened her eyes and saw him gazing down at her, his eyes glistening, his teeth clenched as if he were in the grip of the sweetest pain in the world, Tia did merge with Jeremy. She did, she did, she really did.

Tia's cell phone was ringing. Mark must have called five or six times; the strains of *Die Valkyrie* sounded shrill, almost desperate. Noelle paced back and forth down the hallway outside Tia's room. Should she or shouldn't she? Mark wasn't one to give up. The phone kept ringing, on and on, until Noelle finally decided that she was justified in answering it. There was only so much electronic Wagner a woman could take. She burst into her roommate's bedroom and snatched her phone off the dresser.

'Hello?'

'Tia, where the hell have you been?' Mark's voice exploded into Noelle's ear, so loud and exasperated that she had to hold the phone at arm's length. 'The ballet starts in an hour. Forget dinner – we won't have time now. Just meet me downstairs in fifteen minutes.'

'Mark, it's not Tia. It's, um, me.'

Baffled silence. 'Who's me?'

'Noelle. I wouldn't have answered Tia's phone, but it kept ringing. She forgot to take it with her when she left.'

'Left where?'

'I wish I could tell you. I haven't seen her around much.'

'What's she been up to, anyway? I haven't been able to reach her. I just got back into town. Maybe it's egotistical of me, but I thought she'd be waiting by the phone.'

A tremor of hope shook Noelle's heart. She wanted to scream, 'My roommate's a big flake! She'll never make you happy. Pick me, pick me!' Instead, she waited for a diplomatic pause and said, in her most lawyerly tone, 'I'm not privy to Tia's activities. Maybe she's been enlarging her circle of friends.'

Mark gave an irritated snort, as if he didn't want to imagine the kinds of people that Tia would hang out with when he was gone. 'Whatever. She was supposed to meet me at six thirty. We should be on our way to the theatre. Where is she now?'

'I don't know, but it must have been something important if she forgot her phone.'

'Well, I'm at a loss. Should I drive over and hope she's there to meet me? Or should I just forget the whole thing?' Mark asked. 'Where could she have gone?'

Noelle knew what she was going to say. She saw the evening spread out in front of her like the arc of that high dive she'd never executed, like the race she'd never won, but she needed a second to steady her nerves.

'Look, Mark, if you've got the tickets, I'd be happy to buy one of them from you. I'd love to see *Coppélia*. I've loved that ballet since I was a little girl.'

She cringed as she waited for the inevitable 'no'. What the hell – life wasn't worth living if you didn't take a risk, even if you ended up lying face down in a mud puddle of rejection.

'Why not?' Mark said. 'But no way will I let you buy the ticket. You'll be my date. See you in fifteen.'

'Can we make it twenty? I need a little time to get ready.'

'No problem.'

Sparkles rained down around Noelle, the effervescent magic dust of her long-absent fairy godmother. Steel-plated land sharks didn't get to feel the kiss of fairy dust very often, but this week had been filled with the stuff. First she'd had sex with Kevin, now the ballet with Mark. Sure, Noelle was Mark's second choice. So what? It wouldn't be the first time that a brilliant understudy had stolen the spotlight.

But Noelle wasn't anybody's understudy. With twenty minutes to get ready, she didn't have much time to strategise. Best not to play the artsy ingénue; that was Tia's role. For once, Noelle was going to play herself.

First stop: the shower, where she reluctantly washed off Kevin's earnest scent. Kevin had stopped by this afternoon on his way to class, just to give her flowers and a kiss, and the kiss had turned into a quickie on the kitchen counter top. Such a considerate guy ... and a real virtuoso with his tongue. True to Noelle's expectations, Kevin had been as passionate between her legs as he was in front of a mock court. Kevin had only one tragic flaw, as far as Noelle was concerned: he wasn't Mark.

Wrapped in a towel, Noelle jumped out of the shower and rushed to her closet, where she stood on tiptoe to reach the precious shoebox that held her mother's Ferragamo pumps. No question, these were the shoes to wear tonight. It didn't matter what else she wore, or whether she wore anything at all – with those pumps on her feet, Noelle always came out on top.

The first time was just the national anthem; the ball game lasted for the rest of the evening. Once they were done with the floor, and both Tia and Jeremy were smeared from head to toe with his paints, they raced to the shower (Jeremy won), where they washed each other clean in a multicoloured rain. Then they were all over the apartment, making love in every place and position they could think of. A curious eavesdropper would have heard nothing from Jeremy's three rooms but crazy moans and wild squeals, pleas for more and pleas for mercy, and most of all laughter. Tia had never laughed so much while she was having sex; she laughed until her stomach muscles ached, and her cheeks swelled up like pink tomatoes and her lungs couldn't keep up any more. She laughed at herself, and at Jeremy, and at all the crazy things they were doing to give each other pleasure.

By sunset, they were limp, weak and starving. Tia ordered Chinese. She and Jeremy sat on his bed and fed each other potstickers and lo mein out of red-and-gold cardboard boxes, using Jeremy's detailing brushes instead of chopsticks.

'You know what?' Tia said, munching her second fortune cookie. 'There's only one place in this whole apartment where we haven't had sex yet.'

Jeremy scanned the room, from floor to ceiling. 'Where?'

'Right here. On your bed.'

Jeremy grinned. Before Tia could say 'egg roll', he was on top of her again, pushing her legs back, holding her behind the knees. Boy Wonder was a fast learner; after a few hours together, he'd already memorised the angles and depths that she liked best. This time Jeremy's pace was calm, almost languid. Surrounded by his pillows, she felt like she was being rocked in a tiny boat on a limitless sea. Her climax was barely a ripple, a breeze compared to the storms that had happened before. A sweet sleeping pill of an orgasm, it sent her off to sleep in Jeremy's arms.

Tia woke in the darkness, her head fuzzy. She didn't recognise anything around her at first – not the shadows of toppled furniture, or the roll of butcher paper, or the open window where a curtain swayed back and forth in a nocturnal breeze. It wasn't until she looked up and saw the stars overhead, then looked down and saw the angelic male body sleeping beside her, that she remembered whose bed she was in.

Jeremy slept like a child, all splayed out, one arm stretched over his head. His abdomen moved rhythmically in and out, and a wavy lock of hair that had fallen across his face stirred with his breathing. Tia lay down, propped herself on her elbow and watched him. You could learn a lot about a man by watching him sleep. Mark's sleep was deliberate, purposeful. He slept like a man on a schedule, which he was, and he never seemed to go all the way under. Jeremy's sleep was so deep that, when Tia began to draw invisible circles around his belly button with her fingernails, he didn't even move.

She let the circles widen, venturing down along the line of black hair that ran from his navel to his groin. Though Jeremy still hadn't woken, his cock answered Tia's invitation, rising away from his thigh as the shaft hardened. She moved down, straddled Jeremy carefully and took him into her mouth. He moaned in his sleep, but still didn't wake up. Tia didn't want him to; she wanted to have some alone-time with his body, to talk to his flesh without being interrupted by Jeremy's non-stop mind.

Tia took her time, getting to know the way Jeremy's sex tasted as she explored his skin with her fingertips. In the dark, she used her fingertips like eyes. They started at Jeremy's chest, outlining his nipples, then roamed down his belly and all the way to his thighs, taking note of the parts that were smooth and the parts that were furry; memorising the lines of muscles, pausing to investigate scars. Meanwhile, she never let him leave her mouth. By now, the head of his erection was nudging the back of her throat; if Tia could have swallowed him whole, she would have done it gladly. He tasted and smelt and felt so wonderful that she thought she could spend the next ten or twenty years lying in this bed with him, devouring him inch by inch.

'Wow. I thought I was having the greatest wet dream of my life. And then I woke up, and it was true.'

Jeremy's voice was hoarse with sleep. He wrapped his hands around Tia's head, holding her gently, not shoving her down the way some men did. They worked together, Jeremy's moans urging Tia on. When he arched his back and cried out, she felt a bit guilty, as if she'd stolen something from him while he was asleep. But it had been such a delicious theft that she couldn't resist.

'I can't believe you're still here,' he said, stroking the

back of her neck. 'I thought you'd be gone when I woke up.'

Tia rolled off him and nestled against his chest. 'Where did you think I would go?'

Jeremy's shoulder moved under her head as he shrugged. 'I don't know. I guess I thought you'd go home.'

A strange thought, startling and unexpected, streaked across Tia's mind like a shooting star: I *am* home. But she didn't say it. It was just her own secret thought, something to slip into her pocket and save for future examination.

'I'm glad you stayed,' he added. 'I'm...' he thought for a moment, searching for the right superlative. 'I'm exponentially glad. I'm happy to the thousandth power. Is there a number that big? Sure, why not? Numbers are infinite. That's probably actually a pretty small number, compared to some of the others out there. I never really got into maths. Maybe I should do that next.'

'Shhh. Let's look at the stars,' Tia said. 'I've never had the chance to see them with the lights off.'

'I put those stars up for you, you know. Before I even met you. As soon as Noelle told me about you, I knew you'd be incredible. Then, when I saw you, I had a flash of the future we were going to have. I saw myself lying in this bed with you, and I knew you'd never want to leave –'

'Jeremy, hush.'

Jeremy gave a blissful sigh. Lying so close to him, all of Tia's senses were heightened. He'd had that effect on her from the beginning, sharpening her experiences, bringing the world into dazzling focus. She could hear the faint rasp of his eyelashes whisking his cheeks each time he blinked. She could smell the perspiration, fresh and tangy, in the hollow of his neck. She could feel the Morse code of his pulse against her ribs. His heart was saying what she'd always known it would say to her. Tia reached for Jeremy's hand. He wove his fingers through hers, and squeezed them tight. His left hand, her right – mirrored opposites, interlocking perfectly.

'OK,' she said, answering the question that his heart had asked: *Let me in, let me in.*

He turned to look at her in the dark. 'What's OK?'

'Everything,' Tia said.

Noelle had always wondered what it would be like to be Jeremy, when he was soaring on the currents of one of his highs. 'High' was a state of being that had always escaped her; she was too tightly focused to feel euphoria, too cerebral for joy. But tonight, as she strolled arm-in-arm with Mark through the glass-and-steel atrium of the Performing Arts Centre, Noelle had her first taste of pure ecstasy. As soon as Mark stepped through the arched double doors of the atrium, the crowd of elegant culture vultures parted to admit him. His name bounced along people's lips, like the day's hot new buzzword: Mark was the in-boy. And Noelle, who had always had a healthy appreciation for celebrity, was rapturous to be the envy of about 75 women who would kill to be the in-boy's date.

Unlike Noelle, none of those brown-nosing, surgically enhanced social climbers was wearing vinyl. As she swept through the room, Noelle tightened the sash on her shiny black raincoat, making sure her best assets were still well covered. The raincoat, which she'd swiped from Tia's closet, was the perfect disguise for a woman on a mission. With a flared skirt, cinched waist and broad sash with a big shiny buckle, the coat was the last thing a girl would pick to wear on a rainy day – unless, of course, she was looking to get wet in some very intimate places.

Noelle couldn't wear most of the clothes in Tia's closet (not for lack of trying), but this garment might as well have been made for her. The skirt fell almost to Tia's knees, but, on Noelle's long legs, the hemline hit her at mid-thigh. If there was a man in the room who wasn't staring at Noelle's racehorse calves and ankles right now, he was probably attending the ballet with another guy. She'd borrowed liberally from a bottle of Tia's hair gel, which made her black curls gleam and sparkle like the vinyl she was wearing. To offset the frank trashiness of her outfit, Noelle had elected to wear her glasses tonight instead of her contacts. She'd made the right choice. While her clothes said 'Fuck me in the alley behind the liquor store,' her face said, 'Fuck off, I'm so smart you'll never have a chance.' The contrast left a trail of lust-struck men in her wake.

She couldn't read Mark's reaction to her new look. His eyes had widened when he first saw her, but for the most part he'd been in his own world this evening, greeting her with a polite peck on the cheek, tossing around a few pleasantries on the ride downtown. He was thinking about Tia, no doubt, and how her flaky behaviour had cost him an expensive ballet ticket. Noelle was still nothing more than a pinch-hitter. But the night was young.

'I've always loved ballet,' Noelle said with a sigh of pleasure, as Mark guided her into her balcony seat. 'Beauty and discipline, all in one. So much physical control.'

For the first time that night, Mark glanced at Noelle with something more than friendly consideration. 'Interesting. Tia claims to like the ballet, but I think she finds it too stuffy and oppressive. She never really seems to be enjoying herself.'

'What a shame.'

Noelle lifted her nose and made a non-committal noise. Putting down a man's girlfriend was never a smart idea, especially when you were trying to steal him for yourself. The way Mark looked tonight, it was all she could do not to make a grab for his bod. He was the only man in the theatre who was confident enough to wear khakis and a leather flight jacket, but he wore those casual clothes with an arrogant, catlike grace that put the other males to shame. Kind of a macho outfit for a comic French ballet, but Mark managed to pull it off. The rich brown leather of his jacket set off the gold undertones in his skin and made him look mysterious, exotic, like a rugged outback pilot who'd crash-landed his plane in the middle of this elite world. Glamorous women, draped on the arms of prosperous men, were turning their heads to eyeball Noelle's date.

My date, she reminded herself, enjoying a twinkle of possessive glee. She leant in closer to him and let her hand drift on to his forearm. Proprietary but casual, a simple gesture that informed the other women that Mark belonged to her, at least for the night.

'Funny, I'd never have thought you'd be interested in ballet, much less *Coppélia*,' Noelle remarked.

'Why's that?'

'A dance about dolls? Somehow it doesn't fit your image.'

'It doesn't fit my *public* image, no. But there's more to me than meets the eye.'

'Such as?'

'I'm intrigued by Doctor Coppélius. I can relate to his fantasy about making a beautiful mannequin come to life. I might as well come right out and say this: I like to control women. I like to tell them what to wear, what to do for me and, especially, what to do *to* me. I like making them feel incredible things, watching how they're transformed when I give them pleasure.'

'Hmph,' Noelle sniffed. 'You wouldn't have much luck with me in that regard.'

Oh, yeah, right, sneered Noelle's inner slut. *He'd turn you into a panting, grovelling fool, and you know it.*

Mark smiled. 'Should I take that as a challenge?'

'Take it however you like.'

Through the folds of his bomber jacket, Noelle could feel the swell of Mark's biceps, rock hard. The muscle twitched under her hand, and she shivered.

'Are you cold?' Mark asked. 'You can wear my coat, if you like.'

'No. Just excited.'

Mark smiled. 'You look incredible tonight. I thought you'd dress differently.'

'How so?'

'More like the other women.' He nodded in the direction of a couple of long-stemmed beauties wearing evening gowns. 'But I prefer what you're wearing. Very dangerous and illicit. You could be a Bond girl in that outfit.'

'You ain't seen nothing yet. I can be very dangerous, when I want to be.' Noelle kept her tone playful; Mark would find out soon enough that she was lethally serious.

'I'm sure you can.' Mark laughed. 'Tia told me all about you.'

Noelle would have cringed when he mentioned Tia ... if Mark's hand hadn't suddenly found its way to her knee. Instead, her spirits sang out with all the jubilation of a gospel choir: *His hand is on my leg! His hand is on my leg!*

'Has she said anything about me that you could repeat in public?' Noelle asked. Keeping it smooth, keeping it casual, keeping her cool like she'd never kept it before.

'Nope. Otherwise I wouldn't have asked you to be my date.'

The choir in Noelle's head soared to new heights. Her heart leapt into her throat and a rush of warmth washed across her skin. As the orchestra struck the opening notes of the *Prélude*, she settled in against Mark's body, the way she would with any other date. He wasn't responding yet, but he wasn't resisting, either. The last whispers of the crowd died away, as everyone waited in an enchanted hush for the performance to begin. A doll brought to life, a man crazy with love – *Coppélia* had been one of Noelle's favourite ballets ever since she was a little girl. Too bad she wasn't going to be capable of watching it tonight.

The curtain rose on a fairytale stage that could have been crafted in Noelle's dreams, but she couldn't stop sneaking glances at Mark's profile in the dark. She let her fingers wander from his arm down to his hand, which was still resting on her knee. Mark had gorgeous hands, even better than Kevin's, with strong, beautifully shaped fingers that would have looked equally capable holding a Cross pen or a monkey wrench. Or one of Noelle's breasts.

Part of Noelle wanted that hand, warm and firm, to stay on her knee forever. She would just have to go through the rest of her life like that, with the man of her dreams holding her kneecap. The rest of her was already longing for something a lot more intimate than hand–knee contact. And, because Noelle had never been one to wait for a man to make the first move, she picked up his hand, turned it over and kissed his palm. Her lips palpated the hollows and creases, tasting his skin, getting to know the hard and soft spots on the pads of his fingers. She kissed his fingertips, one after the other, and then she wrapped her lips around his index finger and oh so delicately sucked.

Out of the corner of her eye, she sneaked a peek at Mark's face. He was watching the stage, but physically he was focused on Noelle, his body tense against hers. Then she pulled his hand into the folds of her coat, and let him feel exactly what she wasn't wearing underneath. Mark froze. Noelle held her breath, waiting for him to respond, but he wasn't moving a muscle.

In the fifteen or twenty minutes that Noelle had to get ready for the ballet tonight, she had played out this scene in her mind. She'd calculated that the perfect moment to let Mark feel her up would be Act II, when Swanilda reveals to her fiancé Franz that she isn't the doll Coppélia, but his one true love, trying to rescue him from the evil doctor's plot to steal his life energy. Noelle had planned to bide her time until intermission, teasing and tantalising Mark with subtle ambiguous signals. Instead, they'd barely got into Act I, and Mark's hand was all the way up her coat, pressed against her left breast. Her heart was hammering against his palm, giving away her whole game plan.

Mark didn't take long to figure out his counter-move. He freed his hand from Noelle's fingers and went on his own exploratory mission, roving all over her skin, which she'd softened with lotion and baby powder. Though he never took his eyes off the dancers, he was studying Noelle's body with more attention than any man had given her visually. His fingers crossed the tops of her breasts, and the silky underslopes, the tight flesh of her areolae, the hardened peaks of her nipples. They danced along her rib cage to the dainty tune of the *Valse Lente*, playing the ribs like the keys of a velvet-covered instrument, then moved to her waist. Lower, lower, tickling her belly button, stopping to knead the soft curves underneath. When Noelle felt the sash of her raincoat being loosened, a shiver of alarm ran through her.

This wasn't what she'd planned. Not even close. At this moment, she'd imagined herself holding Mark's hand firmly in place while she reached for his fly, groping him to see how hard she could make him. Noelle was supposed to be leading the dance at this point; it wouldn't be until much later, when she'd set a few ground rules in authoritative body language, that she'd let Mark take over.

But here she was, trembling in her seat, trying not to moan, while Mark caressed every inch of her that he could reach. She didn't know if the people around them could see his hand tunnelling under her coat, but no one was crying out in shock or indignation. Not yet, anyway. The thought of being caught made her stiffen. She closed her eyes and tried to pretend she was lying with him in a locked bedroom with all the lights off, but the potent aroma of French perfumes and the sound of dignified gentlemen sucking breathmints killed that fantasy.

'Mark, I don't think –'

'That's right. Don't think,' Mark interrupted under his breath. 'Stop being so self-conscious. Just experience what I'm doing to you. You'll love it.'

He was right. Noelle did love what he was doing to her, especially when he reached down to push her legs apart, so that he could fondle the thick damp pelt of curls in between. Noelle turned towards him, giving him even more access and hiding herself at the same time.

'Cross your right leg over your left,' Mark whispered. 'That's it. Let your thigh rest on my hand. It's OK. You aren't going to hurt me.'

Mark knew exactly what he was doing. The weight of Noelle's leg, scissored over the other and resting on his wrist, created a rhythmic, insistent pressure that reminded her of her teenage years, when she used to lie in bed with a rolled-up pillow between her thighs, rubbing against it and pretending it was a man's firm body.

'You're a nasty girl, you know?' Mark said. 'You come off so brilliant, so aloof and sarcastic, but, deep down, you're a horny little wench, aren't you?'

Noelle couldn't even manage to say the word 'yes'. She was too far gone in the feelings that Mark was creating inside her: the muscular waves of pressure from his hand, the illicit tingle of knowing she had an audience, the thrill of being revealed as the 'horny little wench' she'd always known she could be. And, if all that weren't enough, there was the vertigo of falling in love with a man who was exactly what she'd always wanted, and more.

She answered his question with a frantic nod. When Mark leant against her to murmur a question into her ear – 'Are you ready to come for me?' – she nodded again, making a guttural noise that no lady should ever make at the ballet. She was dimly aware of the pretty scenery on the stage below, and the clocklike pirouettes of the costumed dancers. The ballet and the audience, her life and her career, all seemed a million miles away. Noelle had never been so delirious that she'd forgotten about law school, but tonight, in this very public place, she let all her concerns and stresses slide away in a river of delight.

When she was done, Mark wrapped her limp body in the raincoat. He tied her sash carefully, like the ribbon on a gift that he intended to reopen later. Noelle couldn't believe that the orchestra was still playing, the dancers still dancing, the audience still watching the stage. Were these people really oblivious to the fact that she'd had an earthquake of an orgasm, right in the middle of the Performing Arts Centre?

'It's your turn,' Noelle whispered, reaching for Mark in the darkness.

'Not yet,' he hissed back. 'Not tonight.'

'What do you mean? Why not?' Noelle had trouble keeping her voice from rising to a squeal.

Mark held both of her hands in his lap, exactly where she would have wanted them to be, but his grip made it clear that he wasn't going to let her touch him yet. Tia had always said he had supreme self-discipline. Noelle had assumed she'd been exaggerating.

'I think you know the reason,' Mark said. 'Now hush. Watch the ballet.'

Noelle didn't know Mark's reason, but she guessed that it had three letters, red hair and the world's biggest collection of sleazy lingerie. Tia was a major roadblock in Noelle's agenda. But, in spite of everything that had happened tonight, and in spite of all that Noelle wanted, Tia was still her friend.

Later, Noelle promised herself, settling back in her seat with a restless sigh. Later, she'd get her revenge. She hadn't got this far in life without learning a thing or two about the sweeter forms of retaliation.

Chapter Nine

Build Me a Bridge to Jump Off

First there was the sex. Then came the wall. Making love, falling in love, set off creative sparks between Tia and Jeremy, and for the next few days, when they weren't rolling around naked in each other's arms, they were poring over books and websites about painting murals. Tia hadn't painted anything that couldn't fit on an easel since she finished the indoor mural at the Java Dive. Jeremy's wall paintings had been mostly 'unsolicited', as he liked to call them. Tia called them illegal.

'If we're going to do a mural together, we're going to do it right,' she insisted. 'I want us to make art together, not graffiti. More importantly, I don't want either of us to end up in jail.'

'Graffiti is considered an urban art form, and jail's not so bad,' Jeremy said blithely, munching an apple. 'Been there, done that, got out on bail. Thanks to my big sister, of course.'

He was lying on his stomach on the grass in City Park, as he sketched out ideas for their public masterpiece with a 2B pencil. Tia, lying next to him, smacked his rear end with an illustrated book of Italian frescoes.

'Well, I haven't been there or done that, and I don't want to. Besides, if we went to jail, we couldn't have sex. Not with each other, anyway. Or with anyone of the opposite sex, for that matter.'

'What's the matter? Don't you like girls?' Squinting in the sunlight, Jeremy grinned and kicked his heels. 'I think bi chicks are hot.'

'Of course you do. You're a man,' Tia said. 'But I don't

think I'd be attracted to the kind of girls I'd meet in jail. Anyway, this is all beside the point. We need to make a final decision on the walls we could use. And then we need to get permission to use one of them.'

'How are we going to do that?' Jeremy yawned. Legalities bored him, especially when they involved getting permission to do something that he would just as soon do without asking anyone at all.

'I don't know yet. But I'll figure something out. Leave that part to me.'

'Gladly.'

'You concentrate on how we're going to transfer the art to the wall.'

'That part's easy.' Jeremy tossed his apple core into the grass. He rolled into a sitting position, flipped his tablet to a fresh sheet of paper and quickly sketched a series of lines. 'After we figure out how big we want the painting to be, and sketch out our final idea, we'll make a grid. It'll look like this, only more exact. Each square on the grid will be a certain size, say an inch square. But, on the wall, the inches will translate into feet. That's the most accurate way to get a bigger rendition of the picture you've got on paper.'

He picked up the tablet, hiding it from Tia, and scribbled more lines, smiling to himself. Then he coloured in his sketch with pastels and, when he was done, he held the tablet out to her.

'This is what I want to do,' he said.

Over his grid, he'd drawn a portrait of a naked man and woman, intertwined, surrounded by the rooftops and bridges and skyscrapers of an imaginary city. Against the background of modern structures, the sensual embrace was primitive, raw in its frank passion ... exactly like the murals that Tia used to dream about painting. The image corresponded to everything Tia had fantasised about creating, right down to the vivid blues and purples and yellows he'd chosen.

'I think this would be a bold statement to make in

the middle of downtown,' Jeremy mused. He tilted the tablet, added a few more dashes of red. 'Cities are temporary. Sex lasts forever. Well, maybe not forever, but at least for five or six hours, if you're lucky,' he added, winking at Tia. 'This could be awesome.'

'How do you know?' she asked.

'How do I know what? That this would be awesome?'

'No, Jeremy. How do you know *me*? I think you know me better than anybody. And we only met a few weeks ago. I keep telling myself this can't be happening, but it is, and I don't get it.'

Jeremy smiled. 'That's not so hard to understand. When most people meet each other, they're strangers. It takes them a while to get to know each other and, if they like each other, they might fall in love. Then there are people like me and you, who know each other and love each other before they even meet. People like us are two halves of a whole that get split apart and have to find each other again. Getting those halves together is just a matter of things arranging themselves the right way. Like you and my sister meeting, and moving in together, so that me and you could meet each other, because we were meant to meet each other. See how it works?'

'Um, I think so,' Tia said.

'Read Plato if you have any questions,' Jeremy said loftily. 'He's the one who wrote about that kind of stuff. It's all in this book called *The Symposium*. I read it in my Western Civ class, the semester before everything fell apart and I ran away.'

He turned to a fresh sheet of paper and started to draw again, whistling under his breath. Tia felt a chill in the air, and she shivered. Summer wouldn't last much longer. The sun was slanting through the trees at a lower angle. If she and Jeremy were going to paint an outdoor mural, they'd need to get started before the snow fell, or else they'd have to wait till spring.

'Jeremy,' she began, knowing that her question would

be impossible to answer, but needing to ask it anyway, 'do you think you'd ever run away from me?'

Jeremy didn't look up, but his hand stopped moving on the page. 'Why are you asking me that?' he said.

He rolled the violet stick of pastel between his thumb and forefinger, and looked straight at Tia. For the first time since they'd met, she couldn't meet his eyes. She yanked a dandelion out of the ground and began to peel at the stem.

'Because,' she said, 'I want to know what kind of chance we have. I mean, I know we have great sex. And we inspire each other creatively –'

'And we love each other. Did you forget that part?' Jeremy broke in.

'No. I didn't.'

Jeremy pulled the maimed flower out of Tia's fingers and squeezed her hand. 'I'm good at a lot of things, Tia. Art, music, sex, running – lots of stuff. I'm good at loving people, too. Ask Noelle. When I love someone, I always love them. Even when I'm crazy.'

Tia cringed. 'I wish you wouldn't use that word, Jeremy.'

'What word? Love?'

'No. Crazy.'

'Hey, that's how I feel when things go wrong. What do you think it feels like, a trip to Disneyland? Listen, I know why you asked me that question, because you think I might screw things up for us. I've made a mess of my life a couple of times, but I've also come back and fixed it again. Haven't I?'

'Yes,' Tia admitted.

'So don't worry about us. You're the first woman I ever loved who made me feel quiet inside. I mean, you also make me feel high and happy and excited but, under all that, I get calm when I think about you. It's kind of like . . . it's like this pond I used to go to when I was a kid, in the summer. When the sun shone on it, and the wind was blowing, the water would get all sparkly and dazzly, millions of colours exploding in the light. There was a swing over the pond, and when I swung out over the water and thought about falling, I'd freak out and get scared. But it always turned out OK because, no matter how I swung, I'd always land in this deep quiet part of the pond, where you could just keep falling and floating and never have to worry about hitting the bottom. That's how I feel about you, Tia. That's what loving you is like. It's sparkly and brilliant but, under all that shininess, it's quiet and cool and safe. I kept going back to that pond till my feet were too big to fit on the swing. Do you think I'd run away from that?'

Tia shook her head. She couldn't say a word.

'I promise you, Tia,' Jeremy said, with a blue-eyed sincerity that seared her heart, 'that my feet will never get too big to fit on you.'

Tia leant over to kiss Jeremy, but she missed his mouth and her lips landed on his nose. She couldn't see him clearly through the warm smear of tears that blurred her vision. Jeremy licked the tears off her eyelids, her cheeks and the bridge of her nose. Then he gave her the kiss she'd been trying to deliver in the first place, straight on the lips. Jeremy's kisses were super-expressive; his mouth had its own language that had nothing to do with speech. The way he was kissing her now, direct and serious, was completely different from the way he'd kissed her early that morning, when they were taking a shower together, or the night before, when he'd come up behind her in his kitchen while she was cleaning out his refrigerator. This kiss said that he really did love Tia, that he wasn't going to leave her ... at least not intentionally. His tongue tasted tart and sweet, like the apple he'd finished earlier.

But she didn't get to savour that taste for long, before his mouth left hers and moved on to her throat. As he sucked and nibbled at her neck, she knew that the pressure of his teeth was going to leave monster hickeys on her pale skin, but she couldn't care less. At the age of thirty, a woman could either be mortified by love bites, or flaunt them with pride. She just laughed, threw back her head and let Jeremy ease her on to the grass. He was lying on top of her now, sliding his hand under her shirt so he could caress her breasts under her bra. His breathing went ragged. His urgency was contagious. Tia was getting hot and bothered too, and she decided to help him out by wriggling out of her shirt and bra altogether. Jeremy caught his breath when he saw her breasts, as if he were seeing them for the very first time.

Suddenly, Tia was seventeen years old again, a senior in high school, lying in the grass with a 22-year-old she'd met at a fraternity party she wasn't supposed to attend. He was a football player, buff and beautiful, the kind of guy who'd never given Tia a second glance before her breasts belatedly grew, only a year earlier. As if they'd been thrown under a spell, the guys who had ignored Tia all wanted to grope her. She wasn't too young to see the irony in this miracle.

She definitely wasn't too young to see the irony in comparing that long-ago lover with the young man who was making love to her right now. Both of them were 22 years old, but there was a universe of difference between Jeremy's sensitive, adoring touch and the crude manhandling that the football player had given her. She felt sorry for the seventeen-year-old Tia, who'd been so unaware of the workings of her body that she hadn't known whether she was having an orgasm.

'D'juh come?' grunted the football player, mostly as an afterthought, as he was hoisting himself into a vertical position.

'Oh, yeah,' Tia had lied enthusiastically, although she had no idea what coming felt like. Not yet. And now, with Jeremy, it was as if the sexual encounters she'd had before were all relegated to the same status as sex with that long-ago guy. Sex before Jeremy was a trailer, a preview to the main feature, and all her other lovers – even Mark, sad to say – were only stand-ins.

Jeremy pushed her breasts together, played with them, tasted them. His soft curls tickled her nipples, brushing the pink-brown borders of her areolae. He moaned into her skin, making her flesh hum. When he slid his hand under her skirt, her flesh gave way under his fingers, no more resistant than a dish of custard. Still, she stiffened and clamped her thighs shut. They were half-hidden under the heavy branches of a low-hanging oak, but the park was full of kids and moms, joggers and dogs.

'It's OK,' Jeremy insisted. 'We can do it here. Aren't you ready?'

He pushed against her with his hips, letting her feel how ready *he* was.

'Jeremy, people are going to see. Let's go back to your place.'

'You think they won't know what we've been doing when they see how I'm walking?'

'Well, I just don't see how –'

'Like this.' In one lightning-fast motion, Jeremy had Tia's skirt up around her hips, and he was inside her. Just like that. She hadn't even heard him unbutton his jeans.

'You really are a boy wonder.' Tia laughed.

'That's right. A sexual super-hero,' he said breath-lessly. 'I won't last very long, though. All that love talk got me too turned on.'

It was flash sex for both of them, as startling and unexpected as heat lightning. A few vigorous thrusts made Tia forget her inhibitions. She wrapped her legs around Jeremy's back, feeling the draft of a cool August afternoon on her bum, and let him have his way with her.

All of a sudden he rolled over, pulling her on top of him. With his cock lodged inside her as deep as it could go, Tia rode him slowly and watched his eyes change colour. Each time she shifted her weight, his face was transformed. A forked vein in his temple throbbed minutely in time to Tia's movements. She liked this – being in control of him, shaping his responses, making his body express his pleasure in a dozen subtle ways.

But Tia couldn't hold the reins forever. Before long, Jeremy found just the right angle, slanting up against some soft inner place with a honeyed friction that made her whimper. Coming was just a matter of waiting for that friction to spread to all her nerve endings.

Tia's nerves were always stimulated these days; ambient arousal was her normal state of being. Pushing her over the edge didn't take much more than a deep long kiss or a quick tumble in the grass. Jeremy knew how to make her body shudder and shake, buck and rise. He'd found all her secret pleasure spots so fast that she couldn't help wondering if he was right, that meeting him hadn't been like encountering a stranger, but like finding her lost half.

The mural gave Tia a million details to consider: surface materials, the porosity of the wall, exposure to soil and sunlight and plant life, cleaning techniques, graffiti protection. She didn't have time to worry about the fact that Mark's six o'clock calls had diminished to every other night. Mark was a busy man, Tia rationalised. He'd come back from that conference with a million new ideas. When he did touch base with Tia, it was usually to reschedule plans he'd made with her the day before, or to remind her of the meeting that she dreaded more than a root canal.

'Don't forget cocktails with my parents,' Mark said ominously over the phone. 'This Saturday, at four.'

'Couldn't we put them off for another week?' Tia whined. Now, more than ever, she wanted to avoid this encounter. After the past week with Jeremy, she'd not only feel tacky and low bred around Mark's illustrious mother and father; she'd feel guilty, too.

'Absolutely not,' Mark said. 'We've cancelled on them twice already. You can't keep putting this off, Tia. My mother can't wait for me to get serious about a woman and settle down. If you put her off any longer, she'll hunt you down and introduce herself by force.'

'Guess I don't have a choice, then,' Tia said, wondering what Mark's mommy would do if she knew that Tia was spending more time getting it on with a 22-year-old than picking out china patterns with Mark.

'No, you don't. Listen, Cherry Bomb, I've got another call coming in, and I've got to take it. Can I call you back in five?'

'Sure,' Tia said.

The phone went dead. Tia set it down on her bed and went back to what she'd been doing – painting her toenails. She'd decided to use ten different shades of pink, ranging from barely there pearl to fuck-me fuchsia. This was the kind of thing she'd liked to do in high school, an elaborate way of postponing something unpleasant and inevitable.

'Hey, sweetie.' Noelle popped her head in the door and waved at Tia. 'Whatcha doing?'

Tia looked up from her pedicure. Noelle's eyes, without their glasses, sparkled like a couple of brand-new bottles of Windex. Her cheeks were flushed the same colour as the third toenail on Tia's right foot. She was grinning like a fool and smelt like gardenias.

'Who are you and what have you done with my roommate?' Tia asked.

'Stop it, silly.' Noelle laughed. 'What's up? Got plans for tonight?'

'No. Come to think of it, I don't,' Tia said.

'That's a surprise. You and Mark used to have something going on every night.'

'Guess he's busy.'

'Too busy for you?'

'Yep.'

Noelle's fingers trailed along the top of a bookshelf that stood beside Tia's door. 'Wow,' she said, examining her fingertips. 'You've even had time to dust. You really must have a lot of time to yourself nowadays.'

'Well, no. Not exactly.'

Tia thought about telling Noelle how that bookshelf had got dusted. Just last night, when Noelle was out with her study group, Jeremy had planted Tia's bottom on top of that shelf while pinning her shoulders to the wall so he could kiss her as he slid into her from a standing position. That was probably the most fun Tia had ever had doing housework, she thought, smiling to herself.

'Well, anyway, wish I had time to chat, but I've got to run. I've got plans of my own,' Noelle said.

'Where are you off to?'

'I've got a date, believe it or not.'

'With that guy from your class? Kelvin?'

'Who? Oh. You mean Kevin.' Noelle waved her hand and wrinkled her nose, as if the memory of Kevin were an unpleasant smell. 'I'm not into him any more.'

'I knew he'd turn out to be too left-wing for you.'

'His politics weren't the problem. I met someone else.'

'Really? Who?'

Tia glanced up at her roommate. Noelle's face wore a creamy Cheshire-cat smile.

'You'll find out, when the time is right,' she said. 'Oh, by the way, I defrosted the fridge this morning after my seminar. Cleaned the bathroom, too. I found this wonderful French lavender-scented cleanser that's totally biodegradable.'

'Great. Close my door on your way out,' Tia said.

Mark wasn't the only one acting differently these days. Noelle's behaviour was so strange that, if Tia had bothered to analyse it, she might have wondered whether her roommate was on drugs, or if she had been possessed by a bubbly demon. Noelle had never been so giddy or affectionate. She hugged Tia for no reason when they ran into each other in the kitchen in the mornings. She took her turn scrubbing the bathtub without being reminded, and never griped about red hairs in the drain any more. She borrowed the opera CDs that Mark had bought for Tia (most of which Tia had left in their plastic wrappers), and played them at all hours of the day.

Something, or someone, had transformed Noelle into a magnanimous hug-o-maniac who loved housecleaning and opera. As she sat mulling over the mysterious changes in Noelle, and touching up the pink spectrum of her toenails, Tia didn't notice that Mark hadn't called her back. She picked up the cell phone and punched in a familiar number.

'Hello? Who's this?' Leo's voice, nasal and perpetually irritated, buzzed over the airwaves.

'It's Tia. What are you doing?'

'Exiting Hellhole Hospital. I just finished evaluating a patient. The poor sucker's a complete mess. He needs to be admitted, but there's not an empty psych bed in the whole state. The world must be going crazy.'

'Still doing your ER rotation?'

'I'll be doing this rotation till the end of time,' Leo sighed in despair.

'Want to meet me for a drink?'

'Darling, I would love to meet you for a drink. Preferably numerous drinks. Where and when?'

'Happy hour at Racine's. I'm already on my way.'

Jeremy had a meeting with his case manager that afternoon. Tia was happy for the break. Starting with Jeremy's first kiss, Tia's world had started whirling on its axis, the old familiar objects and places turning into streaks of colour. She felt like she needed a dose of cerebral sedation, something to give her space and time to think. Leo Baines, with his impenetrable green parka and eternal scowl, was the perfect antidote to delirium.

'So tell me everything,' Leo began, when they were installed on matching barstools at Racine's. Racine's was a popular watering hole among the more mature singles of the neighbourhood. Tia never went there after dark, when it turned into a hunting ground for the marriage minded. She only frequented Racine's at happy hour, to partake of their deadly martinis.

'I'm in love with my roommate's brother,' Tia announced. Happy hour was a good time for confessions, she thought, especially when they involved true love.

'What?' Leo's eyes boggled behind his glasses.

'I'm in love,' she repeated. 'With Jeremy. Why do I get the feeling you're underjoyed?'

'Are you sleeping with him?'

'Of course I'm sleeping with him. We're in love. That's what men and women do when they're in love.'

'Not necessarily. And he's not a man. He's still a child.'

'Leo, he's twenty-two!'

'That doesn't matter. Emotionally, he can't be more than fifteen.'

'How on earth do you know that?'

'Your *petit ami* may be precocious in some ways, but emotionally he's no different from any other male. He's going to be confused about his own feelings for at least five more years. Having sex with a man under thirty should be considered emotional statutory rape.'

'Oh, for goodness' sake,' Tia scoffed.

'This has got to be the worst thing I've ever heard,' Leo said. 'Honestly, Tia, what were you thinking? More importantly, who were you thinking about? Not Jeremy. You're going to break that kid's heart.'

'No, I'm not!'

'Yes, you are. You'll have a few weeks of staggering passion, but as soon as you come to your senses you'll dump him, just like that.' Leo snapped his fingers about an inch from Tia's nose.

She curled her shoulders, making herself a shell to hide in. She fixed her gaze on the empty martini glass in front of her. She'd downed one of these potent puppies already and, with Leo castigating her like an outraged Pilgrim father, she was already longing for a second. Her rejected olive, impaled on its toothpick, stared up at her from the glass with an accusing red eye.

'*Et tu*, olive?' she sighed. 'Does everyone around here think I'm a lecherous old heartbreaker?'

'This isn't just about age. It's about Jeremy's mental health. He's been through enough of an emotional hurricane; he doesn't need a disastrous love affair on top of everything else.'

'Why do you assume it's going to end in disaster? I know we'd never be the typical upwardly mobile urban couple, but what if we worked out, in our own weird way?'

'Think about it for a moment. Jeremy doesn't have a job, and you're not exactly Miss Stability, yourself. This is a tragedy in the making.'

Tia put her hand on Leo's arm. 'Leo, please. Calm down. And stop insulting me, while you're at it. Do you need another drink?'

Leo nodded. Tia searched for the bartender, who was already on his way. Leo's distress was attracting attention. If there was one thing he'd learnt from his patients, it was how to make a scene. A few more sips of chilled vodka calmed him down. At least he wasn't hyperventilating any more.

'Look, Tia, I hate to be a bastard, but the hospital could scrap its art-therapy programme with the next round of budget cuts, and then where would you be? Teaching macramé at summer camp? You're thirty years old; you're not married; you don't have a reliable source of cash. And, I might add, you have a very pricey taste in underclothing. As reactionary as it may sound, you need a man with a steady income to keep you stable and secure.'

'Someone like Mark, you mean,' said Tia.

'No. I mean someone like me. I'd be honoured to take on that responsibility. I'd even assume the onerous task of financing your lingerie habit – as long as you'd model the fruits of my labour for me.' Leo sat up straight on the barstool. At his full height, he was barely a shade taller than Tia.

'Leo, that's sweet, but –'

'I'm serious. You should consider me. I might be a starving resident but, once I get into private practice, I intend to rake in the dough. I'm extremely attracted to you, Tia. I would have no problem falling in love with you. I've just refrained until now.'

Tia buried her face in her hands and groaned. 'Please. Don't complicate things even more.'

Leo slid off his barstool, adjusted his parka and straightened his bow tie with a savage little twist. 'If your perceptions weren't fogged by lust, you'd see that my offer isn't complicated at all. It's supremely simple. You marry me; you learn to love me; you're set for life.'

'Leo, I do love you. As a friend. Not romantically.'

'Romance is a pile of shit, Tia. Love isn't something you fall into, it's something you build. That's an honest statement from something all women claim to want: a mature male.'

'Fair enough. I don't want to "build" love with you. OK?'

Leo cringed as if she'd slapped him. Then he turned and stalked out of the bar. Tia hated herself when she saw the wounded stiffness in his walk, but she couldn't call him back. They could kiss and make up; they could talk and drink all night; but they'd never agree on the one subject Tia cared about: Jeremy.

She looked up from her empty glass, searching for the bartender. The place was starting to fill up, and Tia couldn't see the pierced hipster who had poured her martini. But she did see someone else in the crowd –

two someones, in fact – who killed what was left of her buzz.

It was Mark. With a woman. They were both wearing running clothes, but they were still the most striking couple in the bar. The willowy brunette leant against Mark's arm, staring adoringly into his face as he ordered drinks from the bartender who had deserted Tia. She would have looked familiar if her lips had been compressed with determination, and if her mass of gypsy curls had been scraped back from her face and restrained in a French braid. Tia should have known that Noelle could be breathtaking, if she allowed herself to be. She was Jeremy's sister, after all.

And suddenly, as if a veil had fallen away from Tia's eyes, she saw everything with shocking clarity: the mysterious loss and reappearance of her cell phone, Noelle's ecstatic mood, Mark's run of late-night meetings. Tia leant against the bar. She felt like the wind had been knocked out of her. She knew that she didn't have a right to feel betrayed, but emotions didn't quibble over rights. Noelle was gaga over Mark, and Noelle always got what she wanted.

'Need another drink?' asked the bartender. His smirk looked oddly sympathetic. Maybe he was in on the conspiracy, too.

'Yes, I do. I need many, many drinks,' Tia said. But not here, with Mark standing less than fifteen feet away. She would stop at the liquor store on her way home, buy a bottle of something clear and cheap, and self-administer analgesia in the privacy of her bedroom.

Clutching her purse, Tia slipped off her stool. The seat was instantly filled by another woman, an athletic blonde supermodel type wearing skintight shorts and a Lycra sports bra. Feeling short and dumpy all of a sudden, Tia let the crowd shove her towards the door. She ducked outside, hoping Mark hadn't noticed her.

Of course he hadn't noticed her. He'd been wearing Noelle around his neck like a Velcro scarf, Tia thought bitterly. Arms wrapped around her chest, she walked down the street, conducting an inner dialogue with herself.

Tia: I can't believe I let myself lose Mark. He was the best thing in my life.

Tia: Wait a second. What about Jeremy?

Tia: Well, I love Jeremy, too ... I *really* love him. It scares me how much.

Tia: Easy choice, then. You can't have two men. That would be greedy.

Tia: So which one do I choose?

Tia: I can't believe you have to ask me that. You know which one.

Tia: Then I should let Noelle have Mark. It's only fair. Now that I think about it, they're perfect for each other.

Tia's mother: Wait one red-hot minute! You go back to that bar, Tia, and tell that hussy to step away from your man. I'm going to see you married to someone handsome and successful if it kills me.

Tia (with a groan): No one says 'hussy' any more, Mom. And stop interrupting my tormented mental conversations. I have to figure this out for myself.

Lost in her interior dialogue, Tia had walked past her building and had wandered into City Park. She found herself standing on an ornamental footbridge over the creek, looking down at the trickle of water that was trying to make a path for itself through the dry rocks. Still brooding, she didn't hear the man who came up behind her. When he put his hand on the small of her back, she screamed, wheeled around and came face to face with her best friend.

'Leo! My life sucks,' she sobbed, throwing her arms around his neck.

'I know, darling. So does mine.' He rubbed her shoulders soothingly, giving her tender brotherly pats that gradually brought her back to reality.

'What are you doing here, anyway?' she sniffled.

'This is one of my favourite places in the city,' he said. 'I like to come here and mull things over. This bridge has a special meaning for me. I actually talked a guy out of committing suicide here.'

Tia broke her embrace with Leo to glance sceptically over the bridge, at the six-foot drop to the trickle of water below. 'Someone was going to kill himself in that?'

'It's the ideation that matters,' Leo said defensively. 'But let's not talk about the suicidal guy. Let's talk about you. Are you finally having that breakdown that I've always predicted?'

'I don't know where to start. Everything's a mess. After you left the bar, I looked up and saw Mark – with Noelle. I'm supposed to meet his parents this weekend, and he's out at a bar with my roommate! And I'm having an affair with her brother, and I'm crazy about Jeremy, and I have no idea what to do.'

Leo stepped back, holding Tia by the shoulders so that he could study her face. 'Are you honestly in love with that kid?' he asked. 'Don't even try to lie to me. I'm on my way to becoming a damn good shrink.'

'Yes,' Tia said. 'I'm in love with that kid. I know it's not practical, and it doesn't make any sense, but being with him is like skydiving. I feel so free and open, like the world doesn't have any limits. I know what you're thinking, Leo; that's just the secondhand high of his mania, and someday he'll crash, and I'll go straight down with him. But he's not manic. I swear he's not. This is just *him*. Isn't it possible that a person could just live life on a different key than most other people?'

Leo nodded ruefully. 'I'm afraid it is. I don't hear that key, myself. I suppose that's why you couldn't ever love me.'

'Oh, Leo. This isn't about *you*. I'm trying to tell you how I feel about Jeremy.'

'I know.'

'So is feeling that way enough? Could we make anything out of it, or should I break it off before things get too serious?'

Leo cleared his throat. He shuffled his feet.

'Well?' Tia pressed. 'Tell me.'

'Remember back at the bar, when I said that romance is shit?'

'How could I forget?'

'Only a die-hard romantic would say that. I believe in true love, Tia. I believe in profound and mysterious connections. I believe in passionate fireworks, and thunderous bolts of ecstasy, and wild dirty sex that opens windows on to eternity. And, though I'd never admit this to anyone but you, I believe in taking risks for all that. The only reason I'd settle for a humdrum, build-it-yourself affection is that it's the best I can probably hope for.'

Tia reached out and ran her hand across Leo's precious head, caressing his mixing-bowl hair. 'I do love you, Leo,' she began.

'But not like that,' they concluded in chorus.

With infinite gentleness, Leo dabbed the tears off Tia's cheeks with his fingertips. 'Listen,' he said. 'Here's how you'll make your decision. Pretend you never saw Mark and Noelle together.'

'How am I supposed to do that? This isn't a soap opera, it's my life.'

'I know, I know. But we're only talking about a couple of days here. Unless Mark approaches you with a break-up speech, try to wait it out until Saturday. Then you'll go and meet Mark's parents and pretend that everything's hunky-dory.'

'But why?' Tia cried. 'I never wanted to meet them in the first place. Mark's parents scare me to death.'

'Before you break things off with Mr Perfect, you

should get a glimpse at what you'll be giving up. The Whartons aren't so bad. In fact, Beth and Carl are a delightful couple. At the worst, you'd make two very influential friends.'

'Beth and Carl,' Tia repeated. 'You mean you've met Mark's parents?'

'Sweetheart, everyone in this city has met the Whartons, except you, apparently. I met them last Christmas, when Beth organised a dinner for the Department of Psychiatry. She's stunning, she's gracious and she's got great taste in art. The two of you should get along like two rubber duckies in a warm bath.'

'What if we don't?'

Leo shrugged. 'At least you'll know for sure. Then you can take the big leap into loving your wonder boy. The dive might turn into a belly-flop, but I can promise you that it'll be the thrill of a lifetime.'

'Thanks, Leo,' Tia said.

She leant in to kiss him on the cheek, but he turned his face at the last second so that her kiss landed on his mouth. She didn't pull away, just let his lips find hers and rest there for a moment, before she broke away, took his hand and led him off the bridge.

Chapter Ten

A Fate Worse than Beth

'I'm sorry, sweetness,' Mark said, kissing Tia on the lips. 'I've been neglecting my precious pet. My poor little Cherry Bomb. Did you miss me?'

'Sure,' Tia said. *Once more, with feeling.*

She kept waiting for that familiar throb of lust to kick in when Mark touched her, but her libido was dragging its feet today. Mark cupped Tia's chin in his palm and covered her face with feathery kisses. He looked and smelt and felt so good, in his bomber jacket, jeans and boots, that she shouldn't have had any problem responding, but she felt herself turning to wood in his arms.

'You're mad at me, Tia. I can tell. Damn committees. Those meetings took up all my time this week.'

'I know,' Tia said. 'You couldn't help it.'

'Maybe this will make up for the time we lost.'

Mark handed her a flat gift-wrapped box, creamy-white cardboard decorated with familiar gold script. He'd bought her more lingerie from Delana's, in a box with a bow, no less. Tia should have been ecstatic, but the truth was, she wasn't thinking much about under-wear any more. Her bras, panties, garter belts and teddies used to be the most important articles in her wardrobe, signs of her secret self. Now, when she got dressed in the morning, she grabbed anything clean and yanked it on without thinking. Leo probably would have said that Tia didn't need a secret identity any more; she was wearing all her passions boldly, in Tech-nicolor. Tia would have said it was because she was too busy thinking about sex and art to worry about bras and panties.

'Thank you, Mark.' She set the box down on her coffee table and stood on her tiptoes to give him a polite hug. 'It was sweet of you to buy me something, but you really didn't have to do that.'

And speaking of things we don't have to do, could we skip the forced encounter with your parents tonight? Tia thought.

Mark laughed. 'Aren't you going to open it? Wake up, Tia. There's a box from Delana's sitting two feet away from you.'

'I thought I'd open it later, after we have drinks with Carl and Beth. I'm kind of nervous right now, if you know what I mean. Feel.'

Tia pressed her hands against Mark's face so he could feel how sweaty her palms were. She was perspiring so much that she could have watered half the city's parks. She hadn't chosen the crisp white sleeveless blouse she was wearing because it was cool or conservative, but because it was less likely to show sweat stains than anything else she owned.

'Wow. You're not kidding. Are you really that scared, sweetheart?' Mark's forehead furrowed in concern, and Tia felt a rush of affection for him. He really did care about her. This reunion would have been so different if he were Jeremy.

'Yes. I really am.'

'Come on. Let's sit down and talk about it.' Mark circled Tia's shoulders with his strong heavy arm and led her towards the sofa.

She balked. 'If you don't mind, I'd rather just leave and get it over with.'

'Get it over with?' Mark echoed, with a stiff laugh. 'Look, Tia, this is a casual meeting. Drinks in a private home, not a public execution. Is there something else going on here?'

Silence stretched out between them, full of potential.

Tia could have told Mark everything then: about her mural dreams, about her dwindling interest in expensive underwear, about her love affair with Jeremy.

'No,' she said. 'It's just a very bad case of stage fright.'

'You won't be performing, sweetheart. You'll be surprised. Mom and Dad are very down to earth.'

'Down to this earth? Or some alternative superior one?'

'Down to the earth you're standing on,' Mark said. 'Now come on. Let's go. Bring the box – you can model that for me later, at home.'

At home, he said, as if he and Tia were going back to a cosy cottage they shared, instead of to that draughty loft that always left Tia feeling overwhelmed. She couldn't help comparing her memories of Mark's large luxury dwelling to Jeremy's cramped apartment, with its profusion of colours and engulfing impressions of creativity and passion.

'Couldn't we come back here for once?' Tia asked.

Mark gave her an odd look. 'Sure. Why not? As long as I get to see you in that overpriced scrap I just bought, I don't care whose bed we sleep in.'

The problem wasn't Mark himself, Tia realised. It was the canyon that yawned between his definition of home and her own. The thought left Tia feeling light and airy, as if a dismal fog had lifted. Suddenly she saw her choices clearly, and that clarity made her happier than she'd been all day.

She grabbed Mark by the elbow and dragged him towards the door. 'Let's go,' Tia urged. 'Let's get this show started.'

'Now that's the girl I know and love,' Mark said, giving Tia an approving pat on the rump.

But Tia wasn't that girl at all. She hadn't been that girl since Jeremy's first spinning kiss, and it wasn't very likely that she'd ever be that girl again.

* * *

Noelle and Jeremy sat on a platform next to the river, sharing a six-pack of rootbeer as they watched the water. The rapids were running low this year, but there was still a gaggle of thrill-seekers trying to wade out in the shallows. Noelle could tell, by the way Jeremy was jiggling his knees and twitching his shoulders, that he wanted to roll up his jeans and wade in, too. She wasn't in any mood to stop him.

'What's wrong with you tonight?' Jeremy asked his sister. 'You look like your best friend died.'

'Unfortunately she didn't,' Noelle sighed. 'I was just thinking.'

'Me too,' Jeremy said. 'But I'm happy, 'cause I'm thinking about Tia.'

Not much of a coincidence there, Noelle thought. How ironic, that a sister and brother were each getting shafted, in their own way, by the same cute redhead. The only difference was that Noelle knew what was going on behind the scenes: Mark had swept Tia away in his manly black coach to meet his parents. Cinderella's big night, the metamorphosis of a poor little therapist into a rich man's fiancée. Such a perky, feel-good tale. If Tia's life story had been a movie, Noelle would have puked into her popcorn.

'Betcha don't know where your girlfriend is tonight,' she taunted. Jeremy's buoyant mood was making her feel small and mean.

'I don't have to know where Tia is every second of the day. We're not joined at the liver or anything.'

'But you're in love, right? You should at least know where your true love is on a Saturday evening. What if she's out on a hot date with Mark?'

'She's not! If she was going out with that dweeb, she would have told me.'

Noelle shook her head and laughed. 'You know, Jeremy, you are so naive.'

'Shut up. You don't know what you're talking about.'

Jeremy's shoulders sagged. Noelle had poked a pin

into the bright-red balloon of his happiness, and he was starting to leak air.

'I'm sorry,' she said, propping him up with a big-sister hug. 'I didn't mean to be a bitch. I just am.'

'I know you are. It's OK.'

'No, it's not. Look, Jeremy, I've reconsidered this thing with you and Tia. I think you two could be good for each other. It might actually work out. Just be careful. And don't rush things.'

'Why is everyone always telling me not to rush things?' Jeremy complained. But his face brightened up again.

'Because your loved ones don't want you to be impulsive.'

'I'm not that much more impulsive than anyone else. Everyone's got impulses. I just obey mine. That's because I trust my intuition, where most people don't. Look at you, for instance. You're always rational about everything. You take forever to make up your mind. You use your judgement, not your intuition. You're not any happier than I am. In fact, I think you're less happy than I am.'

Noelle started to come back with a sharp retort, then her mouth snapped shut. 'You could be right,' she said. 'I'm not saying that you *are* right, Jeremy, but I'll think about what you said.'

'Good. Because I think you should try to live on the edge more. Take risks, like me. I took a big one, when I met Tia. And just the other day, I took another risk, and look what happened.'

Jeremy pulled a folded rectangle of pale-blue paper out of his pocket and handed it to Noelle. She opened it. It was a cheque for five hundred dollars, made out to Jeremy. When she saw the name on the account, Noelle's circulation ceased. She felt all the blood drain out of her face, straight into her ankles.

'How did you get this?'

'This cool lady gave it to me. It's for a painting that I

did. My first real sale,' Jeremy said. His chest puffed out with pride. 'Five hundred bucks! Can you believe it? I can't decide if I should keep it as a souvenir, or buy something I can keep to remember this.' Jeremy's forehead wrinkled as he studied his prize. 'Do you have to have a bank account to cash a cheque? Or would any bank give me money for this?'

'How did you meet this woman?' Noelle interrupted.

'Well, it's a long story. An extremely long story.'

'That's all right. Tell me.'

Jeremy swung his feet and stared wistfully at the waders out in the river. 'The other day, after my support group at the hospital, a guy was waiting for me in the hall. Kind of a weirdo. He was wearing a grungy coat, even though it was about eighty degrees outside. He said he was a friend of Tia's, that Tia had told him all about me and that he wanted to take a look at my art. I thought to myself, Maybe this guy's a perv but, if he tries to grope me, I can easily kick his ass. So we walked back to my place, and he asked me all these questions on the way over.'

'Such as?'

'Questions about me. And about Tia. About how I felt about Tia. I told him I was crazy about her, that I'd do anything for her. That I loved her more than anyone else on earth . . . except you, Sis,' Jeremy added dutifully.

'What else?'

'He asked me how long I'd been painting, where I was trained, et cetera. I told him how I'd started out as a realist, but that my paintings got to be less about reality and more about the visions in my head. By that time, we were at my apartment. I showed him some of my older paintings, and the new stuff I've been working on.'

'And?'

'He didn't say anything for a long time. Just walked around and frowned at everything. Then he looked at me and said he thought I might be a genius. Isn't that wild?'

'OK, whatever. So get to the part about the cheque.'

'Well, he said he knew this woman who was a big collector in town. Said she buys all kinds of art by real pros, but her favourite thing to do is to discover brand-new artists, like me. He asked if I had slides, or a portfolio. I said I hadn't had time to put that kind of stuff together. So he said that, if I'd let him take a few of my canvases over to her place, he was pretty sure he could sell her something. I said, is it that easy? He said, sometimes. When an artist has talent, things can happen fast.'

'So then what happened?'

'He took one of the new canvases and a few of my older ones and left. I didn't think anything would happen. I figured Tia had set the whole thing up, as a favour, just a boost for my self-esteem. But the guy came back the next morning with this big cheesy smile on his face, and he handed me a cheque. The one you're holding, right there.' Jeremy studied Noelle. 'Why are you so white, Sis? Are you in shock or something? Want me to start CPR?'

Noelle shook her head. She folded the cheque exactly the way Jeremy had folded it, and gave it back to him. 'I'm not sure what this means,' she said.

'I got paid for a painting. That makes me a professional artist. I can pay my own rent this month. What else could it mean?'

'I don't know. But I'm going to find out,' Noelle said. She set down her can of soda with a determined thud, clambered to her feet and brushed the dirt off the seat of her shorts.

'Hey, you going somewhere?'

'Yes.'

'Where?'

'None of your business.'

Noelle marched away, leaving Jeremy to stare after her. Apparently, he didn't waste much time staring. Before she'd walked twenty yards, she heard a splash as he took his first step into the river.

'Interesting. Very interesting,' she said to herself as she hustled down the asphalt trail that ran along the river. The joggers and cyclists were a blur around her. She didn't know what she was doing, or where she was going. All she knew at this point was that Jeremy was in possession of a cheque from Mark's mother. This could mean that Noelle's dreams were about to blossom into fabulous reality.

On the other hand, that cheque could mean her strategy for nabbing Mark had just taken a fatal nosedive.

Beth and Carl Wharton lived in a museum. Literally. Their brand-new condo was part of a development of residences that had been built as a wing of the city's Museum of Modern Art. *Imagine ... living in your own art gallery*, read the seductive promotional text in the Sunday real-estate ads. *So private, so exclusive, you'll never want to leave.*

Standing in the austere glass lobby, waiting for Mark's parents to buzz them upstairs, Tia already wished she could leave. She'd been watching the ultra-modern structure take shape for months, but she'd never dreamt she'd know anyone who lived there.

'Welcome to our home,' said the towering blonde who opened the door. Beth Wharton had one of those commanding throaty voices that scared Tia to death. She wore a chunky platinum choker around her neck, the perfect accent for her ash-blonde hair, and a sublimely simple cream pantsuit, with long flowing trousers that pooled around her sandals. Tia, who felt too awkward in those first ten seconds to look Mark's mother in the face, stared at her gorgeous feet instead. Beth Wharton had an impeccable French pedicure and a sapphire ring on her third right toe.

A French pedicure. A sapphire toe ring. Tia was definitely in over her head.

Carl Wharton hovered three steps behind his wife, holding a martini pitcher. Shorter than Beth by several inches, he had an alert, observant air that suited his background as a nature photographer. Tia could feel him sizing her up, like some new species of field mouse.

'Come in, come in.' Beth extended a graceful arm, her sleeve falling like a wing.

'Hi, Mom.' Mark pulled the elegant beauty into his arms and air-kissed both of her cheeks. 'You look gorgeous, as always.'

'I'm surprised you recognise your old mom,' Beth scolded. 'It's been so long since we've seen you. I never thought we'd get to meet your fiancée.'

'Er, I'm not –' Tia stuttered.

'Mom, you know we're not engaged,' Mark said smoothly. 'We're still in the dating stage. I wanted to bring you proof that I do something besides work.'

Beth pouted. 'I can dream, can't I? Come with me, dear. Let's get you a drink and a place to sit. If we have any practical furniture in this place, I'll find a chair for you. We just moved in last month. Carl is still getting us unpacked.'

She put her arm around Tia and led her into the living room. The condo reminded Tia of a glass box, with exposed scaffolding and white pine hardwood floors. If you'd always dreamt of living in a museum, this was the place to be. Especially if you liked the way museums looked between installations. Carl must still be unpacking his wife's famous art collection. There were only a few paintings on the walls, subtly illuminated by soft white lights.

Only a few paintings.

And one of them was of Tia.

'You know, there's something about you that's familiar,' Beth said, narrowing her eyes at Tia. 'I can't put my finger on it. Are you involved in the arts?'

'I'm an artist,' Tia squeaked.

She was also a model, apparently. Tia couldn't take her eyes off the canvas hanging on Beth's north wall. It was Tia, no doubt about it. A curvy redhead, wearing nothing but splashes and spots and stripes of colour.

'Really? What do you do?'

'She doesn't do enough,' Mark stepped in. 'Tia spends more time with her patients than she does on her own art. It's too bad. She's very talented.'

Tia forced herself to turn away from the painting. Carl handed her a martini, and she gulped the icy gin at an unladylike speed. Mark still had his back to the painting. If he never turned around, the canvas might never enter his field of vision.

'Have a seat,' Carl said, motioning to a circle of metal objects arranged around a glass table. On the coffee table sat a fan-shaped arrangement of magazines about art and architecture. The cover of the first magazine showed Beth Wharton herself, standing with her arms folded in front of the city's art museum. The photo made Tia feel like Alice in a looking-glass world, faced with multiple reflections of an intimidating queen.

'Sit, sit,' Beth commanded. Her spare steel chairs looked more like miniature coat racks. Tia wasn't sure how to sit on them, so she followed Beth's example. They felt like coat racks, too.

'Mom, these chairs feel like torture devices. What did you do with all our comfy old furniture?' Mark asked. Tia felt a rush of gratitude towards him.

'I sold all that junk at a yard sale before we moved. I'm reinventing our décor,' said Beth. 'Don't you like it?'

'It's kind of austere, isn't it?' Mark asked.

'Well, it won't seem so spartan once Carl gets around to hanging our collection.'

'You know, Mom, you could always help him out.

Dad's back isn't as supple as it used to be when he was climbing mountains.'

'Oh, I'm fine,' said Carl, laughing and pouring himself another drink. 'I'm not about to let my lovely wife ruin her manicure doing something as mundane as hanging pictures.'

'Carl's so full of it. He just doesn't trust me with anything expensive. I've got butterfingers like you wouldn't believe,' Beth explained to Tia, waggling her slim, competent hands. 'I would have waited to have you over until the place was more presentable, but I was too impatient. All I've got now are a couple of pieces I bought within the past month. New artists, both of them. Nothing gets me going like the scent of fresh blood.'

Beth grinned and gave Tia a distinctly dirty wink. Tia was starting to like this woman. She might have been able to relax and enjoy herself if she hadn't been face to face with her own naked self. Though she didn't want to stare at the picture head on, Tia kept it in the corner of her eye, as if it might hop off the wall, stroll over and introduce itself to everyone.

'So tell me, Tia. What do you do when you're not being bright and adorable?' Beth asked, leaning forwards at a hostessy angle.

'I'm an art therapist,' Tia said. 'I work part-time on the adult inpatient ward over at City General. Just recently they assigned me a group on the adolescent unit.'

'You didn't tell me you had a new group, Tia,' Mark broke in with a frown. 'I thought you were going to cut down on your hours at the hospital. We were going to transition you into something more rewarding.'

'Hush, Mark. Let her talk.' Beth's commanding tone sounded exactly like Mark when he was in his dominant mode. Tia smiled. She really liked Beth now.

'Anyway, the teens are great. They put on a tough front at first, but they're starting to warm up to me.

They're so expressive under all that hostility, and some of them are very talented. The point of working with patients isn't to discover talent, but it's always a nice surprise when you meet someone who's got a true gift.'

'I agree. Like the artist who did the most recent painting I bought. This young man has potential. I haven't met him in person yet, but I intend to.'

Beth rose from her chair and walked towards the painting. Tia's heart sank like a rock, landing with a thud in the pit of her belly. There was no way she'd be able to wriggle out of this; she was trapped on all sides. Mark, his father and Tia all watched as she approached the painting, stood in front of it for a few long moments, then slowly turned around. When she looked at Tia again, Beth's eyes were sparkling with evil glee.

'I knew you looked familiar,' Beth crowed. 'You little minx! You posed for this painting, didn't you?'

Now everyone was staring at Tia, especially Mark. She sat blushing furiously, trying to consider her options. She could have denied everything, chalked it all up to coincidence. Jeremy's painting was abstract enough that the model couldn't be clearly identified. Or she could come out with a big messy confession that would hurt everyone in the room, in one way or another. Or she could tell a polite, watered-down version of the truth.

'I didn't pose for that painting,' she wavered.

This was true. She hadn't knowingly posed for Jeremy's painting. She'd posed for his digital camera, when he took pictures of the work he'd done on her body, but, if she'd had any clue that he was going to translate one of those photos into a painting, and somehow sell it to Mark's mother...

'Then how did you end up in it, exactly?' Mark glared at Tia, then at the painting, then back at Tia. The whole room was focused on Tia. Beth looked curious and delighted. Carl looked startled. Mark was turning purple under his beard.

'Carl, I think we need to walk the dog,' Beth announced. She grabbed her husband's arm and pulled him to his feet.

'But, my love, we haven't had a dog since 1989,' Mark's father pointed out.

'Then this is a perfect time to go out shopping for one. Come on, Carl. I think these two need a moment alone.'

Poor Carl barely had time to set down his martini glass before his wife dragged him out the door. Watching Beth, tall and striking and self-assured, lead her husband off, Tia wished she could beg her to stay. Meeting Beth Wharton had been a wonderful experience, compared to what was sure to happen next.

Mark got up and went over to the painting, so he could study it up close. Tia let him take his time. No sense rushing the confrontation. Jeremy had chosen to paint her in one of her most provocative poses, with her arms stretched over her head and her hips twisted to the side, one knee raised to show the glories in between her thighs. You didn't have to be a seasoned art critic to read between the lines of this piece; it was as clear as day that the artist had a hard-on for his subject.

'You want to tell me who painted this?' Mark asked.

Tia took a deep breath, closed her eyes and counted to three. 'Jeremy.'

Mark made a snorting noise. 'Noelle's crazy brother? That kid you've been babysitting?'

'I haven't been babysitting Jeremy.'

'Apparently not!'

'He's not a child, Mark. And he's not crazy.' Another deep breath. 'We're in love with each other.'

Mark fixed her with a look of sheer disbelief. 'You're joking.'

Tia looked down at her fingers, which were worrying a handful of her blue madras skirt. 'I'm not joking. I love him. He loves me. I don't know how to make it any more serious than that.'

'Does this mean you're choosing that kid over me?'

An eternity seemed to tick-tock by before Tia nodded.

'Let's see if I've got this straight. You'd give up everything I can offer you – fantastic sex, security, status, a much better career than the one you've got now – for a kid who's barely out of diapers, who's mentally ill and unemployed. What does he have that I don't?'

'He loves me,' Tia said. 'And he loves the things I love.'

'You don't think I love you?'

'Not the way Jeremy does. Not even close.'

Mark crossed his arms over his chest. 'Sounds like you've made up your mind.'

Tia looked up from her lap for the first time since this confrontation started. She expected to see pain on Mark's face, but he only looked irritated. Impatient. Incredulous. Leo's voice echoed in Tia's mind, reminding her to take a good look at what she was giving up. So she did. She studied Mark's perfect haircut, his expensive clothes, his skier's tan, his killer body and his expression of sheer disgust. Behind him, Jeremy's painting hung on the wall, the colours so vibrant that they sang to Tia from all the way across the room.

'Yes,' she said, lifting her chin so that she could match Mark, glare for glare. 'I have.'

Without waiting for Mark's response, Tia stood. She collected her purse, which was hanging off the back of Beth's dysfunctional chair, and walked out of Mark's parents' condo. She walked at the same pace all the way back to her apartment, her steps swift and weightless. If there'd been a soundtrack to this scene, the tune would have been upbeat and groovy, like the theme song to a sitcom from the 1970s. Tia wrinkled her nose experimentally, to see if there might be a tear or two lurking in her eyes, but nothing came out. She was happy. That's all there was to it. Later, she'd write an apologetic note to Beth and Carl, explaining everything (well, maybe not *everything*). But, for now, she just wanted to get back to her drab, cosy apartment and fix herself a bowl of Top Ramen.

It wasn't until she unlocked her front door and saw the gift from Delana's sitting on her table, still unopened, that Tia felt a glimmer of regret, not because she'd lost Mark, but because she'd never know what was inside that package. Tia picked up the box. Under the crisp gold bow was a card that read, 'To my gorgeous sex slave – I can't wait to see you wear this while you obey my every command. Love, Master Mark.'

Perfect. Tia giggled. She took the box into Noelle's empty room and laid it in the centre of her roommate's bed.

Noelle had met Leo Baines three or four times, in the course of her life with Tia. The last time was at the Halloween party that she and Tia had thrown last year. Leo had been dressed as Napoleon; Noelle had been dressed as Cleopatra. She remembered thinking that those two historical figures really ought to get together for a torrid one-nighter but, before she could make her move, Noelle had been swept off her feet by a guy wearing a Grim Reaper costume (it wasn't the length of his scythe that made her choose him over Leo).

So Noelle wasn't surprised when Leo fixed her with a stare of irritation mingled with curiosity when she rang his doorbell that evening. She'd found his address in an old tattered Hello Kitty address book that Tia kept in the drawer of her nightstand. Snooping through her roommate's belongings made it a lot easier to locate Tia's best friend.

'I know you,' Leo said, squinting at Noelle over his glasses. 'Wait. Don't remind me. I'm trying to improve my visual memory.'

Noelle tapped her foot while Leo wracked his brain. She gave him 45 seconds, then she supplied him with her identity. 'I'm Noelle. Tia's roommate. Remember Halloween?'

'Ah, yes. Cleopatra,' Leo said. 'I didn't recognise you without your bangs and your ankh. Please come in.'

He stood back and ushered Noelle into his basement apartment. The room was dim and damp and smelt like an old used-book store. Books stood in precarious mountains on the floors and countertops. Noelle wrinkled her nose. She hated underground apartments. They made her think of centipedes.

'I'll have a much nicer place when I get into private practice,' Leo said defensively, noting Noelle's expression.

'I'm sure you will,' Noelle said.

'Can I get you anything? Tea? Beer? Xanax?'

'No, thanks. I can't stay long.'

'At least have a seat.' Leo cleared a stack of books off his sofa. The stack left a deep indentation that remained after the weight had been removed. Noelle didn't want to sit in the pit the books had left, but she didn't want to be a total bitch, either. Leo sat down in a folding chair directly across from her. He propped his chin on his hands and looked at her expectantly.

'What brings you here?' he asked.

'My brother,' said Noelle. 'His name's Jeremy. You sold one of his paintings. I want to know why you suddenly decided to act as his agent.'

Leo's face went as blank as an egg. Noelle couldn't tell if he was playing the inscrutable shrink, or if she'd actually caught him off guard.

'Do you really believe that Jeremy has talent? Or were you being Machiavellian? Tell me the truth. I'm extremely protective of my little brother,' Noelle warned.

'I can see that.' Leo shrank back in his chair and folded his arms over his lap. 'I do believe that your brother has talent. Considerable talent. Trust me, Beth Wharton wouldn't have bought his work if she didn't agree with me. But I'd be lying to you if I said there wasn't an element of manipulation in the deal.'

'Who – or what – were you trying to manipulate?'

Leo sighed. 'Would you mind if I made myself a cup of chamomile tea? If I'm going to be interrogated, I think I deserve something warm to sustain my courage.'

'Go ahead.'

While Leo made tea in his cluttered kitchenette, Noelle studied the spines of the books on his coffee table. Mostly philosophy and psychology, with a few religious texts thrown in and several slim volumes of poetry. At the foot of the pile were thick, heavy art texts, covering everything from the Renaissance painters of Northern Europe to bleeding-edge sculptors who had just emerged into the public eye.

'So you do know something about art,' Noelle commented, when Leo returned with his tea. He had made a mug for Noelle, too. Though she wasn't in the mood for a hot drink, she took the offering, anyway. She wasn't sure if she liked Leo, but she was definitely warming up to his library.

'I do, thanks to Tia. She's the one who got me hooked. Galleries, museums, we used to do it all. Every weekend, we'd be out searching for new discoveries. But Tia hasn't had any interest in doing much of anything with me since she met Mark.'

Leo's mouth puckered when he said Mark's name, as if he'd taken a swallow of sour milk. Ah, Noelle thought. So that's it. Unrequited love would turn you into a ruthless schemer every time.

'Does Mark have anything to do with you selling Jeremy's painting to his mother?' Noelle asked.

Leo nodded glumly. 'I encouraged Beth to buy a very special piece of work. One of Jeremy's best. I'm assuming he told you which painting it was.'

'No. He didn't.'

'Beth bought a painting of Tia. A semi-abstract nude. Glorious work. Of course, it's not like seeing the real thing, but it's the closest I'll ever get. And now she's hanging in Beth's living room, where anyone could see her.'

It wasn't hard for Noelle to fill in the blank in that statement. 'Like Mark?'

'Exactly.'

Noelle couldn't respond to that; Leo had left her mute with admiration. She'd always considered herself to be a master of manipulation, but this ploy was brilliant. Leo had set the stage for a break-up between Mark and Tia, and Noelle hadn't had to lift a finger.

'You know, Leo, I think I love you,' Noelle said.

'But you're not *in* love with me, of course,' Leo replied dryly.

'I'm afraid that wouldn't be possible.' Noelle took a deep breath, prepping for her confession. 'You see, I'm in love with Mark, myself. I had accepted the fact that I'd have to steal him. But now that won't be necessary. You've done the dirty work for me. You've left me free to be a bitch and chase Tia's man.'

'I wish that statement didn't summarise my whole existence,' said Leo.

'Don't you see how perfect this is? As soon as Tia and Mark have broken up, you'll be able to go after her yourself.'

'But, Noelle, I didn't dream up this plot to get Tia for myself.'

'Then why would you do it?'

Leo's smile was sad. 'So that Tia could be an artist again. And so that she'd be free to be in love with Jeremy. At first I hated the idea of Tia and Jeremy. I accused Tia of being everything from an unethical tart to a cradle-robber. But she truly loves the boy. And he loves her. I may be a manipulator, but I'm not an ogre. I don't destroy true love. I don't need that kind of karmic debt, thank you very much.'

'Leo,' Noelle said, leaning forwards, 'would I be taking advantage of you if I asked for your professional opinion?'

Leo's eyes caressed Noelle's long calves, her tanned, athletic arms. 'You can take advantage of me whenever you want.'

Noelle ignored his lechery. 'What do you think about my brother and Tia? I mean, I'm assuming you know something about his history.'

Leo nodded, his gaze still fixed on Noelle's bare knees. 'I do.'

'Is it stupid of me to let those two have an affair? I'm so afraid Tia's going to leave him and break his heart. Jeremy's wild. It's not easy to keep him under control.'

'Maybe that's why they get along so well. She doesn't try,' Leo suggested, a hint of reproach in his voice.

'You know, it hasn't been easy, being Jeremy's sister,' Noelle huffed. 'People criticise me for trying to run his life, for wanting him to behave. I didn't do those things for my own satisfaction, believe me. When other girls were gossiping on the phone, or getting dressed for the prom, I was visiting Jeremy on the teen psych unit, or helping him track his meds. No one appreciates the people like me, who work so hard to keep the wild creative crazies under control.'

'I do,' Leo said. 'Don't forget, I'm a member of your anal-retentive tribe.'

For the first time since she'd entered Leo's lair, Noelle smiled. 'That's right. You are. You of all people should understand why it's so important to keep Jeremy's heart from being broken.'

Leo held up his hand. 'No. I can't follow you there. You can support your brother, but you can't protect him from love. Most importantly, you can't save him from a broken heart. That's part of life, Noelle. Everyone has to risk it, even those with mental disorders – which as far as I'm concerned, includes all of us to some degree.'

Noelle's right hand was rising towards her mouth; her teeth were already bared to chomp down on to her thumbnail. The hand stopped in mid-air. Then she lowered it to her lap, covered it calmly with her left hand and breathed.

'You're right, Leo,' she said. 'Thank you.'

Leo tipped an invisible hat. 'At your service,' he replied.

Chapter Eleven

Grabbing It

'Let's work with paints today. Not crayons,' Tia suggested to the four patients who showed up for art therapy on Monday morning. She walked around the room passing out large sheets of butcher paper, cheap brushes and bottles of tempera paint.

'Why?' asked Perdida, a plump woman in her fifties who carried a white straw purse with daisies everywhere she went. Tia happened to know that the purse was filled with Saltines and packets of peanut butter that she'd swiped from the unit's kitchenette. A bruise was fading on Perdida's temple, the aftermath of a head-banging episode in the ER several nights ago. Hard to believe that this motherly lady with the fleamarket purse was the same howling, self-injuring patient who'd been admitted to the unit last week.

'I wanted to draw with crayons today,' said Perdida's roommate Susie, with a melodramatic sigh.

'We've used crayons for the past three weeks. I think you should all try something new. Spread your wings,' Tia replied. She couldn't have told the patients the real reason why she didn't want to bring out the baskets of crayons. Crayons reminded her too much of her failure with Belle.

'Does this mean we can't use the glitter tubes, either?' asked Susie, who had been exhibiting hypersexual behaviour recently. Last week, she had pocketed a tube of golden glitter, painted her nipples and strutted out into the milieu wearing nothing but sparkles and a smile.

'You can use the glitter tubes, if you promise to give them back to me at the end of the session. You can even use the sequins, if you want. You just can't use the crayons today,' Tia said. 'That's the only rule. Other than that, anything goes.'

'This sucks,' said Cory, a bass player who was about Jeremy's age.

Tia didn't pay attention to his comment; Cory thought everything sucked.

'You look pretty today,' Perdida remarked, when Tia gave her bottles of blue, yellow and green paint. 'Do you have a new boyfriend?'

'Just happy to be here,' Tia said.

'Why?' Cory's question dripped with scorn.

'Because I can't wait to see what you make for me today.'

'Yeah, right.'

Cory wore a sneer so caustic that he made Sid Vicious look like Mickey Mouse, but he was the first one to crack open his paints. Within seconds, he was slathering his butcher paper with hostile strokes of colour – black, of course. Tia kept a sharp eye on Susie, who was toying with the cap of her glitter tube as she eyed the two males in the room. Besides Cory, there was Ned, a chronically depressed retired professor in his late sixties who was a regular patient on the unit. He'd never been married, still lived with his 89-year-old mother and showed up on the acute ward every so often when he was decompensating. Ned never said anything in group. Tia had given him the smallest brush she could find. All of Ned's paintings were intricate, detailed and approximately the size of a playing card. His favourite subjects were insects, birds and frogs.

No one was talking much today, and that was fine with Tia. Her favourite times with her groups were the moments of golden peace, when everyone was so focused on their art that they didn't have time to chat with each other, or to react to the voices in their heads.

Cory was scowling in ferocious concentration as he added bold squiggles of orange to his field of black. Ned's tongue was rooted in the corner of his mouth as he dabbled his tiny brush in the bottle of blue. Circling the room, occasionally pausing here and there to peek over someone's shoulder, Tia lost track of the outside world. She hardly noticed when the door opened and a mute, slender figure wearing a hospital gown slipped sideways into the room.

When Tia caught sight of the newcomer, her jaw dropped. Belle Doe stood in the corner of the room for a moment, then, with one ghostlike movement, she slid into an empty chair. Though her heart was pounding, Tia tried to act indifferent as she laid a piece of butcher paper in front of Belle, and provided her with a basket of crayons.

'Hey!' Susie shouted. 'How come *she* gets to use the crayons? No crayons today. That's the rule.'

Belle froze. Tia prayed to all the gods and goddesses of art therapy that the girl wouldn't close up. Belle's thin unsteady hand had been reaching for the basket of colours when Susie let out her squawk of indignation. Calmly, Tia picked out a handful of crayons and laid them in front of Belle.

'It's OK, Belle. You can use these. We can all use the crayons now.'

'But the rule was –'

'Susie. That rule was not set in stone,' Tia said. 'I decided to change it. Besides, you're the one who wanted to use the crayons this morning. So please, be my guest.'

Tia handed Susie her own basket, heading off any more of her complaints. Changing rules was never a wise move around here, but it wouldn't be fair if Belle were the only one who could use the crayons. Besides, Belle was worth bending a few rules. She looked like a different person today, with her hair combed into a long blonde shawl, and her pallid cheeks washed with a hint of pink. Her china-blue eyes were huge and watchful, but at least they were focused. Something had brought Belle back into the present. Without having to ask her a single question, or administer a test, Tia could tell that she was oriented. Maybe not to person, time *and* place, but one or two out of three wasn't bad.

'Let's all get back to what we were doing,' Tia suggested. She was careful not to look at Belle, whose hand floated over the basket of crayons. A delicate frown drew her eyebrows together. Belle was showing signs of concentration, Tia thought, fighting off the urge to give a jubilant shout. OK, so maybe her meds had been changed. Maybe she'd had a breakthrough with her psychiatrist that morning. It really didn't matter who or what had caused Belle's metamorphosis; Tia was just happy to see her here.

'I need help,' Perdida said. 'My flowers turned into trees. How can I make them small again?'

'What do you think?' Tia asked. 'It's your painting. You have to decide.'

Perdida chewed the end of her paintbrush. 'I could make something bigger next to them. Like a carton of milk. That way it would fix the . . . what do you call it?'

'Perspective,' Ned said glumly. 'The size of things is relative.'

He went back to his own painting, where all objects were perfectly proportionate, equally minuscule. Watching Ned's painstaking brushstrokes, Tia thought of Jeremy, and the mural that they were planning together. What was it that made one artist want to reduce the size of the world to three or four inches, while another wanted to enlarge everything, make the universe bigger and bolder than life?

Tia felt a pang of desire for Jeremy. She'd gone upstairs last night to confront him about the nude painting that he'd sold to Beth Wharton, but no one had answered when she knocked on his door. Two hours later, he still wasn't home. Neither was Noelle. Tia had spent the evening by herself, in an apartment that felt more bland and lifeless every day. Her familiar rooms didn't feel like home any more. Any space that didn't contain Jeremy was defined only by the fact that he wasn't there. Even rooms like this one, where Jeremy had never been, were made smaller by his absence.

Someone was pulling at the hem of Tia's blouse, a tug so faint that she almost didn't feel it. She'd been doing what she always did during therapy sessions, walking in a slow neutral circle around the room. She hadn't been aware that she'd paused next to Belle, or that Belle's fingers were clasping a handful of her shirt.

As soon as Tia looked down, Belle's hand dropped into her lap. Though her head was lowered and her hair fell over her cheek, Tia could see a hint of a smile curving the corner of her mouth. Belle's piece of butcher paper wasn't blank any more. In the centre were a pair of intertwined lines, one yellow, one red. The lines were long and graceful, curvy, and, though Tia didn't dare read too much into them, they made Tia think of two strands of hair: one from a blonde, one from a redhead.

'Two colours, Belle?' Tia said. 'That's incredible.'

The girl didn't respond.

'It really *is* incredible, you know,' Ned added. 'She hasn't interacted with anyone.'

'That's because she knows you're all freaks,' Cory said matter of factly.

'Isn't Belle pretty today?' Perdida beamed with an almost maternal pride.

Tia looked at Belle, and nodded in agreement. Then she looked around the room. For the first time in months, everything she saw made her happy. She loved the mismatched outcasts sitting at the battered crafts table. She love the cinderblock walls, and the musty smell of old pee, and the baskets of crayons and glitter tubes.

I'd never work anywhere else, Tia thought. There's no other place, besides this strange, special planet, that I'd rather spend my time.

Belle had retreated again, pulling back into her private inner room and closing the door behind her. But that was all right. As far as Tia was concerned, a slow miracle was just as spectacular as a sudden one. Slow miracles made you wait; when they finally took wing, you were already soaring on expectation.

Walking back to her apartment, Tia saw the first hints of autumn on the narrow old streets of her neighbourhood: yellow leaves, a thoughtful slant to the light, children trailing colourful sweaters as they raced home from the schoolbus. In the distance, the mountains wore a dozen shades of blue, from smoke to slate to midnight. Tia strolled along the sidewalk, kicking leaves. She was so busy watching the yellow swirls and eddies that she didn't see the metaphysically cute boy waiting for her on the brick wall outside her building.

She shrieked when Jeremy catapulted into her, slathering her cheeks, lips and neck with wet kisses.

'Do you have to stop my heart every time we see each other?' She laughed.

'God, I hope I do. Let me know if I don't. OK?'

Jeremy bounced on his heels. His cheeks and jaw were shadowed with a 24-hour beard, and his clothes looked like he'd been wearing them for three days straight. After the scene with Mark Saturday night, seeing Jeremy gave Tia a surge of relief and hunger and sheer joy – he'd become air and food and happiness to her, all wrapped in one rumpled, hyperactive bundle. His muscles held so much energy, so much life, that Tia wondered how she'd gone so long settling for anything less.

As he pressed his body into hers, Tia felt a weird bulge in his jeans.

'What on earth is that?' Tia groped Jeremy's pockets

and found a rectangular object. 'I thought you were just happy to see me.'

'It's a harmonica. But, if you feel me up on the other side, there's something a lot harder and warmer . . .'

'OK, OK. I get the point.'

'Wait a second. You do like the harmonica, don't you?'

'I guess. I don't really know anything about it.'

'Awesome.' Jeremy's face lit up. 'A virgin. No preconceived notions. I'll turn you into a harmonica slut. Think about it. I spend hours practising mouth and tongue control. Any girl who doesn't love the harmonica doesn't know what she's missing. Imagine hearing this in bed every night, after we've made love.'

He let go of Tia, pulled the instrument out of his pocket and played a few bars of a sweet, low, throbbing tune. The music flowed from Jeremy's lips into Tia's blood, where it pulsed through her veins, perfusing her with longing. She imagined the scene that Jeremy had painted for her: the two of them lying sweaty and sated, their legs roped in sheets, Tia's arm wrapped around Jeremy's chest as he played his harmonica in the dark.

'Every night,' Tia said.

He lowered the harmonica. 'What?'

'Every night,' she repeated. 'You mean that, don't you?'

'Duh, Tia.' Jeremy grinned. 'For a smart chick, you can be pretty dense.'

'I know,' she said, thinking of how long it had taken her to see as clearly as she was seeing at this moment.

'By the way, I should tell you a few things about me that you probably don't know,' he said. 'I mostly eat corndogs, I drink too much rootbeer, and I don't like to wear clothes. I've been pretty civilised since I moved into your building, because I didn't want my sister to freak out. But the way I like to be is naked. Just so you know, when you start spending a lot of time with me, you're going to see a lot of my bare ass. '

'Thanks for the warning,' Tia said.

Jeremy scratched the back of his neck and chewed the corner of his lip. 'Also, I'm not good with money. I mean, I don't know anything about cheques or bank accounts or stuff like that. My dad tried to teach me, but he's not very patient. And my sister, well, if I ask her for help, she just does things for me.'

'I'll teach you,' Tia said. 'I'll teach you everything you need to know.'

Jeremy slipped his harmonica back in his pocket so that he could use both hands to cradle her face while he kissed her. His lips moved with the assurance of a grown-up lover, but his tongue tasted like the watermelon Jolly Ranchers that he was addicted to. That pseudo-fruit flavour, familiar from her own childhood, made Tia laugh into Jeremy's mouth.

'It's such a turn-on when you laugh,' he said. 'It makes your whole body shake. You're like my own carnival ride, Tia. I want to ride you *now*.'

His hands were under her light cotton sweater, working at the clasp on her bra. Her nipples tightened under his fingers, but the breeze against her belly brought her back to reality. 'Jeremy, we're outside,' she reminded him. 'On a public street. People are watching us.'

'They're just jealous because they want to ride you, too,' he said, grazing on her neck. 'But they can't. You're mine.'

There were still tender spots on Tia's throat where he'd sucked too vigorously the last time they'd made love, spots that she'd been secretly palpating ever since. At the hospital, in her kitchen, at the grocery store, Tia could touch one of the marks his mouth had left and relive a cascade of sensations.

'No, really. We should go upstairs. Noelle could be coming along any minute.'

'It's OK. She knows I'm in love with you. She's getting over it.'

'That doesn't mean she wants to watch us making out. Come on. Let's go inside.'

Through her haze of arousal, Tia had a vision of Noelle marching down the street, her lips pursed in distaste as she saw her roommate groping her little brother. Tia broke away from Jeremy, took his hand and pulled him up the stairs. But, instead of letting Tia stop at the door of his apartment, Jeremy took the lead and kept going, climbing two more flights of stairs. He stopped in front of a peeling wooden door that looked like it hadn't been opened since the Carter Administration.

'I thought this building only had three floors,' Tia remarked. 'What's up here?'

'You'll see.' Jeremy dug around in his pocket until he found his keys. After a few minutes of wrestling with the lock and yanking the warped door, he finally wrenched it open. Taking Tia by the hand, he led her on to the rooftop.

'Wow,' she said. 'I had no idea this was up here. I've never seen this view before!'

Down below, Tia could see the streets and alleys of her neighbourhood: the cars and buses driving by, the meetings and conversations and illicit transactions taking place. But, when she looked straight ahead, she saw the sky, and the mountains, and the shaggy gold carpet of trees stretching as far as she could see.

'Mrs Crouch gave me the key,' Jeremy said proudly. 'Noelle was wrong about the landlady. She really likes me.'

'Of course she does. Your charm works on women of all ages.'

'Does it work well enough to get you to take your panties off?' Jeremy asked.

He was already fulfilling his own request, lifting Tia's skirt and pushing her pants down around her ankles. Then he got down on his knees and, under the tent of Tia's dress, Jeremy kissed and licked and nibbled her while she gazed out at the city. The ripples Jeremy was creating with his lips and tongue were like extensions of the warm sun-drenched afternoon. She couldn't help comparing Mark, who had preferred to fuck her in closets or locked rooms, to Jeremy, who was making love to her under the open sky, high above the ordinary world.

When her knees began to buckle, Jeremy held Tia by her thighs so that she wouldn't fall. She loved the way he ate her, as if her lips were literally a food, a pomegranate with tart seeds and a succulent inner rind. Under the influence of his mouth, Tia's colours began to appear: pink and blue, yellow and green, purple and red and chartreuse and tangerine. All the colours she'd ever loved were suffusing the sky. Some of those shades, she knew, had never existed before Jeremy. Those hues belonged to the rhythm of his tongue, the pressure of his lips and the edges of his teeth against Tia's velvet flesh.

'Jeremy? I'm coming.'

She heard her own words through a fog, and she was amazed that she remembered what they meant. Her voice didn't seem connected to the rocking explosion of sweetness that brought her to her knees. Jeremy's shoulders broke Tia's fall, and she and Jeremy toppled over together in a heap of legs and laughter. Soon his jeans were around his knees, and Jeremy was gliding into her, so that he could take his own turn on the colour wheel. He rocked his hips back and forth until he found the tempo that pleased him most, and then he began to ride.

Jeremy always made sharp, puffing sounds when he got close to his climax, like a kid pumping his bicycle up the steepest street in the neighbourhood, eager to see what lay on the other side. Tia hoped he'd never stop making those noises when he made love to her, or calling out her name when he reached the top of the hill.

* * *

Noelle didn't know what to do about the package. The heavy white box wrapped in gold ribbon had been sitting on her bed when she came home last night, waiting like a lover. The moment she saw the gift, she knew one thing for certain: Kevin hadn't left it there. Kevin couldn't afford to buy presents like that and, if he could, his anti-consumerist principles would have stopped him. When she opened the card that was tucked under the ribbon, Noelle went cold all over.

The box was undeniably real, but the card had to be a joke. Or a mistake. Mark wouldn't have written those sleazy phrases: 'sex slave', 'obey my every command', 'Master Mark'. Someone had been sneaking around in Noelle's head, teasing out her submission fantasies. Suddenly paranoid, she slammed her bedroom door shut and threw the box on the bed, as if it held a hidden transmitter that was broadcasting all the tawdry spanking scenarios that she played and replayed in her mind.

But she couldn't negate the possibility that the gift was sincere. Mark might have some kind of radar that had picked up on her inner longings. The only way she could find out if this gift was really meant for her was to open the box.

On the other hand, if the gift wasn't hers, if the package had ended up in her room by mistake, she was committing a violation of privacy by opening a present that belonged to Tia.

Oh, what the hell, Noelle thought, tearing off the gold ribbon. Privacy violations were her speciality. As soon as she opened the box, a profusion of tissue paper exploded out. She had to paw through mounds of the flimsy stuff to reach whatever was buried inside.

'My, my. What do we have here,' Noelle muttered.

Using her fingertips like pincers, she pulled a scanty garment out of the box. Noelle, whose preferred brand of underwear was Jockey for Her, had no idea what she was looking at. She wasn't even sure which part of the anatomy it was meant to cover, if any. A tiny gold lock, in the shape of a heart, dangled from a slim band of white satin. Noelle held up the contraption and stretched it out between her hands. If nothing else, it could function as a slingshot.

'Chastity belt,' said a male voice. 'I bought that for Tia. Never knew irony could cost so much money.'

Noelle threw the thing down as if it were on fire. She wheeled around to find Mark himself standing in the doorway. He wore running shorts, a Big Dogs T-shirt and a wry smile – not exactly lord-and-master garb.

'How did you get in?' Noelle cried.

'Your front door was unlocked.'

'Shit! I must have left it open.' Carrying an armload of books upstairs, Noelle kicked the door shut behind her, forgetting to go back and turn the deadbolt.

'This isn't the best neighbourhood, Noelle. Anyone could have come in and robbed you blind.' His eyes surveyed the wreck of the box from Delana's. 'Looks like you've done a bit of robbery, yourself.'

'I was just ... I found ... the package was sitting on my bed,' Noelle sputtered. She grabbed Tia's present and frantically tried to put it back together, mashing down the tissue paper and shoving the lid back on the box. 'I thought it was for me,' she added in a meek little voice.

Mark shrugged. 'Maybe it is. Do future attorneys wear chastity belts?'

'Only the future public defenders,' Noelle said, making a stab at a joke.

Desperation was probably flashing across her face like a highway construction sign. On the floor beside her bed sat Noelle's well-worn copy of *Urban Pace* magazine, the one with Mark's picture on the cover. Noelle had dug the issue out of her closet the night after Mark took her to the ballet (or took her *at* the ballet). She'd been using it as a prop for her private pleasure sessions ever since. Now the magazine was lying there in plain sight, proving that Noelle could never be too mature or too successful to be a complete and total dork.

She wished Mark would go away. She wished she could replay this whole scene, minus the magazine on the floor and the ransacked gift on the bed. Mark was always so calm, so in control. Chastity belts might not be her thing – not yet, anyway – but control turned her on.

'I stopped by on my way to the park. Thought I'd see if you wanted to go running and have a few beers afterwards,' Mark said. 'But if you'd rather model that for me, we could stay here.'

'Yes. No. I mean, I don't practise chastity. I'm not chaste.' Noelle's rhetorical skills were breaking down altogether.

'That's good to know. Because you still owe me for the other night.'

Noelle's throat had something large and dry in it, like a big rock. 'What other night?'

'At the ballet. Remember?'

Mark had moved across the room and was standing only a few inches away from Noelle. At the same time, she'd been unconsciously backing towards the bed. She couldn't go any farther; the edge of the mattress was butting into the backs of her knees.

Noelle nodded dumbly.

'Good. I'm glad you haven't forgotten what I did to you. I know I haven't. All that silky naked skin, under that tacky black raincoat. I had to keep reminding myself I was out with a brilliant prosecutor-in-training. Nothing like that has ever happened to me before.'

'Really?' Noelle's mouth was so dry now that her tongue stuck to the roof of her mouth when she tried to speak.

Mark was touching her now, the way he'd touched her at the ballet, only there wasn't anyone here to stop him or slow him down.

'Really. I've been with a lot of women, but no one like

you. You've got a combination of qualities that drives me crazy, Noelle. I was thinking about you just this morning, when I was alone in the shower.'

'What were you thinking about?'

'About the various ways you could pay me back.'

Somehow, Noelle's shirt had been lifted over her head. Mark's hands were moving all over her, refreshing the claim he'd staked the other night. She felt paralysed, as if she'd been hit by an arrow dipped in curare, like a captive virgin in an old movie. She could feel everything Mark was doing – she just couldn't move. Had no desire to move.

'To start with, I'd like to tie you up,' Mark said. 'Nothing fancy; I'll just use your bra.'

Noelle was so weak with lust that it only took a small nudge to get her on to her back on the bed. Mark tied her wrists over her head, not securing them to anything, just softly binding one hand to the other. For once, Noelle was at an advantage wearing a worn-out sports bra: no underwires, lace demi-cups or heavy-duty padding to get in the way of Mark's intentions.

Noelle's skin was on fire, and she couldn't lie still. Mark hadn't touched her breasts yet, but the ruby peaks were already forming. When Noelle was this aroused, her breasts were all nipple – twin zones of sensation that could bring her close to orgasm at the slightest stimulation. Mark had his shirt off, too, and the sense of his weight bearing down on her was enough to make her whimper. When he tugged off her sweatpants, she felt another lurch of embarrassment. She was wearing a pair of comfortable old cotton boxer shorts that she'd stolen from her brother – a far cry from the exotic spiderwebs that Tia called underwear.

Mark didn't seem to notice; he was too busy admiring the black fleece between Noelle's thighs, before positioning his body between her long legs. But, before he got down and dirty, Mark did something that Noelle found so endearing that it flattened the last of the barbed-wire fences she'd put up around her heart. He carefully pulled off her glasses, folded the earpieces and placed them on her night table, in the lacquered Chinese tray that she used for that very purpose.

'You have the most incredible eyes. Blue and green, and is that gold in there?'

'I guess so,' Noelle said. Jeremy was the one who was always getting compliments on his eyes. Noelle rarely thought about the colour of her own.

Mark kissed Noelle's eyelids, her nose, her lips. His short blond beard set off electric sparkles up and down her neck as he nuzzled her throat. Then his mouth was roving across her collarbones, across the hollows under her arms, down into the smooth groove between her breasts. Her nipples rose higher, begging for his mouth. When he finally kissed them, Noelle made a noise that hardly sounded human. She didn't want to wait for Mark to torture her any more. There would be plenty of time for spankings and other sensuous torments; right now she just needed him inside her, to prove that he was really hers.

Luckily, Mark was thinking the same way. He didn't waste any time getting out of his shorts and into Noelle. She usually wasn't ready this fast but, with Mark, she'd been waiting so long that his entry was as easy as slicing warm butter. When Mark began to move in and out of her at an urgent tempo, she realised that he wanted this just as much as she did. Noelle wrapped her muscular thighs around Mark's back. They bucked together like a well-lubed machine, never stopping or faltering, two overachievers going at it with all the competitive lust of an Olympic event.

We're perfect for each other, Noelle thought blissfully, just before the fireworks went off. There was that moment of singing tension in her whole body, then the blossoming of sparks that burnt all the way down to her toes. Mark was hot on her heels, finishing soon after. A gentleman to the end, he untied her wrists –

even rubbed the skin to make sure it hadn't chafed – before he fell back and collapsed on one of her pillows.

'I need to ask you something, Noelle,' Mark said. His voice sounded foggy, and his head was heavy in the curve of Noelle's shoulder. Noelle was spent, too, but there was no way she was going to lose consciousness with Mark in her bed. She would watch him every second, just to make sure he didn't vanish like a golden mirage.

'Ask me anything,' Noelle said.

'Why is that magazine lying on your floor?'

'What magazine?'

Noelle stretched her right leg towards the floor. She felt around with her foot until her toes made contact with *Urban Pace*, then she kicked it under her bed.

'The one with my picture. I never wanted to do that interview in the first place. My mother talked me into it,' Mark yawned. 'That reminds me, you need to meet my parents as soon as possible. No delays this time around.'

'Don't worry,' Noelle said. That gospel chorus was going off in her mind again. *He wants me to meet his parents! He wants me to meet his parents!* Suddenly, everything that had happened in the past few weeks, all the turmoil and weirdness with Tia and her brother, seemed insignificant. What mattered was that Noelle was going to grab that ring. She could see the brass circle twinkling in the distance, floating towards her; all she had to do was sit up high on her wooden horse and stretch out her hand . . .

'Mark, wake up,' she said urgently, straddling him and bracing her hands on his shoulders. 'I have to be on top.'

'Already?' He laughed, but he was already hardening underneath her.

'Yes,' she announced. 'I'm grabbing it.'

'Grabbing what?' he asked, but his question dissolved into a groan as Noelle mounted her handsome steed.

* * *

'OK. Stop here.'

Jeremy and Tia were standing in the heart of downtown. He'd brought her here after they'd had their fill of sex on the roof, but he hadn't yet told her why. Commuters flowed around them, as if they were a rock in the middle of a river, while he produced a blue bandanna from his pocket and tied it around her head.

'Jeremy, I can't see.'

'That's the point. Haven't you ever been blindfolded before?'

'Not in the middle of traffic.'

'You're not in the middle of traffic. You're on the sidewalk with me. You have to trust me, Tia. I know where I'm going.'

Blind, she held his hand and followed him down the street. With the rumbles and groans of the cars surrounding her, she let Jeremy lead her. She had to hustle to keep up with him. At first she panicked, jostled by the impatient shoulders of the passersby, but soon they were walking down streets that gradually became less noisy. The sense of chaos fell away, and she heard nothing but the squabbling of city sparrows and the melodic beep-beep-beep of a truck backing down an alley.

'Here we are. You'll have to wait a second.'

Jeremy took Tia by the shoulders and positioned her, first in one spot, then another. Once he had her exactly where he wanted her, Tia had to stand still while he arranged the rest of his surprise. She heard banging and clattering, and the sound of him swearing under his breath.

'How long is this going to take, Jeremy? I'm dying of curiosity.'

'Just long enough for me to take your blindfold off.'

Jeremy stood behind her, untied the bandanna, and let Tia look.

Tia blinked a few times, getting used to daylight, before she realised where she was. She was standing in front of a wall. Not just any wall, but the one that she and Jeremy had chosen weeks ago, on their first investigative mission. The wall had been transformed. The old sandstone surface was covered by the faint lines of a grid, and within those squares were the figures of two lovers, embracing against an urban skyline.

'It's ours. It's our mural!'

'Not yet. We haven't even started,' Jeremy reminded her, but he was as excited as she was, moving around her, burying his face in her neck, hugging her from behind. Against the wall stood a stepladder, an assortment of cans of acrylic paints, buckets, trays, brushes and a drop cloth.

'We've got everything we need,' he said. 'We can start right now. The weather's perfect. Nice and warm and dry.'

'We don't have any kind of permit yet. We can't paint on this wall.'

'Yes, we can. It wants to be painted on. It needs to be painted on. Look around you – the whole street needs this. Who knows what could happen? Next week there might be a hundred guys in this street, bulldozing this building. We have to take the chance while it's still here.'

Tia surveyed her surroundings. She saw the broken asphalt, the buildings run down and forgotten or abandoned. There used to be life in this shaded strip of space – light and colour and sound. Small private businesses had operated behind these walls, people had lived in the apartments across the street. Tia had made love in one of those apartments, with a musician she'd forgotten long ago. Everyone had since moved on. Jeremy was right; these buildings would be torn down soon. Anything she and Jeremy painted here would be destroyed when this neighbourhood was renovated. So what did it matter if two lovers grabbed the opportunity to leave their mark, before this tiny piece of the world went away?

'Come on,' Jeremy coaxed. He held her hips and swung her back and forth as he teased her earlobe with his tongue. 'You've done this before. Crimes are always easier the second time around.'

'I'm not a criminal!'

'OK, maybe not a criminal. But you're a rebel. You and me are alike that way. We get to make our own rules. My rule of the day is that any building that gets neglected too long is fair game for painting.'

'What if the city doesn't agree with us?'

'The city does agree, Tia. It's the guys in the three-piece suits who don't. And they're not here. Right?'

'Right,' Tia said. All of her old rules were melting – a process that had begun the first day she laid eyes on Jeremy. She would probably keep melting until there were no old rules left, only the new ones that she and Jeremy were making together.

Jeremy chose a paintbrush. He opened the first can of paint, pomegranate red. The colour was so lush that Tia could almost taste it on her tongue, tart and sweet, faintly dangerous. Jeremy held out the brush. Tia took it.

'Just close your eyes,' he said, repeating the words he'd said to her at the courthouse, 'and lay the colour on the wall.'

So that's what she did. She braved it alone this time, her hands untied. Totally unrestrained, the way she'd been in her dreams, Tia painted.